DRUID ARCANE

A NEW ADULT URBAN FANTASY NOVEL

M.D. MASSEY

MODERN DIGITAL
PUBLISHING

Dedicated to M.D. Massey, Sr.
Rest in peace, Pops.

AUTHOR'S NOTE

To my Welsh readers, please forgive Click's accent. Due to the character's history, I had to assume that his first language was Old Welsh. However, he would necessarily be fluent in all Celtic languages, having lived throughout the Middle Ages and into Modernity all over the British Isles. Thus, I thought his accent might be a mix of Goidelic and Brittonic. For that reason, Click's manner of speech is an amalgam of Celtic language accents. The result admittedly bears little, if any, resemblance to a modern Welsh accent, and is more akin to James Doohan's portrayal of Montgomery Scott in the original *Star Trek* series. As always, all errors are my own, and in this case, intentional.

1

The semi-immortal wizard known as Click and I were at the edge of the Highlands in Southwest Iceland, waiting to meet with a valkyrie, one of Odin's chosen. It was a bright sunny day in April, but still cold. I shivered as the wind cut like a knife through the layers of clothing I'd worn. As I scanned the hills all around, I stamped my feet and rubbed my arms in an attempt to drive some warmth back into my extremities.

Despite the cold, my companion was dressed in a thin black t-shirt, an old-school leather motorcycle jacket, and jeans cuffed over black boots polished to a high shine. He wore his short dark hair slicked back on the sides, with a single lock artfully dangling down the center of his forehead. His boyish face was both clean-shaven and blemish-free, and despite being thousands of years old, he didn't appear to be a day over seventeen. In short, he looked like a teenage reincarnation of James Dean, plucked straight out of some fifties-era feature film.

"Ya' have'nae been in a fight until ye've tussled with a valkyrie."

"Huh?" I replied distractedly.

"Valkyries. Mean buggers, but lookers, every one. Tough as nails in a scrap."

"Right." Click was nuts, so I dismissed his offhanded comment as I continued to search for our contact. "Click, didn't you say she was supposed to meet us here at noon?"

"Well, I did'nae exactly say the lass was *meetin'* us," he offered with a distracted shrug. "'Twas more like we were s'posed to come out here, an then ye'd scuffle, an after she'd decide whether or not yer worthy of any assistance she might offer. 'Tis, if yer not dead after said row."

He pronounced "row" like "cow," referring to a fight, not a canoeing excursion. "Wait a minute," I said, scowling as I gave him a sideways glance. "I thought we were coming out here to *talk*, not get jumped."

"Oh, I'm not gettin' jumped," he replied as he tilted his head quizzically. "That's yer purview, lad. Might even say it's yer own specific area o' expertise."

"Click..."

Ignoring the warning tone in my voice, he snapped his fingers and produced a pack of cigarettes from thin air. In the past, I'd often wondered how he could create such a complex object with magic. Eventually, I realized he wasn't just conjuring them from the aether. Somewhere in Iceland, a tobacco shop owner was probably wondering how the hell his stock was disappearing and considering whether he should call an exorcist.

"Oh, 'tis not as though ye've not fought demigods

afore," he said as he pulled a cancer stick from the pack. "By this juncture, ye've had plenty o' experience, have ya' not? I'd think the entire ordeal would be old hat ta' ya' by now. But if ya' want ta' pack it in an' head back ta' the oak—"

I exhaled in frustration but kept my comments to myself. Complaining did absolutely no good. We'd been in Iceland for six months now, searching for the Celtic god of healing, Dian Cécht. And for all our searching, we had nothing to show for it. Moreover, I'd made enemies of the local fae, also known as the *huldufólk*, and they'd done all they could to make my life miserable ever since.

"Alright, five more minutes, then I'm calling it." I paused, cocking my head as I looked up. "Do you hear that?"

Click patted his pockets, oblivious to my concerns. Why he didn't just use magic to light his cigarette was beyond me. Having grown accustomed to his idiosyncrasies to the point of prescience, I reached in my Crane-skin Bag and tossed him a cheap disposable lighter. He snatched it out of the air, looking at it with surprise before lighting up. After taking a few puffs, he pocketed my lighter before turning his gaze overhead.

"Oh, ya' mean that high whistlin' noise?" he said, his cigarette dangling from his lower lip as he spoke.

"Yes, that would be the sound I was referring to."

"Hmm. I'd say our valkyrie is about to make her presence known. Good luck, and if ya' survive I'll see ya' back at the Oak." With a snap of his fingers, the Welsh master magician once known as Gwydion disappeared.

"Click, wait!" I yelled, knowing I was wasting my breath. The youthful-looking trickster was like the wind; he came and went as he pleased. I kicked a clump of frozen snow, stubbing my toe on a bowling ball-sized boulder hidden beneath. Growling in frustration, I cursed the day Click was born. Then I began seeking the source of that whistling noise, which grew louder by the second.

The sound morphed into an ear-piercing, high-pitched whine that reached a screeching crescendo, just as a blinding ball of light crashed to the ground twenty yards in front of me. As it struck, a thunderclap reverberated from the point of impact, causing a shockwave that sent me staggering. I clapped my hands to my ears, but too late— between the whistling sound and the thunder, my sense of hearing was toast.

As the light and smoke faded away, I saw a tall, regal female figure standing on the spot where the lightning struck. She was dressed from head to toe in shining armor, with a winged Viking helm on her head and a round shield on her arm. Large, hawk-like wings snapped out from her shoulders, spanning at least fifteen feet from tip to tip before folding behind her back.

There was another blinding flash of light. When the spots cleared from my eyes, the valkyrie's appearance had changed completely. The blonde who stood there now wore modern clothing, including yoga pants, a light blue puffy vest over a tight thermal shirt, hiking boots, and a tasseled knit cap. She was almost as tall as me, maybe six feet, and she had the body of a fitness competitor. Flaxen hair fell in braids from under her hat, and piercing blue eyes stared at me from beneath a curtain of bangs that nearly covered her eyebrows.

To say that she was attractive would be an understatement. She had the fine, angular features that so many Icelandic women possessed. High cheekbones, wide-set eyes that were slightly upswept, and a sharp, dainty nose above bow-shaped lips that would've been attractive had they not been drawn into a frown. In short, she looked like some sort of European fitness model, the kind who make their living posting workout videos and makeup endorsements on social media.

She opened her mouth to say something, but I couldn't make it out. All ambient sound had been replaced by a sort of muffled whooshing noise, accompanied by my own heartbeat hammering inside my head. The girl certainly knew how to make an appearance, but if she wanted to have a conversation, it might've been better if she'd forgone all the theatrics.

I tilted my head toward her as I held a hand up to my ear. "What's that?" I yelled. "You'll have to speak up—that thunderclap screwed up my hearing."

The valkyrie's frown deepened as she blew hair from her eyes. She reached over her shoulder and pulled a wicked-looking longsword from thin air. She pointed the sword at me, then gave me an arch-eyed look as if to say, *Ready or not, here I come.*

With a sigh, I pulled Dyrnwyn from my Bag. As I held it aloft, a flicker of flame ran up and down its length before sputtering out. So, this valkyrie wasn't pure evil—but she wasn't pure as the driven snow, either. That was good to know.

It'd make what I had to do next a bit easier.

I'd tangled with fae, vampires, 'thropes, giants, demigods, Fomorians, and even the spawn of an outer god. Yet, nothing I'd faced before came close to the ferocity the valkyrie displayed as she pressed her attack. This chick might've looked like a snow bunny on holiday, but she fought like a rabid honey badger with a grudge.

Fortunately, I was ready for it. Well, not necessarily ready for *this* specific encounter, as Click had failed to provide enough warning for me to properly prepare. But I was ready to handle her in a general sense, having gotten into the habit of stealth-shifting whenever we made contact with supernatural entities. Here in Iceland, we were the outsiders, and I never knew when some fae creature or monster might try to eat me for the hell of it.

The upside was, I'd gotten even better at shifting quickly, cutting my time from human to half-Fomorian down to under ten seconds. A full shift took twenty, which wasn't as great an improvement—but it was still better than the thirty or forty seconds a full, voluntary transformation used to take. When the gods had it in for you, ten seconds could mean the difference between life and death.

I blocked a low slash at my knee, leaning out of the way just in time as the valkyrie's lightning-quick reverse, circular thrust whistled past my face. As soon as the blade cleared her midline, I took the opportunity to thrust Dyrnwyn upward at her eyes, angling the sword to reduce the profile. Keeping your blade aligned with your opponent's line of sight made it harder for them to judge distance, and I'd likely have scored a cut against someone less-skilled.

But the valkyrie was no such opponent. She casually deflected the stab, following with a riposte that I just barely turned away from my chest. I leapt out of range, using a bit of superhuman speed and strength to hasten my momentary retreat.

"We don't have to do this, you know!" I said, louder than I'd have liked. My hearing was returning, but slowly, since my Fomorian healing factor wasn't as robust in my stealth-shifted form.

She danced back, shaking her head as she responded in a breathy, pixieish voice slightly reminiscent of Björk. "The Valkyries can only gauge a man's measure in battle— that is our way. The magician should have warned you. Now, fight and prove your mettle—or die. It makes no difference to me, Irlander."

Oh, it's going to be like that, eh? Fine.

My first sword instructor had been Maureen, half-kelpie and erstwhile girl Friday to my druid mentor, Finnegas. She was deadly with a blade and could've mopped the floor with your typical Olympic fencing champion without breaking a sweat. More recently, I'd trained under a Japanese swordmaster by the name of Hayashi Hideie, who happened to be a tengu. Hideie had devoted his very long life to perfecting the ways of *kenjutsu*, and he also possessed some unique talents that made him a very difficult opponent in battle.

Between the two of them, I damned sure knew my way around a swordfight. I also knew when I was outclassed. I might have spent the last several years training under two of the finest sword masters in the Austin demesne, but this valkyrie had spent millennia studying blade craft. Thus, I was as likely to defeat her in a straight-up swordfight as I was to sprout wings and fly.

Time to cheat.

Although we'd spent six months Earthside here in Iceland, the time I'd spent in the Grove training with Click could be measured in years. It was hard to gauge time inside the Grove, as it passed much differently there. However, based on my own sleep cycles and how far I'd progressed in the arts of chronomancy and chronourgy, I estimated that I was several years into my apprenticeship under the magician.

Half a year ago, Click had referred to my talents as "paltry," although they'd certainly saved my ass when I dueled Diarmuid, a psychotic demigod. Since then, I'd devoted considerable effort to improving my control and expanding my repertoire. While I'd never be able to warp time and space as easily as the quasi-god formerly known as Gwydion, I now possessed enough skill to have an edge against your typical demigod—or valkyrie.

Slowing my breathing and quieting my mind, I entered the calm, still mental state required for performing time magic. Entering that state was second nature to me now, and I could cast minor time cantrips with relatively predictable results. Casting time magic wasn't my issue now. The main challenge in using this particular school of magic was not letting anyone know I was doing it.

There was a reason the gods had outlawed the practice and hunted chronomancers into extinction, and that was because fucking with time was dangerous as hell. Get caught using it, and you'd be branded as enemy number one on every pantheon's list of The World Beneath's Most Wanted. No thanks. I had enough gods wanting my head on a platter as it was.

Besides, I didn't have to humiliate the valkyrie; I only needed to fight her to a draw in a convincing manner. I scanned the immediate time streams, looking ahead several seconds and focusing on the branches and outcomes that showed the highest probabilities of victory. After choosing a course of action that would most likely end the fight without getting me killed, I took a deep breath, and waited.

Although it took only milliseconds, my brief glimpse into the future revealed a myriad of possible scenarios. In one, I slipped on a patch of ice while retreating. In that variant, the valkyrie stabbed me through the chest, pinning me like a bug to the rocky earth below. In another, I just barely missed a parry and got a longsword through the eye. And in a third, I overcommitted to a thrusting attack, losing my sword arm at the elbow.

Time and again, I'd watched myself die as similar

scenes played through my mind like movie clips. Needless to say, it's a bit disconcerting to observe your own demise once, never mind dozens of times. However, doing so proved my hunch that she was the better swordsman, and that I'd likely lose to her in a fair fight.

But as I watched myself expire a thousand different ways, one scene appeared over and over again as I flipped back and forth through alternate futures. In it, the valkyrie attacked with a very specific flurry of slashes and thrusts, a combination of moves she'd likely practiced so often they'd become habit. On identifying that probability pattern, I ran the scene forward and backward in my mind, focusing on her first few movements and looking for the trigger.

Aha—there it is.

Each time she chose that attack combination, I'd allowed the tip of my blade to drift left just a hair, leaving my right upper quadrant exposed. Each and every time I did, the valkyrie thrust high where my guard was weak, pressing her attack in a flurry of motion that left me playing catch up on every stroke and gradually losing ground until she scored a killing blow.

Now, I knew how to defeat her. She was quick, so my timing would have to be perfect to make my plan work.

We stared each other down like a couple of cowboys in an old spaghetti western flick. The valkyrie's piercing blue eyes met mine, and I couldn't help but give her a little wink. Her eyes narrowed and her forehead creased, signaling that I had goaded her into action, just as the events had played out in my mind's eye moments before.

She lunged at me without warning, covering a ten-foot distance in a single bounding step. As predicted, her first attack was a lunging thrust that revealed itself to be a feint at the apex of the movement, just after I committed to the parry. Seeing that I'd taken the bait, she pivoted on her lead foot, bringing the sword up and over her head for a short, quick, slashing attack at my neck. The movement was intended to be a killing blow, although I'd blocked it and a few others in every future scenario I'd seen.

But I had the upper hand now, because I knew what she was about to do. As she redirected her blade, spinning it around over her head toward my neck, I released my sword and burst forward, tapping my Fomorian speed to make my movement much more explosive. As our bodies collided, I grabbed her around the waist, clasping my hands behind her back just at the point where her floating ribs met her spine.

Then, I squeezed, using every bit of my Fomorian strength. First, I heard cartilage snap, then her ribs cracked, one after another. I continued to crush her, anaconda-like, pulling her spine toward me until she was bent backward over my arms in a grotesque imitation of a circus contortionist.

With my head tucked under her left armpit, I was too close for her to do much more than slap me on the back with her sword. That was the thing about longswords—they were great at long and middle range, but not so much in close. Not unless you reverted to half-swording, that is. Even then, your timing had to be perfect, else you would end up in a grapple with two hands on your sword while your opponent stuck a dagger in your gut.

The valkyrie struggled valiantly to escape the hold, but I wasn't having it. I spun and pivoted, lifting her overhead as I arched my back, driving her headfirst into the ground in a classic suplex. It was the type of attack that people didn't expect in a hand-to-hand fight, but one that was incredibly effective if you could pull it off without knocking yourself out.

I'd executed the move countless times in the gym, using a grappling dummy to get thousands of reps in on the mats, and dozens in sparring matches with live opponents. Thus, my form was perfect. The valkyrie's head collided with the rocky ground, my weight and our combined momentum serving to drive her at speed into the unforgiving surface of the Icelandic landscape.

On impact I felt her go limp, and that's when I pressed the attack. If I gave her any chance to recover, she'd most definitely pull a shorter weapon out of some pocket dimension and shove it in my back. I wrapped myself around her like a boa constrictor, using my jiu-jitsu training to transition my way to a full back mount. Once there, I sunk in a deep rear naked choke with my legs wrapped in a figure-four body lock around her waist.

It took no more than a second for my opponent to regain consciousness, but by that point, I was already choking the shit out of her. However, I'd failed to notice that she still held her sword. I watched over her shoulder as the valkyrie flipped her sword around, grabbing the blade with one hand

and one end of the cross guard with the other. Without a moment's hesitation, the shieldmaiden drove the tip of her sword through her stomach, out her back, and into my torso.

Okay, that's fucked up.

I'd been stabbed many times before, both in practice with Maureen and also in real-life battles. Yet seeing your opponent stab themselves through their own body in order to attack you was more than a little unnerving. And the pain was exquisite—first a sharp, piercing agony, and then a kind of dull ache accompanied by a nausea that I'd rarely felt outside of an all-night bender barhopping on Sixth Street.

Ignoring the throbbing torture in my gut, I squeezed even harder, cutting off all blood flow to the valkyrie's brain while producing a few pops and crackles from her cervical spine. She responded by using the cross guard of the sword to twist her blade, widening the wound in her abdomen and mine, and increasing my nausea and pain to levels I'd previously thought impossible.

I choked down some bile and tried to find my happy place as I squeezed her neck with renewed urgency. The valkyrie continued to grind and twist her sword, but with every motion, she was expending oxygen that she could not spare.

Meanwhile, the wound in my abdomen was leaking blood and other body fluids at a surprising rate. Hot liquid seeped out around me, soaking the rocky earth in a puddle beneath us both. I soon became weak with blood loss, and while the valkyrie was fading much quicker than me, I preferred to end the fight before it resulted in our mutual demise.

"Yield," I growled.

"Nay," she croaked back.

"Yield, or I'll snap your neck."

She considered it for a few moments, then with a hissing exhale that could have been a sigh, she relaxed and released her blade. "I yield, druid. You have proven yourself worthy of the Valkyries' assistance."

I pushed her off me, removing both her and her blade as a loud groan escaped my lips. Clamping both hands over my wound, I began shifting into my full Fomorian form just as things started going dark. Then, I blacked out.

2

I was only out for a moment, but it was enough to make me nervous, considering that the valkyrie was within striking distance and armed. As I recovered, she stood up and pulled her sword from her abdomen, a small grunt the only indication of her discomfort. She stood over me, watching me shift with a look of casual curiosity—the kind of look a child might give a bug before they burned it with a magnifying glass.

"You have jötunn blood," she remarked, her voice neutral.

"Fomorian," I rumbled, while the "other" part of my brain considered potential ways the valkyrie might attack, calculating various countermeasures on the fly. While I was fully in control of myself in this form, I thought more like a Fomori—and violence was always at the forefront of a Fomorian's mind.

"It is the same," she said with a hitch of her shoulders.

"All giantkind share similar ancestry. They came before the gods, you know."

"And, in every case, were conquered by them."

"I'm curious why you didn't assume that form for our battle," she asked, ignoring my comment.

Based on the tone of her voice and her seemingly casual indifference, I figured she was irritated that she'd lost to a human. No sense telling her I could partially shift —that info was need-to-know, as it provided me a distinct tactical advantage against supernatural creatures. I kept my deep, booming voice neutral as I replied.

"It takes too long to shift, so I would've needed advanced notice to do so. Besides, would you have respected me if I had?"

She pursed her lips, pausing for a moment before she replied. "Not as much. But we Valkyries are accustomed to fighting the jötnar. It would've mattered little to me either way."

Yep, she's pissed.

Already well on my way to being healed, I pushed myself to my feet. "Are we good? I'd prefer to have this conversation while in my human form, but if you're going to attack again..."

Her upper lip curled back in a sneer. "The Valkyries are of their word, druid. You will not be attacked—not by my kind, anyway. Take the form you wish."

I checked my abdomen to ensure that the wound had closed, probing it with my thick, calloused fingers. It was still tender, but it'd have to do. Seconds later, I'd shifted back to my human form, but my clothes were shredded. I took the time to change into a fresh outfit that I'd pulled from my Craneskin Bag while the valkyrie looked on

"You obviously know who I am. What's your name?"

"You may call me Gwen."

"Strange name for a valkyrie—I'd expected something with way too many consonants and syllables. But it fits, I guess." I laced my boots as we observed each other with the caution expected from two people who'd been trying to kill each other moments before. "Mind if I start a fire?"

She tsked. "If it suits you. I do not mind the cold."

Despite Iceland's valiant reforestation efforts, trees were a rare sight on the island, giving rise to the Icelandic saying, "Where there are three trees, you have a forest." For that reason, I'd taken to storing firewood in my Bag, which I resupplied from deadwood provided by the Grove. I pulled several foot-long pieces of split firewood from my Bag, arranging them in a teepee before lighting them with druidic magic.

"What else do you carry in that Bag?" she asked, a hint of amusement in her voice.

"Liquor, for one. Would you like a glass?"

She gave a single nod and grunt in reply, so I produced a bottle of Reykja Vodka—I called it "wreck ya'"—and a couple of glasses. I poured two fingers in a glass, handing it to her before I served my own.

After capping the bottle and nestling it between two stones, I took a seat on a small boulder, sipping my vodka as I eyed Gwen across the fire. She downed her glass and then gestured that I should pass her the bottle. I did so without remark.

"You drink like a little girl," she remarked.

"Maybe I like the taste."

"Then you should drink more of it," she stated, pouring her glass nearly to the rim. She took another healthy slug, topping her glass off before tossing the bottle back to me without bothering to replace the cap. I caught it one-handed, only slightly bobbling it before setting it down.

She chortled and shook her head. "You obviously are no good drinking companion. So, tell me what you need, druid, before I grow bored of your company."

Fucking Vikings.

I took a swig of vodka, swishing it around before swallowing so I could savor the light vanilla notes and peppery finish. Despite the quality of the liquor, it still burned as it went down. Warmth spread through my throat and chest as I considered how to broach the topic. Many failures and rejections had led me to this point, and I damned sure didn't want to blow it.

"I'm looking for someone," I said, deciding to take the direct approach. Considering Gwen's blunt manners and brusque temperament, it was probably my best bet. "A god, actually."

"One of ours?" she asked, her eyes narrowing.

"No. I'd rather avoid yours, if possible. I have enough problems with the Celtic pantheon as it is."

"Ah, you seek the Physician," she said as she scratched

her nose with a knuckle. "He was welcomed with open arms on his arrival, some centuries ago."

"Because you lack a god of healing," I observed.

"Eir used to serve in that capacity, but she is no more. And believe it or not, even gods require healing sometimes."

Sipping my drink, I stared into the fire. "As I'm aware. I understand Loki avails himself of Dian Cécht's services on occasion."

Gwen frowned, deeply. "We do not speak of that one. After being poisoned and weakened, he was banished here and cannot leave the island. Despite his diminished state, we Valkyries of the island find his presence to be quite —vexing."

"So, there is some truth to the legend. He really was chained to a rock—figuratively speaking, that is."

"Yes. Odin couldn't bear to see his son killed, despite his act of fratricide. While Baldur remains with Hel, we are left to contend with his murderer." She spat in the fire, causing it to flare briefly. "I'll not have anything to do with that one, but I will send one of my sisters to aid you in your search."

Gwen downed her glass and stood. I set my own glass down, following suit. "This is a matter of life and death, so your assistance is appreciated."

"Think nothing of it. We know that one of the Morrígna has set herself against you." She glared at the fire. "My sisters and I have no affection for those three. The one I send will arrange a meeting with the Physician. You have but to return to your camp and await her contact."

With a flash of lightning and a clap of thunder, she was gone.

"Fucking hell, woman!" Cursing both the valkyrie and the ringing in my ears, I sat by the fire and stealth-shifted, sipping vodka while I waited for my hearing to return.

Since trees were such a rarity on the island, it was a pain in the ass to hide a mature oak tree in Iceland. Of course, the Druid Oak's magic was such that people tended to overlook it when it was there and forget about it when it wasn't. That said, a gigantic fucking oak tree would stand out like a sore thumb in the mostly rocky and barren Highlands, so I'd decided to plant it among the wooded slopes of Öskjuhlíð.

Öskjuhlíð was a sort of local landmark in Reykjavik, a sixty-meter-tall, partially-wooded hill topped by a glass-domed edifice that contained a museum, a few restaurants, and a manmade ice cave. At first glance, it seemed to be the most convenient place in the city to plunk the Oak down. But in hindsight, I really wished I'd done more recon before I'd chosen that location for our home base.

The upside to locating there was that it was within walking distance to a great MMA gym and a geothermal beach, and only a mile or so from some of the best dining in the city. The downside was that it was a very popular destination for local hikers and mountain bikers. And apparently it was some sort of holy site for the huldufólk.

No matter where you go in the world, you'll find some

version of the fae. West Africa has the Aziza; in the east you have Yōkai, Mogwai, Peris, Tien, and Yaksha; Latin countries have Duende; while the Greeks have various creatures such as sylphs, nymphs, dryads, satyrs, and the like. Indonesians and Malaysians have the *orang bunian* and *orang halus*; the Maori have the Patupaiarehe; Slavic nations have Viya, Rusalka, and such; and Iceland has the huldufólk.

For the most part, the culture of the fae in each area directly reflects the culture of the local peoples. In less-developed areas, the fae tend to be closer to nature, while in more technologically-advanced nations, the Fair Folk tend to adopt more modern customs and appearances. But as for the huldufólk—well, they were a people with one foot in the present and two in the past. And they were hellaciously picky regarding places they'd claimed as their own territory.

I had no idea the can of worms I'd be opening when I planted the Druid Oak on that stupid hill. Over the years, Öskjuhlíð had been variably been used as a quarry, as a location for bunkers during WWII, and now as a recreation area and tourist trap. And as far as I could tell, the local fae had shown little interest in it prior to our arrival. But as soon as I'd decided to set up camp there, the fucking huldufólk had a conniption fit.

Click said they were just being territorial because they didn't like the idea of some Irish druid putting down roots on their island. I then pointed out that I wasn't Irish except by heredity, and that we were only passing through. His reply was something along the lines of, "Tell 'em that, lad, an' see if they care." Then, he disappeared and left me to deal with them.

Could I have moved the Oak? Sure, but the fuckers wouldn't give me a straight answer regarding where I might find a suitable temporary location. And then they'd started casting curses on us, petty shit like spells that would make your coffee go cold or untie your shoelaces at inconvenient times.

The huldufólk were a far cry from their Álfar ancestors, and they didn't have a lot of magic—they drove modern cars, for fuck's sake. Thus, it was nothing for me to set some wards that reflected their curses back at them. Even so, it hacked me off. I'd decided they were just being dicks, so I said "screw it" and kept the Oak where it was.

So, when I pulled into the museum parking lot at the top of the hill and saw a small contingent of huldufólk waiting for me, I wasn't surprised at all.

Like the fae back home, they looked just like humans at first glance, but anyone with a grain of magical talent would see them for what they were. Never mind that they were tall, model-thin, and supernaturally attractive with straight, coal-black hair that made them stand out from the locals like an ant in a sugar bowl. If the high fae back home were a bunch of self-important, pretentious pricks, the huldufólk were their bureaucratic, officious, meddlesome cousins from afar. And, personally, I could do without them both.

As I opened the door of my rented Land Cruiser, three tall, imperious figures hopped out of a white Škoda Octavia and marched right toward me, hemming me in.

It'd been a long drive back from the Highlands, so I was not in the mood for any bullshit. Even so, I pasted a smile on just to piss them off.

"Máni, Rós, Sigi," I said with a nod, purposely emphasizing a very American pronunciation of their names as I swung my door open and forced the trio to retreat a step. I exited the vehicle, speaking over my shoulder at them as I walked around the back to open the hatch. "To what do I owe the honor on this fine day?"

Máni spoke up first, straightening his light-gray tie, which had been elegantly matched to the charcoal business suit he wore. He looked a bit like Gavin Rossdale in *Constantine*, albeit with a prissier appearance. "Mr. McCool, as you know, you're encroaching on the sacred ancestral land of the huldufólk. You've been warned several times to move your abode—"

"The gall of him, using magic to accelerate the growth of a tree on our lands," Rós muttered behind him.

How someone could be both off-putting and attractive at the same time was beyond me, but the female fae somehow pulled it off. Dressed to the nines in a gray plaid Prada dress and matching double-breasted wool coat with black Louboutin block-heel boots, she looked the part of a European model. But her expensive cosmetics and 500-dollar haircut couldn't make up for the bitchy expression that seemed to permanently mar her fine elfin features.

Máni gave her a sharp look over his shoulder before continuing. "Ahem. As I was saying, you have been warned—"

"Many times!" Sigi chimed in, his mousy hipster

mustache and beard all aquiver as he emphasized his displeasure by shaking his head vigorously. He was the sole slob among them, dressed as he was in gray hiking pants, a grayish knit wool sweater, and an almost black all-weather outdoor jacket. Salewa hiking boots completed his ensemble, making him look like a reject from an REI catalog.

Their nominal leader cleared his throat loudly, looking back over his shoulder. "Do you mind?"

Oblivious to their mutual faux pas, the two shook their heads. "No, do carry on," Rós said.

"Indeed," added Sigi.

"Your shoes are untied," I added, glancing down at their feet.

To his credit, Máni managed to continue with nary a hitch. "And after being warned of your trespass and the consequences, you were given a deadline for removal of said abode—"

"Which he ignored," Rós interjected.

"Numerous times," Sigi added as he knelt to tie his laces.

"—which you ignored, numerous times," Máni finished with a straight face.

"Tell him about the invasive species!" Sigi said apoplectically.

Máni blinked several times as he released a short, frustrated sigh. "I was just about to get to that." Gathering his composure, he pulled out a piece of legal paper, scanning it perfunctorily as he continued. "Additionally, we have found your oak tree to be an invasive species, in violation of HC 6.253.1, subsection 84.11: 'Invasive species prohibited to be used as domiciles by non-native wizards, sorcerers, magicians, witches, warlocks, and enchantresses.'"

"Well, then I've done nothing wrong," I said. "I'm a druid."

"A magic-using druid!" Rós shrieked.

I slammed the hatch closed and turned on the trio, with Dyrnwyn sheathed in one hand and a foot-long birch twig in the other. On seeing the stick, the three of them stepped back with a collective gasp, their skin turning just a bit paler at the sight. It took everything I had to resist cracking up as I observed the looks of distaste and horror on their faces.

The length of birch was just a bit of trash I'd found in the woods. After I learned that the huldufólk knew little of druidry, I'd carved some meaningless symbols in it and started carrying it around with me. They, of course, assumed it to be my magic wand, and since their curses had bounced right off me, they also assumed that I was a force to be reckoned with. All I knew was, pulling out that stick in front of them was always good for a laugh.

"Take it up with the Valkyries if you don't like me being here," I said, pushing my way past them as I headed for the woods.

"The Valkyries?" Máni asked.

"Yeah, Gwen was her name, I believe. Just had a meeting with her, and she's sending a rep to help me out."

"Oh dear," Rós said.

"They stick their noses in everything," Sigi hissed.

"B-b-but—" Máni stammered. "They have no right to interfere with huldufólk business!"

"I'll be sure to pass that along," I said as I twirled the birch "wand" in their general direction over my shoulder. As soon as I entered the tree line, I stole a quick backward glance, smiling with satisfaction as I watched them scrambling for the safety of their vehicle.

"You haven't heard the last of this," Máni yelled from the window of the Škoda as he peeled rubber out of the parking lot.

With a chuckle, I tucked the stick and Dyrnwyn into my Craneskin Bag. "Morons."

Once inside the Grove, I did a quick scan to see if Click was present; he wasn't, of course. Admittedly, I enjoyed the peace and quiet when he was gone, but I wasn't necessarily certain that being alone was good for me at the moment.

Roscoe and Rufus greeted me soon after I arrived, not a bit unsettled at the fact that I'd more or less appeared out of thin air. I'd brought the dogs along with us for several reasons, one being that I was worried they'd be neglected in my absence. Being half-fae, Maureen didn't enjoy being in the junkyard proper. While the touch of ferric metals wouldn't outright harm her, she found all that iron and steel unsettling and therefore preferred to stay in the office whenever possible.

Rather than burden her with their care, I'd had the Oak retrieve the pair shortly after we arrived in Iceland.

And a good thing, too. Click might've been an excellent, if unconventional, magic tutor, but the immortal magician was a horrible companion. Without the dogs for company, I'd be almost completely alone.

Unlike Finnegas, who'd chosen to retain much of his humanity in lieu of gaining true immortality, Click had gone the full monty. And while godhood had its privileges —and advantages—choosing immortality meant losing that certain *je ne sais quoi* that provided mortals with their most human characteristics. Empathy, patience, and even common courtesy were qualities that Click had in short supply. And while he was never intentionally malicious, over time I'd discovered I could only take his quirky, unpredictable personality in small doses.

In short, I missed Finnegas.

Taking a deep, shaky breath, I meandered over to where my mentor lay with Rufus at my heels. Roscoe, on the other hand, let out a low whine before laying down on the soft grass, his head resting on his paws as he watched us from a distance. From the very start, the dog hadn't been comfortable seeing the old man in his current state. I didn't blame him.

I'd not been able to remove Finnegas from St. Germain's coffin, even though I found it morbid and disrespectful to leave him there. Moving him would require breaking the stasis field I'd placed him in, and that was something I wasn't willing to risk, even for a few seconds. So, I'd set the coffin under a large maple tree, arranged and angled to ensure he got just the right amount of light and shade each day.

Of course, in his current state, comfort mattered little to the old druid, considering that he'd been comatose before I cast the stasis spell. Besides, any sunlight that entered the stasis field would take days to reach his skin, and his day and night cycles inside the bubble were so slow as to be nonexistent. But tending to him made me feel better, so I did it anyway.

As always, on approaching the coffin I scrutinized his face and expression, searching in vain for some sign of improvement—and, if I were being honest, to make sure he was still alive. That he wasn't dead was a fact I knew empirically, because I'd instructed the Grove to monitor the old man's condition. Through my connection to the Grove, I'd determined that his heart beat at the ponderously slow pace of one contraction every few weeks. The Grove also informed me that his cells still contained life, although he'd suffered quite a lot of brain damage in the areas affected by the stroke.

I knew all these things, but knowing the facts made it no easier to observe him in his current state. His complexion was pale as ever, save for the color that had returned to his cheeks after I'd tried healing him with water from Fionn's hand. The fingers of his left hand were curled, claw-like, his arm drawn to his side as if he were guarding against a blow. And the left side of his mouth still drooped, a sign of damage to the right motor cortex—or so the Internet had said.

He looked so frail, helpless even. Months ago, the man had been vibrant and relatively healthy, even while entering the final years of his life. Those memories made it hard now to accept his current state. How could I reconcile the defenseless, infirm figure who lay before me with the man who'd been my rock for so many years?

It was an impossible task. Finnegas was like a father to me, filling the void that had been left after my dad had been taken from me. Losing one father had been painful enough.

A reality that was even more difficult to face was the looming threat of failure in completing my task. I'd sworn to find someone to heal the old man, yet we'd been on this island for six months with nothing to show for it. I was starting to doubt that we'd ever find Dian Cécht, even with the Valkyries' help. Weeks prior, I'd suggested to Click that we approach one of the other gods of healing for help.

"Nay, lad—we'd never get it," was his reply. "Even if one were willin' ta' help, the tasks they'd set ta' us and the debt we'd owe'd be so great, it'd likely defeat the purpose o' askin' in the first place. Best we stick wit' the god we know, who were ever a friend ta' Finn Eces, and unlikely ta' turn him away in his time o' need."

In other words, the gods generally didn't mix well with those from other pantheons, except in the case of the tricksters. Apparently, those fuckers got along famously—even to the point of helping each other plan schemes to hatch on their unsuspecting fellow deities. Or, on humankind.

After making sure for the thousandth time that Finnegas' condition was, if not improving, at least not worsening, I plopped down next to him under the maple tree. Exhaling heavily, I leaned back against the massive trunk, staring at the verdant beauty of the Grove's interior while not enjoying a bit of it. Rufus laid down beside me, resting his head in my lap with a small whine of shared despondence.

I scratched him behind his ear, grateful for his presence. "I know, boy. I don't know what I'm going to do if we lose him, either."

3

I fell asleep under the maple tree, but it was a fitful, restless sleep. I awoke hours later to the sight of Click standing over me with his hands on his knees, staring at me like a cow at a new gate.

"Ya' talk in yer sleep."

I rubbed my eyes, yawning as I stretched.

"An' yer breath stinks," he added, waving his hand in front of his nose.

"If you don't like the show, change the channel," I said as I began to work the kinks out of my neck.

Click's presence meant it was time to train, so I immediately went into my warm-up routine, a series of yoga poses and druidic breathing exercises. The semi-immortal magician looked on as I completed the sequence of movements, never showing the least bit of impatience. Time was irrelevant to a chronomancer of his caliber, all the more so considering we were inside the Grove.

"Click, I'm curious about something," I said as I flowed

from downward dog into upward dog, and then into child's pose.

"Yes, lad?"

"Do any of the gods know time magic?"

"Aye, plenty can look forwards an' backwards in time. And a few are capable o' walking the Twisted Paths. Chronos, fer' instance. But none do so. Too dangerous."

"Except for you," I remarked, standing to transition into warrior's pose.

"Ah," he said, holding his index finger aloft, "but I'm no god."

"As you keep saying. But from where I stand, you're the closest thing to a deity from one of the pantheons."

"Gods require worshippers, lad. An' ya' hafta be a first-class horse's ass ta' set oneself up ta' be worshipped, tradin' minor magical favors in exchange fer' the adulation o' the masses. When all is said an' done, I'm jest a magician who stole some o' their tricks."

I clucked my tongue. "Please. You think I haven't figured out that you're the goblins' great and mighty clown god?"

The quasi-god affected a pose of mock indignation, drawing himself erect as he clutched at an imaginary string of pearls. "I'll not stand here an' be accused o' such chicanery by the likes o' ye, lad." He paused with a hint of a smile tugging at the corner of his mouth. "An', theoretically, if I did pose as a minor, obscure deity in such manner as ta' gain the worship o' the goblin clans, I can assure ya' it was merely fer' laughs an' nothin' more."

"Theoretically speaking, of course," I said with a smug grin as I arched backwards into reverse warrior.

"Eggs-zactly," he replied with a wink "Now, are ya' done wit' yer' cat stretches an' ready ta' train?"

"Just a sec'," I said, sneaking behind a red alder tree to take a leak. Then, I walked over to a nearby stream, kneeling to wash my hands and take a few gulps of clear, pure water. Drying my hands on my shirt, I stood. "Alright, now I'm ready."

The magician formerly known as Gwydion looked at me askance. "If ye'd let me show ya' the ways o' immortality, ye'd never have need ta' do such things again."

"As I've said many times, Click, I rather enjoy the human rituals of elimination and taking sustenance. And living for thousands of years doesn't interest me all that much."

"Ya' could be like me, ya' know—ya' have it in ya', lad."

I laughed. "Click, I've hardly mastered the first circle of chronomancy spells. Why you think I'm capable of becoming the next Gwydion is beyond me. But no matter your opinion, the answer is still no."

He frowned and shrugged. "Lemme know if ya' change yer' mind."

"You bet. Shall we get started?"

"O' course." Click snapped his fingers, and suddenly we were no longer in the Grove. Instead of the lush green interior of my sentient pocket dimension, we stood in a scene straight out of Heinlein.

The first thing I noticed was the harsh, hilly landscape, painted in red and black as far as the eye could see.

Obsidian crystalline shards thrust up from the earth in random patterns, like large ebony knives. In places where the red dusty soil clung to those structures, it gave them the appearance of sharp, bloody teeth.

There were mountains in the distance, also ochre red, with black dots that I assumed were the same irregular rocky protuberances that jutted up from the ground all around. On closer inspection, I noticed that smaller shards of the black crystalline substance were scattered everywhere, mixed in with the fine, sandy soil. On a whim, I scuffed the dirt beneath my feet, kicking up a puff of fine red dust that hung in the air like smoke.

"Where are we?" I asked.

"One o' the worlds the Great Race o' Yith destroyed, eons ago. Not even in the same reality, in fact. The fookers fought a war that killed this world, then they cut a rift into our own, castin' their minds forth ta' escape the destruction they'd left behind."

I scanned all around, awestruck. The landscape was completely alien, yet it also felt somehow familiar. Click had taken me to some odd places to train, but never to a place so foreign and un-Earth like. The light was wrong somehow, and what I had thought to be a stormhead in the distance was actually the sky above the horizon.

Spinning slowly in a circle, I made out a dense band of darkness that seemed to hug the edges of the planet where the land met the sky. Then, I craned my neck to look up. Directly above us, that blackness thinned out, allowing a view of the stars overhead. They were also completely unfamiliar, arranged in constellations I did not recognize.

Based on previous such "outings" with Click, I cast a cantrip that allowed me to see the world in the magical spectrum. There was magic here, tons of it, but it was tainted somehow. Also, there was a thirty-foot domed shield surrounding us that had the quasi-god's magical signature all over it.

"Was it a civil war?" I asked, genuinely curious.

"Not exactly." He held a hand up to his ear. "Speakin' o' which, the subject o' today's lesson approaches. By-the-by, air's not fit ta' breathe, lad—leastwise, not in yer current state. I'll be back in about an hour, more or less. Have fun meetin' the locals."

"Click, wait!"

The fucker snapped his fingers and vanished, taking the atmospheric bubble he'd apparently cast along with him. My mouth and throat began to burn, making me wheeze and gag with every inhalation.

Son of a bitch.

Initiating a full shift, I held my breath and strained to detect whatever it was that my substitute magic tutor had brought me here to face. Off in the distance, I heard something approaching. And whatever it was, it was huge.

As I shifted, I turned to face the coming danger. Of course, I didn't empirically know that something dangerous approached, but it was a given considering who'd brought me here. Click's lessons nearly always involved a perilous encounter with some strange new environment or creature. He was the sort of teacher who believed in trial by fire, basing his approach on the assumption that impending doom could spur instinctive leaps in a student's magical ability.

That would've been fine if I had a decent grasp of time magic, or if I was even half the magician he was. Druidry was nature magic, and it worked best on Earth and in dimensions that were modeled after it. However, most of the locations where our lessons took place were so exotic that they made the magic I'd learned from Finnegas nearly useless.

Given enough time to acclimate, I could use the principles of druidic magic to adapt to any environment. Ironically, Click always structured my lessons to ensure I was never afforded that luxury. Clearly, his intent was to force me into situations where I had to use the arts he was teaching me—chronomancy and chronourgy.

Chronomancy was the easier of the two to use, as it was a form of divination. The art simply involved looking ahead into potential alternate futures, scanning probabilities to determine which "fork" had the greatest possibility of occurring. It took skill, certainly, but not a great deal of effort, especially if a chronomancer only looked a short time into the future. However, anything beyond a few minutes involved scanning so many probability branches that only the most skilled chronomancers could know what might happen days, weeks, or months in advance.

Chronourgy was the greater challenge by far, as it involved the actual manipulation of time. All magic defied nature's laws to an extent, even druidic magic, and it required a certain strength of will to perform. Yet wielding the elements and influencing the forces of nature was nothing compared to manipulating time.

All these things ran through my mind as those ponderous, ground-shaking footsteps grew nearer. I was only halfway through a full shift when the creature's footsteps came to a halt maybe thirty yards away, in the direction of a large hill topped with a cluster of those strange shard-like structures. Whatever it was, it had chosen to remain hidden, but I had the distinct sensation that I was being watched.

No matter how many times I shifted, it was always agony, as it required a complete muscular and skeletal restructuring of my body. Adding several hundred pounds of mass along with several feet in height and girth to my lean six-foot-one frame was no walk in the park. Every single time, my skin would split and my muscles would tear away from my bones, reattaching and mending even as they grew denser and more resistant to damage. The pain was excruciating, yet I kept my eyes on the hill as I focused on speeding up my trans-formation.

Considering the furtive nature of whatever stalked me, I'd expected to catch just a glimpse of it—maybe a head popping out from behind the rock, or an eyestalk for that matter. So, when a sixteen-foot tall, black-furred, gorilla-looking thing came running out from cover, I nearly shat myself. It was an absolutely terrifying creature to behold—muscular and hairy like an ape, but with huge dinosaur-like feet and arms that forked at the elbow, resulting in upper appendages that had two muscular forearms and matching clawed hands on each.

Yet those features paled in comparison to the absolutely freakish and utterly grotesque appearance of its head and face. For one, its skull was shaped all wrong, almost like it had grown upside down atop its neck. Pink eyes set on short, bony protrusions stared at me from where its ears should be, and it lacked a jaw entirely, instead displaying a huge mouth that split its skull cap vertically down the middle. When it opened that orifice to reveal a double-row of razor-sharp teeth, I found myself wishing I'd skipped today's lesson.

The thing was coming at me with a speed that contradicted its size, halving the distance between us in a few short seconds. It'd easily reach me while I was still in the midst of my transformation, and while I'd been known to fight in that state, I doubted my chances in doing so against this creature. Thus, I'd need to improvise a strategy that would give me enough time to complete my shift.

A dozen different spells and tactics ran through my mind in an instant. Druidry was out of the question, since I'd had little time to adjust to the strange, eldritch magic of this planet. Besides, Click had obviously left me in this situation to force me to use time magic, and since he was much better at chronomancy, I could only assume that was my best option. A stasis spell would work, but it was hard to cast on a fast-moving target.

By the time I'd worked through that conundrum, the creature was only a handful of footfalls away. I needed to do something, and fast, else I was going to end up in that big hairy fucker's belly. On instinct, I was reminded of the "magic bubble" that Click had cast around us when we first appeared on this plane. That spherical shape had obviously been designed to keep the toxic atmosphere out —could I use it to trap something coming at me as well?

I'd never cast a mass stasis spell, and the largest stasis field I'd ever pulled off was the one that was currently keeping Finnegas alive. That was because the difficulty in casting such spells was directly proportionate to the volume of space affected. Volume was the greatest limiting factor to using time magic; the more matter you attempted to affect, the greater the resistance. Which meant that, in theory, if the volume of the stasis field did not exceed my abilities, the *shape* of the field didn't matter.

The giant four-forearmed ape-thing was almost on me. *No time to think, Colin—just act.*

I exerted my will, perfectly envisioning the shape I wished the stasis field to take. Then, I released the spell. The configuration I'd settled on was a hollow dome approximately fifteen feet across and three inches thick. The construct itself had a rather large surface area, but a relatively small internal volume in comparison to the area it could potentially affect, so it actually wasn't all that hard to cast.

Now, let's see if it works.

The magical effect that I called a stasis field actually wasn't, because stasis fields didn't completely halt time.

Instead, the spell slowed time drastically within the affected area. So, when the giant space gorilla hit the field, nearly all forward momentum halted for the parts of its body that had entered my spell's area of effect.

However, the rest of its body kept moving forward. This caused a rapid and rather spectacular deceleration of the space ape's body, almost as if it had hit a brick wall. The parts of its body that had come into contact with the spell became stuck like a bug in a glue trap. Even better, the more it struggled, the greater the surface area that came into contact with the stasis field, and the more the creature became entangled.

In awe of my own ingenuity, I finished transforming and watched in complete and utter fascination while the creature tried to free itself. As the great beast struggled, opening its misshapen mouth wide to release silent screams of frustration, it occurred to me that the spell had a great many applications. Essentially it worked like a force field, which was kind of like the holy grail of defensive spells.

In druidry, we manipulated physical matter to form protective barriers, but that approach was cumbersome at best. And in standard wizardry, a spell caster could use wards to create a force-field-like effect, but it took a great deal of time to draw the glyphs and symbols necessary, and it wasn't something you could do on the fly. Not to mention powering them up and imbuing them with enough magic to function. Even then, your wards had to be tuned specifically to repel whatever you wanted to keep out, which was another limiting factor to such spellwork.

Thus, effective force field creation was a magical conundrum that had baffled magicians for centuries. In fact, the problem had eventually been named after a famous theurgist who'd spent most of his life trying to solve it—Julian's Enigma. And I had just solved Julian's Enigma.

So, what am I going to call my spell? A stasis barrier? Stasis blockade? Stasis fence? Stasis wall? Hmm... field, shield. Stasis shield. Yeah, that works.

The more I thought about it, the more I realized that I'd created the perfect defensive spell. The only real drawback was that it required the use of time magic, so it wasn't something I could use in front of witnesses. At least, not if I didn't want to be hunted by the gods and demigods of every single pantheon in existence. Meaning, I could never let the world know that I'd just solved one of the greatest challenges ever known to defensive magic users.

Well, shit.

Still, it was one of those spells that I could always pull out of my ass if I got in a bind. But I could worry about that another day. Right now, I needed to decide what I was going to do with Magilla.

Although I could breathe the planet's harsh atmosphere just fine in my Fomorian form, I didn't have a lot of room to move inside my stasis sphere. If I wanted to get out of here, I'd need to drop the spell and fight the beast. I was almost ready to do just that when a dozen more of the giant gorilla thingies showed up to help their friend.

A couple of them tried pulling their friend out of the

stasis field, nearly ripping one of his arms off in the process. Then, they started throwing those black shards at me with deadly precision. Based on the speed with which they were able to throw them and the placement of said shards when they hit my stasis shield, I had no doubt that I'd play hell if I had to tangle with them.

Fighting a baker's dozen of those big hairy sasquatch-looking things sounded like a lot more work than I was willing to take on at the moment. After all, I'd already learned something new—why put myself out unnecessarily? So, I sat cross-legged in the dirt and began to meditate, eyes open so I could monitor the threat in front of me.

4

Click showed up an hour or so later, appearing inside my stasis shield as if he'd known exactly where I'd be at that moment. Of course, he pretty much did, within certain limits of probability. Then again, there was also a chance that I'd be dead when he returned, and that he'd have found me roasting on a spit over Magilla's campfire.

Each time Click placed me in mortal danger for the sake of these "lessons," I tried not to think about how he'd likely witnessed all the gruesome ways I might die, well in advance of said peril. And I ignored the fact that he had weighed the potential risks and benefits of each dicey encounter, sifting the threads of my existence like so much sand in the name of my education as a mage and druid. Or, as he liked to put it, to transform me into "a druid, most arcane."

I set those thoughts aside after he appeared. Else I might attempt to strangle him, and frankly there was no way I could take the guy—Fomorian form or no. Meanwhile, he glanced this way and that, hands clasped behind his back like a math teacher searching for an error in his student's work.

"Ahem," I said, gesturing at my stasis shield. "You're not even going to comment on the fact that I solved Julian's Enigma?"

Click waved my question off, replying with indifference in his voice. "Pfah. I solved that problem 900 years ago. Was curious if ye'd do the same. Surprised ya' made the field so thick. Works just as well with a fraction o' the volume." He frowned as he peered at my work. "Sloppy, but I s'pose it'll do."

"Whatever," I huffed.

Truth be told, I was hacked that I wasn't the first to solve the problem. I thought I deserved some recognition, considering that I'd only started learning time magic a few months ago. Or years, depending on how you measured such things.

"Ya' sound a bit miffed, lad. Did I say somethin' ta' offend ya'?" Click asked as he made faces at Magilla through my stasis shield.

"Well, yeah. What is it with you immortals and the grudging praise? Finnegas is the same way—getting even the slightest nod of approval from the guy is like pulling teeth. I mean, by the time you solved Julian's Enigma, you had, what—a couple of millennia under your belt as a chronourgist? I've been at this only a fraction of that, at most."

"Beginner's luck, no more," he said with a shrug, turning his head this way and that as he examined Magilla. Meanwhile, the space apes were going, well, ape-shit on the other side of the barrier. "Do ya' think they stand on their hands ta' eat? Or do they take turns tossin' food at each other's noggins?"

It suddenly occurred to me that the immortal magician was acting very nonchalant considering the feat I'd just pulled off. I snapped my massive fingers, producing a sound not unlike a gunshot—more than loud enough to startle Click.

"You're jealous!" I exclaimed.

Click stuck his thumbs in his ears, waggling his fingers as he gave Magilla the raspberries. "Nonsense, lad, nonsense."

There was a hint of irritation in his voice, a tautness I hadn't noticed before. "Yep, you're definitely upset I was able to pull off that spell."

"Doesn't take much effort," he replied, feigning indifference as he mimicked the space ape's facial expressions, which was quite a feat considering their anatomical differences. "Just a bit o' ingenuity."

"Was that a compliment I just heard?" I asked, grinning smugly.

The magician formerly known as Gwydion threw his hands up in the air as he turned on me. "Fine, yer a feckin' prodigy, ya' little prick puddin'! Is that what'cha wanted ta' hear? Took me damned near a century to learn how ta' cast simple stasis fields, never mind this construct ya' pulled out'cher arse. Outdone by a feckin' upstart *twpsyn*. Unfeckin' believable."

I wiped the smug smile off my face, partially because I knew it looked hideous when I smiled in this form. "Well, I had an excellent teacher," I said, perfectly serious.

Click blew a stray lock of hair out of his eyes, crossing his arms over his chest. "Stop blowin' smoke up me backside and let's get ya' back ta' yer' damned tree, afore I blow a feckin' fuse."

"Ready when you are, chief."

He waved at the space apes, who were beating their chests and hammering the ground outside the shield. The ones who weren't entangled, that is. "Alright, then drop this shield so's we can get outta here."

"Uh-uh, no dice. The state you're in, you'll leave me here to fight those things."

He arched an eyebrow at me. "It's a stasis field, lad. Magic's stable as a horse's hard cock once it's cast. Ye'll be leavin' these poor beasts ta' suffer 'til they perish o' old age. That is, if those other fellows don't abandon 'em an' let 'em starve."

I thought about it for a moment, rubbing my chin absently as I examined my spell work. It was time magic, after all, and there was no reason why I couldn't add a few weaves here and there to place an expiration date on the spell. I worked through the necessary adjustments in my head then made a series of arcane gestures, mumbling under my breath as I modified the spell. If my calculations were correct, the shield would now dissipate in an hour or so.

"There, that should do it," I said, rubbing my hands together as I glanced at Click.

The magician glared at my shield, tensing his shoulders and arms until he shook. His hands curled into fists, and he sputtered a few unintelligible syllables before releasing a string of Welsh curse words in a tone that could curdle milk. The next thing I knew, I was back in the Grove, and Click was nowhere to be found.

"So, same time tomorrow?" I yelled, only to be answered by another string of curses that faded off into silence.

No sooner had I dozed off to sleep in my Keebler cottage than the Oak sent me an urgent message that roused me awake. It was an image of three large wolves prowling the woods at night. Something dangerous was stalking around near the Oak, Earthside.

The Oak and Grove each spoke telepathically to me through our bond, using images to convey meaning and intent. At first, it had been difficult to interpret their unique method of communication, but I'd learned how to decipher their messages. Time moved differently here, and by now, I'd spent enough time inside the Grove communicating with them to learn their moods—and, to some extent, their personalities.

Although the two had been created from the same magic acorn at the same time, they were two separate entities. I'd begun to see them as brother and sister, the Oak the masculine sibling and the Grove the more feminine of the two. Regardless of the existential nature of the pair, it was clear they were two halves of the same coin. Therefore, any attack on the Oak was an attack on the Grove, and vice-versa.

So, when the Grove sent me an image of an oak tree on fire, I knew that serious trouble was brewing. The two were quite protective of each other, likely because one could not survive without the other. Perhaps their bond went deeper than mere survival, but I wasn't enough of a druid yet to sort out the emotional motivations of a tree. But it was obvious that something had the Grove in a tissy, and it wanted me to intervene without question.

I bolted out of bed, searching for my Craneskin Bag, only to realize it had been strapped over my shoulder the entire time. The thing had a mind of its own, and while it wasn't as intelligent as the Oak and Grove, it tended to respond to my needs and relocate itself accordingly. Instinctively, I reached for my pants and boots, then I thought better of it.

Something tells me this is going to get ugly. Best I go out prepared—no need for a repeat of the fight with the valkyrie.

As I exited the cottage, I pulled the strap over my head, leaving the Bag slung over one shoulder only so it wouldn't break when I shifted. Based on the messages I was getting from the Oak, the danger seemed to be imminent and not immediate, which meant I had time for a full-fledged transformation. Once I was in my full Fomorian form, I reached into my Bag and rummaged around for a few seconds until I found what I wanted.

With a heavy sigh, I pulled Tethra's greatsword from the Bag.

"Oh, there you are, master!" the sword said in a voice that sounded very, very similar to a certain overly-talkative gold android. "I've been eagerly looking forward to the moment when you'd pull me from that dark, dreary sack. Speaking of which, I never did finish telling you about the time Tethra defeated a whole squad of Tuath Dé..."

After slaying the sword's former master, I'd snagged the massive weapon as a bit of war booty. It had been made for a Fomorian's hands, forged in proportions suitable for a twelve-foot-tall giant. While my massive mitts were a bit more misshapen than Tethra's had been, from the moment I'd grabbed the sword, it felt as though it had been tailor-made for my Hyde-side to wield.

Obviously, the greatsword was a sentient object, capable of speech, but with an unfortunate and peculiar quirk. For some strange reason, its maker had placed a geas on it that compelled it to recite the deeds of its former owner after said person had died in battle. Little did I know that I'd trigger it the first time I swung it around, else I'd have left it in my Bag and never touched the damned thing again.

As for how it had learned English, the sword claimed it had been enchanted with the ability to learn its owner's language via osmosis. Why it spoke in an effete pan-British accent was beyond me, although I suspected it had picked it up from my subconscious mind. I'd repeatedly asked it to drop the accent, to which the sword had repeatedly replied, "What accent, master?"

Finally, I'd given up and resolved to only bring it out in emergencies.

With an annoyed hiss, I cut the sword off mid-sentence. "Another time, alright, Orna? Right now, I need you to be quiet. Something is stalking around outside the Oak, and I don't want to give away my position before I know what it is."

Orna replied in a stage whisper. "Certainly, master—mum's the word!"

Once I was fairly certain the sword would be quiet for the next few minutes—it had a short memory, after all—I cast a chameleon spell on myself. Then, I instructed the Oak to send me Earthside so I could see what the hell had the Grove in such a fuss.

———

When I arrived outside, the forest was on fire. It didn't take long to determine the source, as three *eldjötnar*—fire giants—were waging war on my druid oak.

Fucking giants. I hate giants.

I had my reasons for avoiding giantkind—besides getting clobbered by a twelve-foot-tall redneck Viking with a penchant for human and fae flesh.

Reason number one? They were heartless, conniving, murderous, cannibalistic monsters, every last one. To say they were nasty and cruel would be too generous, as their reputation for filling their pots with innocent humans and fae was well-deserved. Not that there *were* innocent fae, but it was still pretty messed up that giants ate other intelligent supernatural species.

Plus, fighting the bastards always brought back painful memories that I'd just as soon forget—and taking on Crowley's *fachen* was one such experience. Fachen are brutish giants out of Celtic folklore that have just one arm and one leg. While a person might think such a creature would be for shit in a fight, that would be a mistake.

A single fachen could fell an entire forest in a night, or so the legends said. Certainly, the one I fought would've killed me if my Hyde-side hadn't emerged to take care of business. Unfortunately, that victory had cost me dearly, and everything that followed after that was a complete and total shit show.

Yeah—if I had to do it over again, I'd skip that night entirely.

Then, there was Elmo, the ogre with a heart of gold. Most people wouldn't know that ogres weren't truly related to giants, as they were almost as large and just as ugly. But size and looks notwithstanding, the guy had been nothing like the bloodthirsty creatures of lore.

Elmo was the epitome of the term "gentle giant," and in the brief time I'd known him, I'd been proud to call him a friend. Sadly, he'd been the lone witness to a brutal murder, and the killer then murdered the ogre in order to cover his tracks. Eventually, I'd avenged Elmo by taking down the person who murdered him, but I still blamed myself for not preventing his death in the first place.

Despite the guilt I felt over Elmo's passing, my most

painful giant-related memory was the time my best friend
Hemi died while fighting a giant during our trip to Underhill. The bastard pulled Hemi off a cliff, and the big Maori
later died in my arms. Even though Hemi's mom had resur-
rected him, it wasn't an experience I cared to dredge up.

As for these brutes, they looked just like the legends
depicted. They were roughly twelve to fifteen feet tall, with
clawed fingers and long, tusk-like lower canines sticking
out of their mouths over their thick, unruly facial hair. One
of them had two heads—he was the largest and ugliest—
and each giant wore iron scale-mail that glowed a dull
orange against their hot, red skin. Their lower halves were
covered in leather cingulum, made from some unknown
material that didn't catch fire despite the heat they put off.

The two smaller giants each wielded large double-
bitted battle axes, while their leader had a sword strapped
to his waist. He was busy tossing fireballs at my Oak as the
two smaller giants hacked and chopped at the many large,
thorny vines that whipped at them from the forest floor.
The Oak was doing a fair job of blocking the leader's
attacks by curling its vines into large, circular shields,
which it moved to intercept each fiery attack. And each
time it did, the vines burst into flames, disintegrating into
ash seconds after making contact with the giant's spells.

Clearly, the tree was fighting a losing battle, as the
giant could toss magical fire just as quickly as my Oak
could deflect it. However, the entire forest was on fire, and
soon the flames would reach my tree. It could portal away,
but I'd instructed the Oak to avoid doing so to prevent the
Celtic gods from finding us.

I doubted that Badb and her compatriots would be welcomed on the Norse gods' turf, but they might ask for special dispensation to hunt us down. And Odin or some other Norse deity might give it, just to see what happened. The gods were fickle like that. But I couldn't let my tree get burned down, so I did what I had to do—I told it to get lost while I dealt with the fire giants.

One second the tree was there, and the next it was not. Meanwhile, my chameleon spell was still active, but it was damned hard for a ten-foot tall Fomorian to move silently through woods this thick. I decided to stay put and wait for an opportunity to cut them all down with Orna before they knew I was there. But before I could make my move, the larger giant began scanning the area with his piggy little orange eyes. One of his heads turned my way, and he fixed his gaze on me like he knew I was there.

"I can see you, druid. Your magicks do not fool Fritjof Hálogison," the large giant's left head said with a faint Scandinavian accent. He spat black phlegm on the ground, where it sizzled before sparking another small fire. "We were told that an attack on the tree would draw you out. The álfar were right."

Fucking huldufólk—I should've known. I'm going to wring Máni's neck when I see him.

The time for subterfuge was over, so I dropped the spell. "Listen here, Fritz—"

"Fritjof," the right head interjected in a slightly deeper voice. "Bah, I should not expect an American to pronounce our names correctly."

"Whatever. You attacked my Oak, and frankly, that pisses me off."

"Who's Frank Lee?" asked one of the smaller giants in a gruff, yet feminine, voice.

"He said, 'frankly,' Tove," the other flunkie said. He was the most human-looking of the three, and if it weren't for his size—as well as a double-row of teeth and six-fingered hands—he could've easily passed for normal. "It's like saying 'honestly' or 'candidly,' you see."

"Then why'd he not say that?" she asked, clearly confused. "Why use such obscure language in conversation with non-native speakers?"

"Seriously, *that's* your beef?" I shook my head as I turned to address their leader again. "Like I was saying, you attacked my tree. Speaking of which, how the hell did you find it?"

"The álfar who hired us told us they suspected you lived in a tree here in their woods," the leader's right head replied. "I was around when your kind ruled Írland, and I know about your druid groves. So, I simply started throwing fireballs until your magic oak reacted."

"Well, shit," I replied, scratching my head. "That was smart, in a way, but stupid too."

"How so?" his left head asked.

"Because now I really can't let you leave. Or live, for that matter."

He laughed, holding his stomach with both hands for effect. "Little jötunn, do you really think you can kill all three of us?"

I lifted Orna in my right hand, pointing it at his face. "Only one way to find out."

Both of Fritjof's heads gave me big, snaggle-toothed grins. "I had hoped you would stand and fight instead of run." He drew his sword in one hand and summoned a trio of bowling-ball-sized fireballs above the other. "Say your prayers, druid, for you go to meet your ancestors this night."

5

"Oh, shut up and fight already," I growled as I charged the nearest giant.

Part of my druid hunter training was learning virtually every practical martial art I could, and one of the arts I took was krav maga. "Krav maga" is Hebrew for "contact combat," and despite being commercialized in the U.S., it was one of the more brutal arts I practiced. Mostly because I trained with an ex-IDF soldier and not at a strip mall dojo, but that's beside the point.

The movements taught in krav maga are actually quite simple and based on the body's natural reactions and mechanics. That's because the art is principle-based rather than technique-based. The goal in krav maga is to ingrain the proper instincts and mentality for survival, and one of the ways they do that is through multiple-opponent training.

For the average person, fighting multiple opponents teaches you three things. First, the key to fighting multiple opponents is don't do it, because you can't fight two people at once, no matter what you've seen in the movies. Second, attitude and aggression matter a lot more than technique. The only way you're going to get out of a multiple-opponent encounter is by taking the initiative and eliminating the opposition quickly and with prejudice.

And, finally, if you can't take the opposition out quickly, then only fight one of them at a time. In krav maga, they teach the principle of stacking, lining up your opponents so only one of them can reach you at once. That's why I went for the nearest giant, so I could use him as an obstacle while I took him out of the fight.

One thing about being in my Fomorian form is that I'm fast. Maybe not as fast as when I stealth-shift, but I'm still hellaciously fast for a giant. So, when I closed the gap between me and the smaller male eldjötnar in less than a second, it took him by surprise. He took Orna through the eye socket before he could lift his axe, which I imagine ruined his day.

The blade itself was supernaturally sharp and durable, meaning I could do things with it that I couldn't with a mundane sword. Fritjof and Tove were scrambling to flank me, so I twisted the blade and lifted, freeing Orna by cutting through the top of the giant's skull. I front-kicked the corpse at Tove with Fomorian strength, and it flew through the air at her while tumbling willy-nilly, arms and legs floundering. When the body impacted the giantess, she released a rather dainty-sounding "oomph" as she tumbled backward, entangled in a mess of limbs and weaponry.

That left me and Fritz.

He'd gotten relatively close, almost within sword range. And if he'd have kept me occupied with swordplay, Tove might've recovered and gotten around my flank, giving them a much better chance at victory. But after seeing me drop his minions like flies, he chose to stand back and toss fireballs at me instead. Against anyone else it'd have been a wise move, since I had the better reach with Orna. He had at least a millennia of battlefield experience on me, after all.

But against me in my Fomorian form, that was a foolish decision.

Fritz slung his first volley of flaming bolides at me with the smug confidence of someone who's seen their magic obliterate dozens of enemies before. When I started batting them away with my free hand as I advanced, his cool composure began to crack. Sure, my left hand soon became a charred, smoking mess, but I didn't care in this form. I liked the pain.

Thing was, pain fed my Fomorian lust for bloodshed. It made me stronger, more resolved, and more eager to rain down hell on whatever or whoever challenged me. Also, it triggered something within my brain that I likened to a computer doing battlefield calculus. Feed me pain in a fight while I was in this form, and I became one devious son of a bitch.

"Stop running so I can end you, jötunn!" I roared as Fritz backpedaled past Tove. She was just getting to her feet when her leader tripped her and pushed her into my path. I cut her down like so much summer wheat, cleaving her in two from shoulder to hip with an upward swing without even breaking stride.

Coward. If he'd have helped her up, he might've stood a chance.

Meanwhile, my bastard of a warrior brain was figuring out the best way to end this guy. I really didn't want to face him in a fair sword fight if I could help it, because he was likely better than me. I'd still win, but I didn't want to spend the time to heal. I had to get back to my Oak and Grove and make sure Badb and the other fuckwit deities hadn't homed in on them.

Fritjof's mistake was choosing the wrong battlefield. He thought the element of surprise would stand him in good stead, and he was wrong. He was fighting a druid with fire magic in a forest that was just a few hundred yards from the ocean. Big mistake. With an almost automatic efficiency, I started casting a spell, mumbling under my breath as I advanced on my opponent.

I was almost on top of Fritz when he finally decided to stand his ground. His sword burst into bluish-white flames, reminding me of my sword Dyrnwyn in a way. The giant brandished his flaming weapon with obvious skill, taking an aggressive stance that indicated he was ready to trade steel.

Too little, too late.

"*Reodóg,*" I said in Gaelic, triggering my spell. Instantly, the air temperature dropped well below zero as my druid magic pulled heat from the air and sent it deep underground, where it couldn't harm any of the locals. At the same time, the spell gathered all the atmospheric moisture in a fifty-yard radius, forming it into long, sharp icicles that flew at Fritjof from multiple angles.

The first few icicles that struck the fire giant disappeared in an explosion of steam. However, that brought down the surface temperature of his skin and armor enough so that those following did not. One took him through the thigh, another through his upper arm, and a third through his neck. They melted almost instantly as they contacted his lava-like blood, but the damage had been done. Fritjof stumbled to his knees, clapping a hand over the hole in his neck.

"The álfar misled me," he wheezed as his hot orange blood poured through his fingers. "Your magic was much stronger than expected. Had I known, I'd have brought a legion of my brethren."

"Live and learn, motherfucker," I said as I lopped his head off.

"Oh, master," Orna said as Fritjof's skull went rolling down the hill. "This reminds me of the time when my *former* master Tethra slew an ice dragon of enormous girth—"

"Not now, Orna!" I growled in my deep Fomorian voice.

"Perhaps another time, then. I shall busy myself by adding your great deeds to the annals."

The blade had a piss-poor short-term memory, and it was sure to start blabbing again in a few minutes. I suspected that had to do with the way it had been enchanted. You could only imbue so much intelligence and memory into an inanimate object, after all. And unless you trapped a living entity inside your magical thingamajig, you had to allocate that limited intellect and memory to specific tasks. In Orna's case, that meant memorizing and cataloging every adventure and battle of those who were unfortunate enough to bear it.

I wondered if someday it might run out of memory and start glitching—that could be amusing. But regardless of how annoying the thing was, it was the best weapon I could hope to find, as far as Fomorian-sized weapons went. So, I resisted the urge to shove it in my Bag, keeping it handy as I contacted the Oak to see where it had gone and whether or not the Celtic gods had zeroed in on it.

Status report.

The Oak responded immediately, sending me an image of a birch forest situated next to a large body of water.

Hallormsstaður National Forest. Has to be.

That was our fallback and rally position, should something happen that forced us out of Reykjavik. Hallormsstaður was the largest forest in Iceland, and it was remote, which made it a great place for us to hide. Unfortunately, it was also all the way on the other side of the island—a full eight hours by car from the capitol. I'd have to take the long way there if I wanted to remain hidden.

The good news was, everything appeared to be copacetic. I sent another message to the Oak, telling it to stay put and await my instructions. I'd left it with specific directions regarding what to do if the Celtic gods discovered us. Our emergency plan was simple: portal me back to the Grove, and then portal us to the Void. Nobody would ever find us there, that was for sure.

Can't run forever, though.

Eventually, they would find us. At the moment, however, that was not my main concern. The only thing I was really focused on was finding Dian Cécht and convincing him to heal Finnegas. Which meant I couldn't head back to the Oak—I needed to stay here to meet whoever Gwen was sending our way. Plus, the forest was on fire, and as a druid I felt an obligation to correct that mess.

I cast a few simple spells, pulling moisture from the air to douse the flames Fritz had lit in his attempts to kill my tree. Then, I borrowed some power from the Grove, using it to help the land heal—and to bury the bodies. Once done, I shoved Orna back in the Bag and shifted into my human form. I'd just pulled on a fresh pair of Jockeys when someone cleared their throat behind me.

"Colin, I assume?" The voice was female but whiskey rough, and it carried a clear note of amusement.

I glanced over my shoulder at the tall, dark-haired woman leaning against a birch tree ten yards upslope. The fact that she'd snuck up on me, and from the high ground, no less, told me a lot about who—or rather, what—she was. It pissed me off that I'd allowed her to surprise me, but I'd been distracted by shifting back into my human form. Vulnerability between forms was one of the drawbacks of being a shifter, after all.

"In the naked flesh." I slipped on some jeans and a

thermal shirt, then I sat on a fallen log to pull on my socks and boots. "I take it Gwen sent you."

"She did, although I wasn't certain where I should find you. At least, not until the eldjötnar started burning down the forest." Her accent was fairly neutral, maybe American midwestern or Canadian, possibly from the Vancouver region—I couldn't really place it. "In any case, Gwen sent me to help you, so here I am."

I took my time getting dressed, mostly so I could get a good look at her, both with my mundane sight and in the magical spectrum. One glance with my magical sight told me she was who she claimed to be, because she practically bled magic. Plus, wings. They were hidden in this form, but still there.

Like Gwen, she was tall, athletically slender, and attractive, although this valkyrie was a lot more Claudia Black than Claudia Schiffer. Unlike the aforementioned actress, the valkyrie's jet black hair had been cut in a short, shaggy bob—more likely a practical choice than one driven by fashion. Beneath that unruly mop she had brown eyes, thin lips, a prominent, slightly crooked nose, and the lean look of a hunter. Individually, her features might've been considered unattractive, but together the sum was greater than the parts.

For some reason, I liked her. Maybe it was her casual, devil-may-care attitude, her easy smile, or the mischievous look in her eyes. Or perhaps it was that she seemed to have a sharp edge to her, like chipped glass—pretty, but dangerous. Regardless, I found her to be both alluring and instantly likable on an instinctive level.

"You know my name, but I haven't gotten yours," I said as I laced up my boots.

"My friends call me Bryn," she replied.

"With a 'y' or an 'i'?"

"Does it matter?"

I chuckled. "No, just curious. Let's see—you're Norse, so I'm guessing with a 'y'." Interestingly, Bryn had not dressed for the outdoors. She wore faded, boot-cut Levis over black biker boots, a black t-shirt, and an old-school leather motorcycle jacket. "Well, Bryn-with-a-Y, based on your sense of style, I have a feeling you're going to get along great with my magic tutor."

"It's more of a fashion statement than anything. Magical clothes, yeah?"

"Again, just making conversation." I slapped my hands on my thighs and stood. "But enough of that shit—on to business. Can you help me find the Physician?"

The wry smile she wore faded into an annoyed frown. "That's going to be a problem, druid. I'm fairly certain he's been abducted."

As it turned out, the clothes weren't just for show. Bryn had arrived on a typically-European BMW R1250GS—a good bike, just a little uppity for my tastes. As usual, I preferred to soften the blow of bad news with liberal amounts of alcohol, preferably the kind that came in pints. She declined my offer of a ride to a local watering hole, thumbing her nose at my rented 'Yota. Likewise, I refused her counteroffer to ride bitch on her Beemer, earning me a nod of approval. When it came to self-respect, it seemed some things were universal.

Boundaries set and manhood safely intact, thirty minutes later we were sitting at a cozy corner table at Ölstofa, a popular local beer joint. They had a good selection of brews on tap and a nice atmosphere, and it was just a short drive from Öskjuhlíð—all definite checkmarks in the "pros" column. But, most importantly, it was a human hangout.

I'd yet to see any denizens of the World Beneath in the pub, which placed it high on my list of places to hang when I needed a break. Thus, it was also a good place to take Bryn to discuss the situation. Less chance of the wrong people—or monsters, or what have you—eavesdropping on our conversation.

I ordered us a couple of pints of Borg imperial stout, a 12 percent ABV liver-killer put out by a small craft brewery that was popular with the locals. No mystery there; it was tasty and strong as hell. Besides, how in the fuck could any self-respecting nerd pass up beer with a name like Borg?

Bryn downed her pint, forcing me to do the same. She paid for the next round, and we drank in silence for a few moments, taking the time to savor the beer. Halfway through the second glass, I set mine down to signal that it was time to get down to brass tacks.

"So, Dian Cécht," I said. "What do you know?"

Bryn leaned in, cradling her beer in both hands while casting me the occasional glance as she spoke. "Apparently, you pissed some people off long before you arrived in Iceland. Then, you ruffled some feathers among the huldufólk. They took a keen interest in your affairs after that."

"Bah. Bunch of prissy busybodies. I can't see why everyone here is so afraid of them. Hell, they don't even remember the old magicks. Pretty pathetic, as fae go."

She gave a noncommittal shrug. "They have more magic than you might think, although most of it is limited to artifacts handed down from the past. They also have their hands in every aspect of Icelandic culture that you can imagine, both mundane and supernatural. Politics, business, entertainment, art—you name it, the Hidden People are involved."

"And I should care about this because...?" I replied archly.

Bryn snorted softly, clearly expressing derision at the dumb foreigner who was definitely not familiar with Norse ways. "Normally, if they wanted to make life hell for someone, they'd pressure them through the standard channels. Get you fired, have your visa revoked, make it difficult for you to do business here. But you—well, you don't operate within the normal boundaries of influence."

I was starting to see where this was going. "And they couldn't intimidate me, either."

"Exactly," she said. The valkyrie examined her glass, which was already empty. "When their magic proved to be ineffective, they resorted to *other* methods."

"The gods?"

"Not quite, thankfully. No, they got the jötnar involved, which is nearly the same thing in Scandinavia. The ones you faced earlier were mere foot soldiers, mostly sent to harass you, although I don't think their master expected you to dispose of them so easily."

I scratched the back of my head as I sucked air through my teeth. "I take it the huldu-fucks didn't send Fritz and his buddies directly?"

"No, they did not. Colin, does the name Býleistr mean anything to you?"

Rubbing the stubble on my chin with my knuckles, I gave her a *mea culpa* look that was halfway between a wince and an apologetic grin. "Um, maybe."

Bryn set her empty glass down, crossing her arms on the table like a sphinx. "Colin, if we are going to work together, we must be honest with each other."

"Okay, okay. So, I may have killed his son. Didn't want to, but Snorri forced my hand."

"Likely so, but that does not change the fact that you killed him. And while he will probably cross the Veil again several centuries hence, such insults are not taken lightly in Norse culture." She signaled for another round of brews, somehow immediately getting the waitstaff's attention on a busy night. "No, they are not taken lightly at all."

Immediately, I thought back to my dust-up with Cade Valison. You know, *Vali's son*, Thor's nephew, Odin's grandson, etc. I still had his magic hammer sitting inside my Bag, and while I'd done a decent job of covering up the evidence after I killed him, deities of that caliber had all kinds of ways to discover such dark, hidden secrets.

But I wasn't worried. Cade was a demigod and immortal, more or less. Among immortals, it wasn't a big deal for one of their kind to get lost for a few years. Heck, if I was lucky, they hadn't even noticed his absence yet. I took a nice, long drink of that stout to cover up the guilt that was probably written all over my face.

Here's to hoping.

"Right. So, there's another giant out there who's pissed at me. No biggie."

Bryn winced and shook her head like she'd just gotten an answer from the slowest kid in the class. "You don't get it. Býleistr is Loki's brother, born of Laufey and Fárbauti. He is very powerful—god-like, in fact. If that doesn't give you pause, consider that he and his brothers are to lead the jötnar armies against the gods at Ragnorak."

"Um, so what's the good news?" I said, snagging a third beer from the waitress before she could even set the glass on the table.

"There is no good news. I am fairly certain that Býleistr has abducted the Celtic Physician, and that he's holding him at his fortress in Jötunheimr."

"Well, shit."

6

W e were leaving the bar when Bryn casually bumped me with her elbow. Her eyes darted across the street and back, where a couple of goth-looking teens lurked in a shop doorway. Day had given way to night while we were in the bar, and the dark kept me from making out any important details. Bryn hooked her arm in mine and guided me north, away from where she'd parked her bike.

"So, your place or mine?" she asked.

It wasn't that uncommon for Icelandic women to be forward about sex, but she was obviously making conversation so the thugs wouldn't know we were on to them. Casual hookups were almost the national sport here, a fact I'd embarrassingly discovered my first night out in Reykjavik. Apparently, my traditional American view of relationships was "cute and endearing, but a bit weird." Go figure.

"I'm hungry, actually," I said, playing along while I

extended my senses outward, eventually locating a rat that was hiding in a fenced-off alley behind us. A slight mental nudge encouraged him to poke his head through the fence, allowing me to surveil the suspicious duo, who I immediately dubbed Jay and Bob. As expected, they began to follow us after we turned the corner.

"They're definitely tailing us," I whispered after casting a night vision cantrip. "Any idea who they are?"

"The Hidden People, most certainly. Come," she said, pulling me toward a darkened cobblestone walkway that passed between two buildings, connecting the streets on either side.

"Are we going to ambush them, or are you trying to lose them?"

"We shall see. Hide us," she commanded. I arched an eyebrow, mostly because she was being bossy. Her brow furrowed at my reticence. "You are a druid, are you not?"

"Fine," I whispered, casting a chameleon spell on us both. "But don't move until you have to, else they'll spot us."

"Hmpf," was her only reply.

Soon, our tail strolled cautiously up the sidewalk and into view, their eyes darting this way and that. I had mistakenly pegged them as goths earlier, but they were dressed more like metal heads—death metal, that is. Lots of black leather and spikes, long, stringy black hair, and ink on almost every exposed bit of skin. Yet one look at their faces told me they were fae, because there was no mistaking those fine, almost alien features and supernatural attractiveness.

The ink didn't bother me, and neither did the way they were dressed, but the long black knives they carried gave me pause. Something was decidedly *wrong* about those blades, and it wasn't just the way they dripped thick black drops of liquid like pus from an infected wound. When I looked at either knife too long my eyes wanted to cross, my skin crawled, and every cell in my body told me they'd been made with dark magic.

Suddenly, one of our pursuers—Bob, I thought—snapped his head around, scanning the walkway where we hid like a hawk searching a field for prey. As I observed their movements, I realized that I'd underestimated these two. They didn't move like a couple of wet-behind-the-ears thugs, stumbling around looking for a few easy marks to mug. Instead, their actions were precise and coordinated, reminding me of a couple of fae assassins I'd recently dealt with back home.

I'd taken Lucindras and Eliandres out by myself, so certainly I could deal with these punks. Granted, I'd almost died when the twins jumped me outside of Luther's cafe, but I wasn't about to split hairs regarding my own victories. The memory of that fight, and the presence of the nasty-looking blades these particular fae carried, almost had me at their throats despite Bryn's cautionary attitude.

Still, those blades looked deadly, and I didn't care to find out what sort of nasty magic poison dripped off them. So, I waited until his gaze swept past, holding my breath to avoid making any sound that could give us away. Moments later, he turned and headed down the street after his partner.

Fuck it.

Having already stealth-shifted out of habit, I drew my cold iron hunting knife from the small of my back. Dropping my chameleon spell, I bolted out of hiding with a burst of Fomorian, vampire-like speed. The fae assassin heard me coming too late, and my knife was sticking out from between his shoulder blades before he had a chance to turn around. Bob was definitely not silent as he died, falling to the pavement with a short, sharp gasp of surprised agony that was loud enough to draw his companion's attention.

One down, one to go.

Jay turned out to be the cagier of the two, squaring up on me immediately in a wide knife-fighter's hunch. I pulled my blade from his buddy's back, stomping on his head and bursting it like a melon as I walked over his corpse. Couldn't be too careful about such things, after all.

Jay's eyes narrowed dangerously at that, but he said not a word, instead closing the distance with supernatural grace as he slashed at my eyes. Fighting with short blades is almost always a matter of who gets cut worse first, which may sound like common sense, but it was the crux of surviving a knife-to-knife encounter. So, the opening gambit against an aware opponent was almost always a feint.

Knowing this, I leaned away without overcommitting, because I knew he'd follow up with a second attack. And attack he did, slashing at my gut, groin, and knee in a finely-tuned combination of cuts that would've taken out your average combatant. Too bad for him, I'd done this dance before a thousand times, first with Jesse, and then with Maureen. And they were both way better than this loser.

Plus, I was quicker. Way quicker.

I parried the gut slash, redirecting it with a quick slap while quickly retracting my hand to avoid a withdrawal cut to my forearm. At the same time, I took a quick retreat step with my forward leg, pulling my groin and thigh just out of the guy's reach. Meanwhile, I ran my blade through the guy's eye socket with my other hand, performing all three moves simultaneously.

Sometimes people don't know they're dead after they're stabbed or shot, so I left my knife in place as I backed away to avoid a lucky last slash from his poisoned blade. But it wasn't necessary. The lights went out in his other eye almost instantly, and he dropped like a sack of potatoes to the street. I watched him twitch, once, twice, leaning over to retrieve my knife only when he went absolutely still.

Bryn's voice spoke from over my shoulder as I was cleaning my blade on the killer's shirt. "Gwen said you were deadly. She was right. But now their employer will have reason to hunt you openly."

"Well, at least I'll see them coming," I said as I dragged the bodies to a small area of grass in front of house that had been converted into a shop. I used druid magic to sink the bodies and the daggers deep underground, covering them to leave no trace they were ever there.

She snorted silently. "Perhaps, but I'd say it's time to go."

"Fine. But fair warning—it's a long drive to my place."

After she turned down my offer of a ride a second time, I gave Bryn directions and agreed to meet her there. Valkyries must've been pretty fast in flight, because the location didn't faze her a bit. I was tempted to call the Oak for a lift, but I wanted time to think and the convenience wasn't worth the risk.

Nowhere was better than my Druid Oak for sheer privacy. It was the one place I could be certain no huldufólk were around to spy on us. The Oak had its own built-in surveillance system, and nothing short of a god could come within a mile of it without being detected. Combine that with my druid senses, and I was confident we'd be able to determine our next steps in peace back at Hallormsstaður.

Still, I didn't intend to share all my secrets with the Valkyries, no matter how much I liked Bryn. Her boss creeped me out, and while I might have earned her respect, that didn't mean she was completely on my side. Besides, Gwen worked for Odin. Word was, the Valkyries had minimal contact with him these days, but I couldn't trust anyone who was allied with the gods.

By way of subterfuge, I instructed the Oak to construct a sort of mock campsite a few hundred yards from where it was located. "Construct" was probably the wrong word, as it would simply grow whatever I asked it to make by shaping earth, wood, and stone like clay. I asked the Oak to make it look like it was manmade, and after a few confusing exchanges, it sent me an image of a rock-lined fire pit, a lean-to fashioned from rough-hewn wood, and a bed made from fresh-cut pine boughs. It was actually a bit more rustic than what I was capable of these days, but it'd do.

Once that task was complete, I had nothing to do but drive. The first leg of the trip to Hallormsstaður was long and boring, and if it hadn't been for the distraction of the Northern Lights, I might've stopped and slept until morning. But I gutted it out and drove straight through, and as night gave way to day, I was treated by vista after vista featuring Iceland's stunning, rugged beauty. That was one thing you could say about the island—the views were never a disappointment.

It was mid-morning when I pulled off the road into the forest, down a dirt road that probably hadn't been there the night previous. As I followed the Oak's directions, slowly cruising further into the depths of the woods, the forest foliage closed in to cover the path behind me. The Oak would also cover up any tire tracks, as that was part of the security protocols we'd established.

I had to assume that the huldufólk would rat us out to their gods or the Celtic pantheon, which was even worse. Once they knew we were in Iceland, it was just a matter of time before Badb, Fuamnach, and Aengus worked out a deal with Odin or Frigg or whoever so they could come after us. The clock was ticking, and while I could steal time inside the Grove, I might only have weeks or days Earth-side to find Dian Cécht and heal Finnegas.

It was all very frustrating, considering that I was finally getting somewhere in my search. If Bryn was on the up and up—and my instincts said she was—she could lead me straight to the immortal Physician. Sure, I might have to kill a few giants, but whatevs. Once the old man was all better, he'd know what to do next about the Celtic pantheon. And once I dealt with them, I'd find Fallyn and take her and the old man somewhere safe.

Yeah, and unicorns shit Neapolitan sherbet.

My vague, half-baked plan was a long shot, and I knew it—but I had to hope things would turn out alright. My life had been one crazy battle after another for too long, and I was ready for some peace. Plus, maybe a little happiness, but I wasn't going to get my hopes up.

I parked the SUV where the Oak indicated, then I grabbed my Bag and headed down a faint dirt path toward the makeshift campsite. I'd only walked thirty yards or so before I heard the faint gurgling of a running stream and Bryn's raucous laughter accompanied by Click's weird Welsh accent.

Click sometimes suppressed his accent in order to conceal his identity, as he had with me when we first met. That he didn't make the effort in front of Bryn told me either the two were already acquainted, or he'd decided she was no threat.

Interesting.

"So, then the boy shifts inta' his other form ta' fight the three *roggenwölfe*, and he rips his trousers from seam ta' seat. So now he's fightin' the *feldgeister* with his *pidyn* an' *cwdyn* flappin' all over the place. Understand, now, he's ten feet tall, so his member is like this—"

I parted a few branches, walking into the campsite just in time to see Click hold his fist and forearm up in the air like he was giving the Italian salute. Bryn saw me enter the clearing, but she was too busy belly-laughing and wiping her eyes to acknowledge me. Knowing that it was impossible to interrupt such a performance when the quasi-god had a rapt audience, I busied myself with settling in while he continued.

"Now, o' course, all the werewolf lasses and female hangers on are more intent on his pecker than the fight— not ta' mention a few o' the males as well. Every time it'd swing back and forth, it was like watching a group o' cats watch a tennis match. I swear, I think he fielded a half-dozen proposals and three times as many propositions fer' a good roll in the hay that day."

Bryn was laughing so hard at this point that she nearly fell off her log. Click had joined in, and the two carried on with their seemingly uncontrollable fits of laughter for a good minute. Finally, the valkyrie and the mage settled down, each choking back a few chuckles as Click acknowledged my presence.

"An' looky what we have here—the man o' the hour arrives."

Despite my embarrassment, I kept my expression neutral. Experience had taught me that the only way to get Click to shut up was playing the straight man to his jokes. "Well, I see you two have already become acquainted."

Bryn wiped her eyes one last time. "Oh, Gwydion and I go way back."

"Now, now, lass—I told ye that I don't go by that name no more."

The valkyrie gave him a rueful yet sympathetic look. "Don't worry, I won't tell anyone." She turned toward me again, casually glancing at my crotch with a barely contained snicker. "I have to say, he doesn't look like much to me."

"Jest wait until he shifts, lass—then ye'll either be droppin' yer panties or runnin' fer dear life!"

That comment resulted in yet another outbreak of riotous laughter. Rather than stand for any more of that humiliation, I headed back to the truck to take a nap until Click was done being an asshole.

Thirty minutes later, the laughter had subsided. Soon after, the smell of eggs, bacon, and sausage roasting over an open fire made my stomach grumble. After a few minutes of deliberation, I decided that a full stomach was more important than salving my bruised ego. Besides, I was eager to figure out our next steps, and sitting around sulking wasn't going to get us any closer to rescuing Dian Cécht.

When I walked back into the campsite, Click was cooking breakfast over a large camping grill that had appeared from nowhere. Bryn sat on the forest floor nearby, sipping from an enameled metal mug with her back against a large log bench. Once I spotted the matching enameled metal coffee pot sitting atop the fire, all of my concerns vanished, replaced by my deep desire for that sweet black nectar.

I made a beeline for the coffee pot, taking time to admire the spread Click was preparing as I poured myself a cup of joe. Atop the grill sat a sizzling assortment of breakfast meats, including several varieties of sausage, and steaks—honest-to-goodness steaks. Intoxicating smells emanated from a mess of bacon and eggs in a cast-iron frying pan, liquid grease crackling and sputtering with promises of profound satiety and early-onset coronary artery disease. But the real treasure amidst all that fatty goodness sat on the griddle that rested on the far side of the grill.

"Holy shit—are those pancakes?" I asked, my stomach rumbling.

"Aye, lad. After the verbal drubbin' I gave ya', I felt I owed you some decent grub as some small means o' recompense."

I took a sip of the coffee—Luther's special roast. "Click, you Welsh pain in the ass, I could kiss you right now."

"Now, now, let's not get carried away," he said, suppressing a smile. "'Sides, fair Brynhild tells me we've cause ta' celebrate."

Bryn cleared her throat loudly. "Just Bryn, please."

"Oh, right, right," Click said as he gave me a wink on the sly. "*Bryn* says she might've found the Physician. Again, cause fer' celebration."

"It's certainly progress, if her intel is correct," I said.

"It is. I'm a valkyrie. We know how to make people talk," Bryn interjected with a self-satisfied smirk.

"Um, that's creepy," I replied. "Anyway, say she's right and Býleistr did kidnap Dian Cécht. Seems like we're going to have an uphill battle rescuing him, based on what Bryn told me."

Click produced a blue enameled plate out of nowhere, deftly flipping meat, eggs, and pancakes on it in a few smooth swipes of a spatula. He handed me the plate, magically producing utensils and a bottle of maple syrup as well. After pouring the sweet sticky stuff over my pancakes, I busied myself with stuffing my face as the magician and the valkyrie spoke.

"I'm certain ye'll be able ta' deal with those giants once we find them, lad. What concerns me is the act o' finding his lair. As I recall, gettin' ta' Jötunheimr is no simple matter."

Bryn stood and sauntered over to the fire, snagging a steak and a sausage, which she deftly rolled inside the steak like a burrito. The valkyrie took a large bite, wiping grease from her chin with the back of her hand. Swallowing a huge bolus of meat with a loud gulp, she gestured at me with her meaty creation.

"Fomorian or not, you know as well as I that Býleistr's a handful. I'm sure that Colin's capable, but a direct confrontation would be disastrous, as Loki's brother has hundreds of his kind under his command. We'll need to use cunning and subterfuge to rescue the Physician—that is, if we want to make it back from Jötunheimr hale and whole."

I swallowed a huge lump of chewed up pancake, washing it down with a generous slug of coffee. "Quick question. Where exactly is Jotunheim, anyway?"

"'Tis its own dimension, lad. Unreachable directly from this realm."

"So, how do we get there? Do we have to climb the World Tree or something?" Bryn and Click glanced at each other, then they both broke out in laughter. "What's so funny?"

"You actually think there's a huge tree that connects the realms?" Bryn set her coffee cup down on a nearby log. She was laughing so hard she was in danger of spilling it. "Oh, that is rich."

"I bet he thinks there's a giant squirrel that scurries up an' down its trunk as well!" Click declared with glee. He danced from foot to foot with his index fingers curled in front of his mouth. "'Oh, look at me, I'm a giant squirrel, out ta' eat young druids fer' a snack.'"

The valkyrie snickered loudly, shaking her head as she looked my way. "There's no 'world tree,' Colin—at least, not in the conventional sense. Yggdrasil is a network of portals and pathways the gods created so their armies and agents could travel from plane to plane."

"Okay," I said, setting my plate down. "Sheesh, excuse me for being ignorant of the realities of Norse cosmology."

The valkyrie gave me a sympathetic smile, the polite equivalent of a pat on the head. "While we're on the topic, it bears mentioning that neither the gods nor the giants are in the habit of leaving those doorways unguarded and exposed. It will be no small feat to make our way to Býleistr's realm."

"Ya' see, there really is a giant squirrel, lad," Click said with a snicker. "It guards the portals from pesky druids who come ta' steal its collection o' golden acorns."

"Sure there is," I said, rolling my eyes. "Hey, Bryn, did I ever tell you about the time Click here got nicked by my friend, Hemi? Grabbed him just like a leprechaun, by the scruff of his neck."

Click's face fell, and his voice grew somber. "Come now, lad—there's no reason ta' be bringin' up such painful memories. 'Sides, I let the great blunderin' lunk capture me. 'Twas the only way I could get ya' ta' let yer' guard down, so's I might steer ya' two in the right direction."

"Whatever you say, Click." I turned to Bryn, who, by the smile on her face, seemed to be enjoying our exchange. "So, let me get this straight. Basically, Jotunheim is in another dimension, and we're going to have to take a portal there, sneak past hundreds of giants and their god-like leader, free Dian Cécht, and make it back to Earth without pissing off the gods?"

"That is an incredibly simplified, but accurate, summary of the tasks that lay before us," she replied solemnly.

I shoved one last bite of pancake into my mouth. "Great, when do we start?"

7

The three of us debated our next steps until late in the day. I was all for storming the gates, kicking Býleistr's ass, and freeing Dian Cécht by force. Bryn continued to advise caution, while Click insisted that we needed to speak to Loki, and that suggestion was a bridge too far for the valkyrie. She spent half an hour arguing with my substitute mentor before disappearing in a flash of lightning and clap of thunder that left my ears ringing.

"Sheesh, warn a guy before you blow his eardrums out," I said while shaking my index finger inside each of my ears in turn.

"That solves that, I s'pose," Click said, cheerful as ever.

"What do you mean?" I asked. "Don't we need her to find Jotunheim?"

Click blew a Bronx cheer. "Pfah! They're all fine drinking companions, ta' be sure, and easy on the eyes. But ya' can't trust a valkyrie any further than ya' can toss 'em in full armor. Their first allegiance is ta' the gods, specifically ta' Odin—never forget that."

"Whatever. Call me impatient, but I just want to get to Jotunheim and kick some giant ass."

Click gave me a disapproving grimace. "That's yer' alter-ego talkin', 'tis. Yer' smarter than that, lad, so think fer' a moment. Sure, ya' waylaid those three tossers that attacked yer' Oak without so much as breakin' a sweat. But what happened when ya' faced Tethra? Ya' blasted the fooker with both barrels, an' he shrugged it off. Býleistr's easily a force ta' match Tethra, ta' be sure. An' with his armies behind him, well—can ya' stand against such might?"

I took a deep breath as I ran my hand through my hair. "Ah, shit. You're right. It's just that we're so close, and Finnegas—"

Click's expression softened. "He's not gettin' any better, and dyin' a slow death in stasis is not how ya'd care ta' see your oldest friend go, is it?" I shook my head, and Click clapped a hand on my shoulder. "I know. Never fear, one day ye'll be able ta' muster such might as ta' shake the foundations o' Jotunheim. Then, such as Loki's kin'll tremble in their boots at'cher passin'. But not today."

"Speaking of which, do you know where to find him? Loki, I mean."

"O' course! He maintains a bachelor pad in Garðabær, a great sprawling modern thing. Hideous, 'tis."

"Wait a minute—you're buddies with Loki? The most hated of all the Norse gods?"

The magician drew himself up in indignation. "Whoa

there, lad, hold yer' tongue now. Loki's not a bad fella', he's jest' had some tough breaks. Sure, he's a trickster, an' prone ta' makin' life miserable fer' his kin. But that's his job after all, an' ya' can't blame a viper fer' bitin' ya' on the arse when ya' turn yer back."

I rocked my head side to side. "I suppose. But if that's the nature of trickster gods, then why haven't you screwed me over yet?"

"Who says I haven't, eh?" He chuckled at my deep frown, mussing my hair like I was his little brother. "Ah, I'm only takin' the piss out o' ya', Colin. Let's jest say that we tricksters have a code an' leave it at that."

I had no idea what he meant, but I'd learned not to pry when Click was being obscure. Pestering him for more info almost always resulted in being sent on wild goose chases, for no other reason than it amused the quasi-god. Since we'd arrived in Iceland, I'd been sent on quests for magic *hákarl,* to find Mimir's well, and, my personal favorite, to track down a hair from Loki's beard.

Hákarl is fermented shark, and it smells as bad as it sounds. After I'd bought the disgusting dish from dozens of stores and restaurants, as well as several sketchier sources, Click admitted that he'd just wanted to see which was the best hákarl in Reykjavik. As for Mimir's well, it doesn't even exist on the mortal plane. Finally, Loki is the only clean-shaven Norse god in history—facts I only discovered after wasting weeks on each task.

The magician stared at me in anticipation, as if waiting for me to take the bait. But I'd had my fill of snipe hunts. If Click said, "leave it at that," that's exactly what I intended to do. I maintained a neutral expression until he clucked his tongue in disappointment.

"Anyhow, we'll need ta' be gettin' ta' Loki's place afore he gets too deep in his cups. Once he gets good an' pissed, he'll be useless ta' us. That means ye'll be leavin' that metal deathtrap behind, lad, as we'll have ta' take more direct means."

"Uh-uh, I can't risk using the Oak. The Celtic gods are probably already on our trail as it is."

"Huh?" he replied, cocking his head sideways. "Nay, I weren't suggestin' ya' use the tree's powers. I kin simply portal us there, quick as a wink, no trouble t'all."

"What the fuck?" I had always known Click could cast portals. However, I assumed there were limits to his powers, as he'd never offered to portal me around on mundane errands previously. "All this time, you could've been portalling me around Iceland?"

"Why so pissy all o' a sudden? It's not as if ya' didn't have suitable transportation."

"But—I—ah, damn it. Never mind. Just take us to Loki's house before he's too drunk to tell us how to get to Jotunheim."

"Which is what I suggested in the first place," Click replied, turning around to cast a portal spell.

With a herculean display of self-control, I resisted the urge to throttle him. Instead I followed him through the oval, shimmering hole in time and space that he'd summoned, cussing under my breath all the while.

Dusk was falling when we stepped out of the portal onto a quiet suburban street. Straight ahead was a massive driveway, easily wide enough to accommodate five cars. It led up to a sprawling glass and concrete structure that looked like a modernist architect's wet dream. It was all cubes, rectangles, sharp corners, and straight lines, broken up here and there with insets of vertical wood siding.

The wood accents were certainly intended to give the building character, and perhaps add a bit of warmth, but they had quite the opposite effect. Those small patches of organic material stood in stark contrast to the glass, concrete, and steel, sticking out like bits of deadwood trapped in a glacier field. It was all very sterile and contrived, and I shuddered to think what it looked like inside.

"So, this is Chez Loki," I remarked. "You were right. It's awful."

"Don't tell him that, lad, else ya' might send him into a funk that'll put him on another bender. He's terribly sensitive about his current state o' affairs, and by Asgard's standards, this place is a pile o' shite. So, keep all such comments to yerself."

I merely nodded, following the youthful-looking magician up the drive. We walked in silence past a Bugatti, a Lamborghini, and an Aston Martin, the last of which had been rammed into a concrete support pillar hard enough to drive the right front tire nearly into the cockpit. How the driver had managed to achieve that much speed while coming up the drive was anyone's guess. An empty bottle of Cristal sat in the passenger seat, along with a lacy red bra, an open pack of Sobranie Black Russians, and an alehorn that practically bled magic.

On realizing that the drinking horn was more than just a kitschy souvenir from one of the local tourist traps, I decided to check it out more thoroughly. When I looked at it in the magical spectrum, the power emanating from the alehorn nearly blinded me, and I was forced to break off contact almost immediately. But in that brief instant of contact, I heard a clear, deep, melodious voice reciting prose in some ancient Germanic language, one I understood perfectly.

On hearing those words, I was moved to right wrongs, perform great deeds, slay monsters, and generally fuck some shit up for the sole sake of committing my name to the annals of history. It wasn't quite a geas, because it was gone as soon as I cut the connection. Yet the absence of that voice left me with a deep longing to hear it again. If I didn't know how to resist such magical compulsions, I'd certainly have picked the alehorn up and claimed it for my own.

There was no telling what sort of mischief might be caused by such an object, were it to fall into the wrong hands. I tapped Click on the shoulder and pointed at the alehorn.

"You think we should, I dunno, hide that thing or something?"

"Pfah, no one's gonna' steal Óðrerir. Fer' one, only someone wit' a great deal o' magical talent can see the damned thing. An' even if they did manage ta' notice it, 'tis more a concept than a physical manifestation o' magic.

Only the gods can grasp such things an' hold them in their hands as if they were real. Ye'll likely see more such items inside Loki's home. Pay 'em no mind, if ya' know what's good fer' ya'."

"Er, right. But if I see Draupnir in there, I'm asking him for a copy."

Click gave me a quizzical frown, likely puzzled as to why I wouldn't just steal such an item. I rarely argued the merits of moral constraint with the quasi-god anymore. It was a lost cause. Click saw nothing wrong with minor acts of theft, since resources such as food and money were infinitely reproducible and replaceable to him.

Once, when arguing with him late into the night, I asked him why he didn't just create money by magical means instead of stealing it from his unsuspecting victims. "Where's the fun in that?" was his reply. That was the exact moment when I stopped trying to convince him to behave. I realized that I might as well have been asking the sun not to shine.

Leaving the cars and alehorn behind, we soon stood in front of a massive glass door, set in an equally massive wall of windows. Although an eight-foot-high concrete retaining wall blocked the view of the home's entrance from the street, there were no drapes or window dressings to speak of, and we could see to the other end of the house from where we stood. The section of the home immediately beyond the entrance included the living area, dining area, and kitchen, all contained in one large open space beneath a high-vaulted ceiling easily twenty feet high.

Each "room" was demarcated only by cosmetic architectural features and the furniture each area contained. The living and dining areas had been decorated in that typical modernist, Scandinavian style so familiar to Americans who shop at IKEA. Except these furnishings had definitely not been purchased at a big box store. My bet was that the ginormous white sectional sofa alone cost more than my entire college education, and that I could make a down payment on a modest home with what he'd paid for the stingray rocker that sat next to it.

Hell, maybe he didn't pay for any of it. He is a trickster god, after all.

As I conducted a quick visual scan of the home, I forced myself to avoid gawking at the insane wealth on display, instead searching for any potential dangers that might be present. Depending on Click to protect me from environmental hazards was an exercise in futility, as he expected me to be fully capable of avoiding magic traps and snares all by my lonesome. As far as he was concerned, if I couldn't keep myself safe from passive threats, how could I ever expect to survive a direct attack from a god?

Starting with the front entrance, I scanned every visible inch of the exterior of that home, moving on to the immediate interior just beyond the doorway. Strangely, there were no wards or protective spells here—at least, none I could see. Besides a few odd magical items of immense power left lying about, Loki had set up absolutely no magical defenses.

As my scan moved on to the next room, that's when I noticed the bodies.

Three figures lay atop the dining table in various states of nakedness, sprawled across the massive art deco wood and steel structure in a tangle of limbs and partially or fully discarded clothing. I hadn't noticed them before because they were statue still and cloaked in deep shadow. Two females, one male. The women were tall and athletically lean—one an olive-skinned brunette, the other the epitome of African beauty. Either could've easily graced the cover of *Vogue* or *Harper's*.

The man who lay between them was about my height, maybe six-two, with long, strawberry-blond hair, a handsome if too-angular face, and the lean, fit look of a triathlete. He was clean-shaven, but not what I might consider "clean" by any means, as he'd apparently thrown up on himself in his sleep. His hair was dirty and unkempt, as were his nails, and his skin had a sickly, pale cast to it as if he were just recovering from a long illness.

"I take it that's Loki." A statement, not a question. "Holy shit, except for the hair and poor hygiene, he does resemble Tom Hiddleston."

"Aye, an' he'll be tampin' when we rouse him." Click let out a long sigh. "Well, I s'pose there's nothin' fer' it."

The magician snapped his fingers, and instantly a bucket of water appeared in midair above the table. As we watched from the other side of the glass, the bucket tipped and spilled its contents on the trio, but mostly in Loki's face. No sooner had he been doused than the Norse trickster god startled and sat up, sputtering water and wiping his face with his thin, almost delicate hands. The god's violet eyes began to glow with a dull lavender gleam, and that's when I knew things were about to get interesting.

We may have been separated by an inch of glass and a good fifty feet of distance, but the stream of curse words that spewed from Loki's mouth came through loud and clear. He cursed in English, modern Icelandic, German, and what I suspected was old Norse. Not only did he say some very naughty words—including some inventive phrases that I tucked away for future use—but his curses were *actual* curses and strong enough to cause physical harm.

Click snapped again, enclosing us in another magic bubble that deflected Loki's magic. Unfortunately, much of it bled over into the neighborhood around us, causing all kinds of mayhem. The sounds of blown tires, crunching metal, and smashed glass echoed over the concrete retaining wall from the street below. A water pipe burst in front of the next-door neighbor's house, blowing a foot-wide hole in the street and spewing water thirty feet high. Birds fell from the sky, and despite Click's magical shield, my heart began to flutter and skip in my chest.

My mentor laid a hand on my arm, but I'd already activated my own wards, casting spells to deflect curses and repel dark magic. I had no doubt that without Click's protection I'd have been toast, but the combination of his magic and mine was enough to keep me from serious harm. After roughly thirty seconds, Loki's stream of invectives trailed off, leaving him wiping and blinking his eyes as he disentangled himself from his companions.

Strangely, both women continued to slumber, even though one of their heads had bounced off the table's surface when Loki sat up. Eventually the god noticed us standing outside his front door, which soon swung open of its own accord. We walked in, and by the time we reached the dining area, the trickster sat on the edge of the table with his head in his hands, massaging his temples while yellow flecks of vomit flaked off his face onto the floor.

I tried to ignore the stench as we stood by in silence, waiting for the trickster god to acknowledge us. Strong odors of sex and magic mingled with the pungent aroma of puke and stale alcohol, causing my stomach to churn. Underneath that smell, another, subtler scent lingered— the sickly-sweet redolence of illness and death.

Immediately I was reminded of Clarence, a pedophilic werewolf Samson had sentenced to a long, slow, painful demise. The alpha had done it by magically inhibiting Clarence's lycan healing factor just enough for him to die from lung cancer over the course of a few decades. I wondered, had the Norse gods done something similar to Loki, perhaps as punishment for his role in Baldur's death?

"Did you bring anything to drink?" the pale-skinned god croaked in a dry, raspy voice.

Click nudged me, so I poked around in my Bag until I found a six-pack of Thirsty Goat. I'd been saving it for a day when I might be feeling particularly homesick, but since that hadn't happened yet, I reluctantly sacrificed it for the cause.

Loki snatched the cardboard carrier from my hand with a growl, pulling three bottles out by the neck with one long-fingered hand. The tops flew off the beers with a pop-hiss, then the deity poured all three down his throat without so much as a single swallow. How he managed that feat was beyond me, and I wasn't foolhardy enough to ask. After he disposed of the next three bottles in like manner, the pale, sickly god released a gloriously loud belch that seemed to go on forever. Once done, he wiped vomit and beer from his mouth with the back of his hand, turning to us with a leering grin.

"Alright, boys—let's party."

8

Loki hopped off the table wearing nothing more than a tattered pair of silk boxers and the vomit that remained on his face. He made a beeline for the kitchen, moving surprisingly well for a terminally-ill alcoholic. I gave Click a quizzical look. The magician gave me a palms-up shrug then followed after his deific friend, leaving me no other option than to follow suit.

I could've split, but that would've been rude, and one thing I'd learned over the last few years was that there were consequences to pissing off gods. Surly, fickle, pretentious pricks they might be, but they wielded prodigious power, and I needed as many of them on my side as possible if I was going to survive my third decade. And, based on the off-the-cuff display of Loki's magic that I'd witnessed moments earlier, I definitely wanted him on my team—drunkard or no.

Loki led us through a side door into the bowels of his home, chattering all the while. "I tell ya', Gwydmeister, the night I had with those two. Couple of hellcats, absolute animals, although the Moroccan chick couldn't hold her liquor for shit. This is her puke on me, not mine, mind you. She tossed her cookies in my mouth, can ya' believe it? Never had that happen before, but it kinda turned me on, ya' know?"

"Er, 'bout our reason fer' comin' here—" Click began.

"And then, that black babe—Odin's missing eye, but does she know how to move those hips. I'd wake 'em up for you, but after a night of passion with the Lokinizer, those girls need their beauty sleep."

The more he talked, the more I realized that Loki's entire reputation and persona could be summed up in three words: frat boy, personified. He might've looked like Hiddleston—or rather, Hiddleston might've resembled him—but his personality was one-hundred percent Steve Stifler. Hell, he even sounded like Seann William Scott a little, what with the sort of nasally way he spoke.

All the while, Click couldn't get a word in edgewise, which was a hell of a thing to witness. "Loki, ol' pal, ya' see, we weren't comin' over ta' get drunk—"

"I get it—you guys want me to introduce you to some first-class Nordic poon," Loki said, not missing a beat as we walked through his concert-hall-sized bedroom and into a bath that was bigger than most New York apartments. "No worries, fellas, consider me to be your guide to the wonderful world of sexually liberated Scandinavian women. Just make sure you tell the kid to cap that Jimmy —these Icelanders share STDs like sixth-graders trade Pokémon cards."

Loki dropped trou right in front of us without warning, stepping into an open steam shower that turned on instantly as soon as he entered. I escaped around the corner into the bedroom, partially because I didn't need to see the trickster wash his junk, but mostly because I wanted to get another look at his bedroom furniture.

"Holy shit—is this a Ruijssenaars floating magnetic bed?" I yelled in the direction of the bathroom door.

"Yep," Loki yelled back over the sounds of running water.

"I saw this in *Robb Report*. What do they run, like $1.5 mil?"

"Two, now," he yelled back. "I call it my Magnetic Panty Removal System. Chicks see it, and next thing you know they're hopping into my bed. Totally worth it."

"This thing is insane! Mind if I sit on it?"

"Um, you might wanna wait until the maid changes the sheets," Loki replied as he stepped through the bathroom door with a towel wrapped around his waist. "I had a naiad in here night before last, and let's just say—"

"Let's stop right there, shall we?" Click interrupted. "No need ta' be corruptin' the lad, eh?"

"Pfft, please," Loki replied. "This kid's been around—I've heard the stories." He waggled an eyebrow at me. "So, tell me, Colinator—is Maman Brigitte as wild as they say?"

While I fumbled for an answer, Loki dropped his towel and turned to face the far wall. There he stood, hands on his hips in a shoulder-width power stance, naked as the day he was born. Meanwhile, a pair of hidden automatic doors slid away in front of him, revealing a massive wardrobe of the kind you might see on one of those "million-dollar listing" real estate shows on TV. Before the doors had fully opened, the frat-tastic deity began picking through the closet for fresh clothes, tossing them over his shoulder onto the bed as he continued.

"That's alright, Colemite—no need to brag. Way I heard it, you did Brigid and Niamh both. Man, that Niamh— hubba, hubba. She has ex-cheerleading squad MILF written all over her, amirite? We should do a threesome with her sometime—that is, if you're into that sort of thing."

"Er, she's kind of like my grandma?" I proffered, instantly regretting it.

"Ooh, kinky!" He turned and raised a hand in the air— still completely naked, of course. "High five, bro."

Click saved me by grabbing a pair of silk boxers from the bed and tossing them in Loki's face. "The lad don't swing that way. So, fer' the sake o' all that's fae, put some clothes on!"

"My bad, my bad," the Norse trickster replied with a shit-eating grin. "Sorry if I made you feel uncomfortable, Colinstigator. But shagging your grandma—straight gangster, bro!"

"I never—" I began before Loki cut me off.

"Heh, sure you didn't. Hell, there's no shame in it. She has to be, what, sixty generations removed? You're barely even related, which makes her completely baggable. Fucking-ay, if Niamh was a lesbian I might even swap genders again to get in those—"

"Loki, enough!" Click roared. "We didn't come here ta'

drink, or ta' shag some bird, or ta' talk about our sexual exploits. Our whole reason fer' comin' over was ta' ask fer' yer' help."

The pale trickster slipped on his boxers, then he spread his hands wide. "Well shit, Gwydmaster—why didn't ya' say so?"

Minutes later, we sat around a poker table in Loki's game room, which was like a Vegas casino and arcade rolled into one. He had pool tables—plural—the aforementioned card table, slot and pinball machines, several classic arcade games, foosball, hoops, skeeball, and a full-sized mechanical bull. The bull looked well-used, and I did *not* want to know how it had been broken in.

The place smelled like cigars, beer, hard liquor, ass, and money. Come to think of it, it smelled a lot like Samson's office—go figure. Soon after we sat down, Loki had gotten distracted by a professional MMA fight that was playing behind me on the largest widescreen television I'd ever seen. Meanwhile, Click and I waited for our host to turn his attention back to the conversation.

"Oh no, bro. He's gonna' get a leg lock if you—ah, you idiot!" Loki slammed his beer down on the table, splashing it all over the green felt surface. "I had sixty-flippin'-grand riding on that fight. Hermes is never going to let me live this down."

"Er, gettin' back to our situation," Click said.

Loki leaned in, elbows on the table. "Alright, Kembros-abe, let's hear it—I'm all ears."

"Ya' already know we didn't come ta' Iceland fer' the scenery," Click began almost apologetically. It was amusing, seeing him alter his speech and mannerisms to manipulate Loki's huge ego. Usually, Click was the one who had to have his ego stroked. "As it so happens, the lad's druid master requires the attentions of a healing god—"

"Done," Loki said, clapping his hands and spreading them wide. "Panacea owes me a favor from way back. That bitch can cure anything, including a severe case of blue balls. And that ass—" Loki gestured with both hands as if fondling a rather large posterior "—absolutely divine. I'll get her on it, and boom! Problem solved."

"Actually, another healing god or goddess jest won't do fer' this particular illness. Ya' see, it was caused in part by a curse from a Celtic deity."

"What?" I said, standing up from my seat. "You never told me that."

"Now, lad, calm yerself down. I didnae' tell ya' on account o' yer' temper—or rather, that an' yer' great bloody beast of an alter-ego. Last thing I needed was fer' ya' ta' go chasin' after Badb—"

"Hold up," I said, waving my hands back and forth. "Badb cursed Finnegas?"

Loki kicked back in his chair, sipping his beer and grinning like the Cheshire cat. "Oh, man, this is getting good."

Click scratched his ear as he avoided my gaze. "Did I nae mention she were at that park in the Big Easy?"

Loki made gun noises as he shot the air with his index fingers in my direction. "Bet you were there ta' tap that voodoo ass, amirite? Shit, Gwydster, you shoulda' brought this kid around a long time ago."

Click turned to his friend. "Actually, the lad turned her down. Twice."

"And lived?" Loki's eyes were wide as saucers. "That's even more badass."

I leaned forward, hands on the table. "Click, stop changing the subject. You're telling me that Badb caused the old man's stroke? And you never bothered to mention this to me, this whole fucking time?"

"Nay, lad, I did not. And I already explained ta' ya' why. An' ya' shoulda' figured this out fer' yerself already. Did'ja really believe that half-arsed excuse I gave ya' 'bout other pantheons givin' us the run around? Ya' know I can outwit any o' 'em with me eyes closed."

"Still, you should've told me," I said as I glared at him.

"Ooh, the Gwyd Kid's in trouble..." Loki said softly.

Fed up, I turned and looked Loki dead in the eye. "If you don't shut the fuck up, I'm going to slap that shit-eating grin right off your silly fucking face."

Click gasped, his face turning pale.

Undeterred, Loki leaned toward Click, whispering behind his hand. "We need to get this kid in a room with Thor and a couple of barrels of ale. I'd pay good money to watch that throwdown, lemme tell ya'." When he turned back to me, the fun-loving frat boy was gone, replaced by the grim gaze of a stone killer. "Kid, I can tell this is a touchy subject—my apologies for upsetting you. I know what it's like to have the gods turn on you, so I'm going to cut you some slack. But if you ever threaten me again, you'd best be ready to back it up. Feel me?"

I nodded because he was serious. And seriously scary. "Yeah, I feel you. Sorry for threatening you in your own house." I slumped back into my chair. "You're both right. I do get emotional where Finnegas is concerned."

"Shit, I wish I'd had a father figure like that," Loki replied. "Me and my dad, we don't get along too well, to say the least. He was always playing favorites and pitting us against each other. I feel for you, kid."

"I appreciate it," I said, meaning it. Loki might've been a turd, but he was a sensitive turd, at least. I looked at Click, who was staring a hole through the table. "We have to find Dian Cécht. And then I'm going after Badb."

"That's the spirit!" Loki exclaimed as he smacked his hand on the table. His devil-may-care grin had returned, as if the last ten seconds of conversation had never happened. "Now, who the hell is Diane Keck?"

"Dian Cécht," Click said, emphasizing each syllable. "He's the fooker who made that silver arm fer' Nuada."

"That's handy," Loki said. "Anyone ever try to steal that arm?"

"Huh?" I asked.

"Never mind," the Norse trickster said. "Just a random thought. Anywho, why do you need me to find this Diane dude?"

Click cleared his throat. "That's jest it, ya see. Seems yer' brother's abducted him and snuck off ta' Jotunheim."

Loki rubbed his baby-smooth chin for a moment as he pondered the situation. "Man, you guys really are fucked."

The Norse god of mischief held his hands up in a placating gesture as he looked back and forth between us. "And before you get all freaked out, yes, I know that the Coal-Train here was the one who fucked up my nephew. Honestly, I always hated that prick, and I'm glad you did it. He was a spoiled smart-ass who was always causing trouble. 'Sides, I warned him not to go fucking around in Niamh's backyard."

"What the hell was he doing in Austin, anyway?" I asked.

Loki frowned and rolled his eyes. "Said he wanted to visit Austin for the live music and barbecue."

"Barbecued red cap, more like it," I replied.

"Colin has a rather—er—*unique* relationship with the local dwarves," Click offered.

"Seriously? That in and of itself is a feat worthy of praise. Nobody ever really gets along with the *dvergr*— foul-tempered, double-dealing bastards, every last one." Loki gave me an appraising look. "You'd stick up for those sneaky little fuckers?"

"They helped me a time or two when I needed it, so yeah. I wouldn't trust them with my checkbook or anything, but I wasn't about to let some jötunn eat them and not answer for it."

"Fair enough," Loki said, nodding to himself. "Look, I

don't mind helping you get to Jötunheimr, but once we're there, you're on your own. Deal?"

"Click?" I asked.

He hesitated, then he frowned and gave a single nod. "Those are acceptable terms. Question is, whadya want in return?"

Loki grinned from ear to ear. "After this is all done, you guys have to sneak me out for a night on the Strip. Vegas, baby! With you two as my wingmen, we'll tear that town a new one."

"An' Honos?" Click asked. "Whadya' mean ta' do about him?"

"That's what your boy is for, Gwyd-o-rama. You'll see."

About that time, the two naked ladies we'd seen earlier came strolling into the game room. They'd gotten dressed —mostly—but had yet to clean up or put their faces on, and frankly they were looking a bit haggard.

"Loki, we're hungry," the Moroccan girl said.

"And we smelled snacks," echoed the other.

"Human snacks," her friend added.

Both of them were looking at me like fat old ladies eyeing the desert cart at Luby's. That's when the smell hit me—that combination of graveyard dirt, dried blood, and the mild yet pungent odor of desiccated human flesh.

"Oh, hell no," I said, leaping to my feet.

"Oh, hell yes," they said in unison as they leapt across the room at me.

In that moment, several things happened at once.

First, I raised my hand and released my sunlight spell, one of the few spells I kept on instacast. I was in my full human form, so there was no way I could fight off a coordinated attack from two higher vampires. That meant I had to unleash the big guns on them, before they ripped my throat out.

Second, Loki grabbed the Moroccan girl by the waist as she zoomed by his side of the table. I'd rarely seen anyone move that fast. These girls were probably a few hundred years old, which meant they were faster than me in my stealth-shifted form. So, for Loki to snatch that girl out of the air like that—it was damned impressive.

Third, Click snapped his fingers, freezing the black chick and my spell in midair. I remained unaffected, but the burst of light that emanated from my hand had been caught in his stasis spell. It hung in the air in front of me, a white blob of brilliant energy that looked a bit like the floof from the inside of a Twinkie.

Since light moves at around 300,000,000 meters per second, there was no way Click could snap his fingers in time to freeze my spell. Meaning, he had to have either foreseen what would happen, or he'd experienced it and then went back in time several seconds to stop it from happening.

"Don't try to wrap your head around it, kid," Loki said as the female vampire fell limp within his grasp. "I've known this dude for ages, and trust me, you'll get nowhere trying to figure time magic out."

"Click, you told Loki you're a chronomancer? I thought the gods would flip out if they knew what you could do."

"They know what I can do," Click replied. "It's gettin'

caught in the act o' doin' the forbidden that'd put ma' arse in a sling."

"And you don't care?" I asked, directing my question to Loki.

"Nope," Loki interjected. "Tricksters have a code."

He looked at me with expectation in his eyes, almost daring me to ask him to expand on that statement. I ignored the challenge, knowing better than to invite disaster by stepping into such an obvious trap. Someday I'd find out what that mysterious code was, but not by outright asking one of these jokers to tell me.

The Norse trickster chuckled. "Fine, be that way. Kid, why don't you suck that magical energy back in before you kill a Vampyri Council member's daughter, yeah? Last thing you need is to stir up trouble with those asshats."

Click stood. "Time fer us ta' go, methinks."

"Shame, I was enjoying the company," Loki replied. "Look, I'll cast an augury and get back to you within a day or two. Then, we'll see about getting you fellas to Jötunheimr, alright?"

"What about them?" I asked, pointing at the female vamps.

"Man, most chicks are usually out for days after a romp with the Lokester, but I guess these two had a little more fire in them than I thought. Don't worry, I'll spell them up real good so they don't remember a thing. Go get some rest. I have a feeling you're gonna need it."

9

As soon as we exited Loki's front door, Click turned and poked me in the chest, his eyes blazing. "Have ya' some kind o' death wish, lad? What the hell were ya' thinkin' threatening a god like that, an' in his own lair, no less? Even in his diminished state, yer' no match fer' the likes o' him at this juncture."

I'd rarely seen the pseudo-god get angry. Even when he'd been ready to throw down with Hideie, he maintained a certain levity in his actions and demeanor. But in this moment, all evidence of the lighthearted, good-natured fool was gone, replaced by a deadly serious, barely contained fury that ran quite contrary to the laid-back Click I knew.

"You're right, it's just—"

"Jest nothin'! It's too late in the game fer' ya' ta' throw it all away by actin' the fool around a god. An' ye'd best thank yer' lucky stars that Loki took a shine ta' ya', else ye'd be a wet red stain on his fancy marble floor 'bout now."

"'Late in the game,' Click? I didn't realize we were running a game—I thought we were just trying to survive long enough to save Finnegas. Is there something you're not telling me?"

His eyes narrowed, then he thumped me with a lightning-fast finger flick, right between the eyes.

"Ow!" I said, rubbing my forehead. "What did you do that for?"

"Fer' bein' an idjit, that's why. Of all people, ya' should know that there's always somethin' immortals aren't tellin' ya'—always! There's always a game afoot, always some dark plan at work, always an ulterior motive. An' until ya' start thinkin' like one o' us, yer' forever doomed ta' be a pawn in the plans o' yer' betters."

"Okay, okay. I guess I'm just not the kind to sneak around or hide my intentions. I've always preferred the straightforward approach."

Click laughed humorlessly as he scratched the tip of his nose with his thumb. "Ah, but yer' capable o' trickery, lad, and some might even say ye've a knack fer' it. Let's recount all the fookers ye've outsmarted thus far," he said, counting off on his fingers. "The Fear Doirich, twice —nay, thrice. Sonny an' his merry band o' feldgeisters. Maeve, a faery queen and goddess in her own right. That right prick Gunnarson. La Onza. Cade Valison. Diarmuid. Tethra. Fer' shite's sakes, feckin' Lugh. Shall I go on?"

"Aw, hell—I was just lucky, Click. I mean, seriously, I

only survived most of those encounters by the skin of my teeth."

"Is that so?" Click said, tapping a finger on his chin. "Ya' know what they say, lad. Once is luck, twice is coincidence, an' three times is skill... or in yer' case, guile an' talent. An' I'd hate ta' see it wasted jest because ya' couldn't control yer' temper around a god."

I pursed my lips, nodding in agreement. "It won't happen again."

"See that it doesn't." He snapped his fingers and a portal appeared behind him. "Now, I'm off. I've things ta' do afore Loki gets back ta' us. Stick close, find someplace ta' stay in the city, an' wait fer' his response."

"Can't you just drop me off at the Oak?" I said, in a tone of voice just short of a whine.

Click gave me a put-upon look. "I get that yer' tryin' ta' steal time, an' believe me, I understand yer' position more than most. But ya' can't cheat time forever, and ofttimes ya' just have ta' let it run its course. Find someplace ta' stay fer' the night an' wait fer' Loki's message."

"Um," I said, glancing over my shoulder at Loki's couch. "Can't I just stay here?"

"Have ya' not been listenin'? Even if he invited ya', it'd be a bad idea. Fer' one, it's a god's home, an' not what it seems ta' be no matter how mundane it might appear. Second, he's a trickster. An' third, he's a womanizing drunk. Ye'd never get any sleep, 'cause he'd have ya' up chasing skirt an' drinkin' till the wee hours, an' then he'd never get around ta' castin' his augury. An' ya' might wake up a goat, or married ta' a frost giantess, or some other horrible an' horribly funny fate that neither o' us has yet considered. Much as that might amuse me, not on yer' life."

I scratched the back of my head, exhaling slowly. "Fine. But don't expect me to stay out of trouble."

He chuckled as he stepped backward through his portal. "Wouldn't dream o' it."

The portal winked out, and I realized I was left stranded in a part of Reykjavik that was completely unfamiliar, at night, with no idea where to go to find a place to stay. I was hungry, tired, and wound up from my conversation with Click. To top it all off, it was colder than a witch's tit in a cast-iron bra, and the huldufólk had probably already sent more assassins after me.

"Well, fuck."

With a frustrated sigh, I stuck my hands in my jacket pockets and headed toward a bright cluster of lights down the road.

———

Since I was mostly operating on instinct—I'd given up mobile phone use for fear of being tracked by the Celtic gods—it was a matter of walking until my feet bled, or until I found a place of respite. After an hour or so, I found Route 40, a major north-south thoroughfare for greater Reykjavik. With no better options, I figured I'd follow it until I found a bar or hotel.

By the time I came to a footbridge that crossed to the east side of the highway, my feet weren't bleeding, but they were in danger of being frostbitten. Several blocks back, a local had told me of a bar just a few hundred meters north on the other side of the road, and that was my destination. I'd almost reached the apex of the bridge when an eight-foot-tall, hairy, somewhat simian-looking creature clambered over the safety rail. He landed heavily in the center of the path before adopting a wide-footed stance that blocked my way forward.

Great.

The beast looked as broad through the shoulders as it was tall, with a thick, muscular upper body and neck and spindly, almost comically thin legs. It wore a hodgepodge of tattered and rudely mended clothing, including a too-small pair of mustard-colored corduroys, a ratty *Frœbb-blarnir* t-shirt, and a military-style wool overcoat that fit so tight, the sleeves made its arms look like malformed sausages.

Damn, he kind of reminds of Elmo.

For grins, I checked the creature out in the magical spectrum. Interestingly, the beast had a glamour on it that would've made it very hard to see with mortal eyes. Why I was able to see it, I hadn't a clue. I also had no idea what it wanted, but I was damned curious to find out. Just to be safe, I slipped a hand inside my Bag, resting it on Dyrnwyn's hilt.

"*Borga vegatollinn,*" it rumbled from behind the Dr. Who scarf that wrapped around its face and head. Unbelievably, it had the hat to match, although it looked to have lost its shape due to years of wear and abuse.

"Say what?" I asked.

"I said 'pay the toll,'" the creature replied in perfect, almost accent-free, English. "You're an American, then?"

"As apple pie. You're a troll, then?"

"That's what people call us now. I am of the mountain folk, and my kind are descendants of the jötnar. Or, rather, we are a mixture of human and giantkind."

If he really was a troll, I should have smelled him a mile off. Trolls back home smelled so awful, to get near them you had to use magic to cover their scent. I took a furtive sniff, but all I smelled was stone and earth. Weird. I guess they had different trolls in Iceland.

"Hmm. No offense, but I thought trolls were supposed to be—"

"Dim-witted and unsophisticated?"

"Something like that, although I intended to be a bit more tactful."

"That's alright, we get it all the time. And, in truth, some of my relatives are insanely stupid. But many of us inherited our intelligence from our human ancestors."

"Huh, you learn something new every day." We both glanced around with forced nonchalance, avoiding the topic at hand. "So..."

The troll fiddled with a loose button on its coat. "Ah, yes, the toll. I'm terribly sorry, but it can't be helped. For one, times are tough. And second, it's not often that someone walks by who can actually see me. Difficult to ask for a toll when you're functionally invisible."

"I can see how that would make extortion a challenge," I observed. "Have you considered scaring people into dropping their stuff? You know—purses, backpacks, and the like?"

"Oh, I gave up on those tactics ages ago. Consider this: The last time you got scared, did you drop what you were holding or hang onto it for dear life?"

I rubbed my chin with my free hand. "I hadn't actually given it much thought. Now that I think of it, I guess people do tend to cling to whatever is in their hands when they're startled."

"No, I didn't say 'startled.' I said 'scared.' If I could startle people, I might *actually* get them to drop their valuables. But again, I'm invisible to most humans. That means the process of frightening them is usually a slow burn. Most humans don't believe in ghosts, so when they hear a disembodied voice, they start looking around and trying to determine the source. After a while, skepticism gives way to disbelief, and disbelief to panic. But by that time, they're typically past my bridge."

"This might be a dumb question—"

"There are no dumb questions," the troll remarked drily.

"Hah, tell that to my current teacher. Anyway, why don't you just grab their shit and run?"

"By 'shit,' I take it you mean their belongings?"

"Right," I said. "Invisibility would seem to make that task a hell of a lot easier."

"Rules," the troll stated simply. "Huldufólk upper management won't allow it. Outright muggings draw too much attention, they say—and don't even ask about stealing children and livestock. Thus, we must resort to trickery or extortion."

"Okay, but this is Iceland. It might not be on the peninsula, but it's a Scandinavian country in all but geography."

"Allow me to stop you there," the troll said. "I can't get social welfare benefits."

"Right, you're invisible." I tsked in sympathy. "Wow, that's rough."

"Which leaves us at an impasse of sorts."

"It does." I thought about the situation for a second, chewing my thumbnail all the while. I might not like having a bit of fae magic running through me, but at times like this, magical intuition sure came in handy. "Okay, here's what I propose."

"I'm listening," the troll said, crossing his arms over his massive chest.

"I'm headed for a bar that's somewhere over there," I said, pointing in a general northeasterly direction. "On principle, I can't pay you protection money or whatever you want to call it. But I can buy you a couple of pints and a meal, if you're interested."

"And when the humans see food and drink floating around, how are you going to explain the poltergeist at your table?"

"Eh, don't worry about that. We'll find a place to sit where you won't be noticed—bars always have back rooms and dark corner tables—and I'll tell the waitress that I'm ordering for a friend who's in the bathroom or something."

The troll drummed his fingers on his arm. "Alright, so

long as you don't stab me in the back with that sword you've been fondling for the last several minutes."

"You're now my guest, so I wouldn't dream of it. C'mon, let's go get warm and fed."

It turned out the troll's name was Ásgeir. "Like the singer," he said, "although you probably wouldn't know him. He composes some very pleasant musical arrangements, but his voice is a bit too sharp for my tastes."

"By the way, I don't 'fondle' my sword," I said after taking a good long draw off a dark ale. "Warriors don't *fondle* their weapons."

"So said the teenager when caught in the act," he said with a straight face. "It's nothing to be ashamed of—as natural an act as any."

I nearly spat beer all over the table. "That's what she said. Oh, wait—food's coming."

Our waitress was a pleasant-looking older woman with a warm smile and manners to match. Typically, Icelanders did not enjoy engaging in idle chatter. This might've made them seem aloof to most Americans, but I actually appreciated that I could avoid casual conversations via ocular aversion and feigned obliviousness.

"Your friend isn't back from the toilet yet?" she said as she set two plates down on the table, both piled high with double cheeseburgers and triple orders of waffle fries. "I hope he isn't ill."

"He's fine. As soon as he finished his pint, he had to take a phone call from work."

She nodded sagely. "You Americans, so obsessed with your careers. Not that we aren't ambitious, but we know how to relax."

"And drink," I said, taking a healthy slug off my beer. "Speaking of which, do you mind bringing us another round when you get a chance?"

"Of course," she said, eager to take the opportunity to break off the conversation.

As soon as the waitress bustled away, leaving us alone in our deserted corner of the pub, Ásgeir dove into his food with abandon. Somehow, he managed to stuff his face and chug beer while keeping his scarf in place. I had no idea how he did it.

"We Norse may know how to drink, but your countrymen perfected the art of eating," he said through a mouthful of waffle fries.

"Some might argue that the French hold that distinction," I said before digging into my burger.

"Yes, French cuisine certainly ticks several gustatory boxes. But the portions are atrociously small." He leaned in, whispering behind his hand unnecessarily. "Tell me, what's it like drinking a Big Gulp?"

"Absolute heaven on a hot Texas day. Sixty-four ounces of sugary, syrupy goodness. Insulin injections not included."

"Ah, I knew it," he replied. The troll took a huge bite of his cheeseburger, downing almost half of it at once. He held his sandwich aloft, eyeing it with his beady brown eyes as if it were a prized gem. "Dairy, meat, and bread. Simply glorious."

"Glad you approve. I'm also happy for the company."

"I as well. It beats ripping your head off, that's for sure."

"Or taking a sword in the gut," I said cheerfully.

"Hazards of the profession, although these days, there's honestly not much danger in it. Occasionally I shake down one of the lesser huldufólk, but they're generally not very impressive. I mean, what could a low-level bureaucrat do to me? Have me fired? Get me thrown out of my housing? Good luck with that."

I hadn't made many friends since I'd arrived in Iceland —none, in fact, and to be honest I was starting to like this troll. My fae intuition hadn't revealed any malicious intent on his part, so on a whim, I decided to risk revealing recent events. "Thus far, I've not been very impressed with them either. But earlier, I ran into a couple that gave me the creeps."

"Let me guess—long hair, fetish for black leather and chrome, and carrying knives that made your skin crawl?"

"You know them?"

He swallowed half his beer in one go. "All the huldufólk's assassins look alike. Scandinavian death metal enthusiasts. Great music, silly aesthetic." The troll scratched beneath his hat with his thick, hairy fingers. "You must have really pissed someone off."

Ásgeir's food had disappeared while we spoke, so I pushed the rest of my burger and fries across the table.

"It's a talent," I said with a self-effacing grin. "Anything I need to know if I run into them again?"

The troll was already licking his fingers by the time I finished that sentence. "They're said to be among the oldest of the Hidden Folk. Some speculate they're *álfur* who were banished from Álfheimr long ago. I couldn't say for sure, but I know they do all the dirty work for their huldufólk brethren."

"Old magic, then."

"Indeed, and much deadlier than those gray-suited bureaucrats who run much of Reykjavik."

I ran my tongue across my incisors as I considered my next question. "Would you tangle with them?"

Ásgeir hitched his shoulders. "They don't frighten me. Once, my name was feared across this land. 'The spear of the gods,' they called me, because I solved problems for a few of the Vanir. Those days are long gone, but I have not forgotten how to do battle."

Suddenly, I had an idea. An evil grin stole across my face as the notion began to take shape in the dark recesses of my devious little mind. "Tell me, Ásgeir—would you like a job?"

10

W orking out the terms of Ásgeir's employment was a fairly simple matter. First, I warned him that several of the Celtic gods wanted me dead and he'd automatically be in danger by entering my employ. He responded by saying that he'd recognized the "godsmark" on me back on the bridge, and that all *our* kind shared enmity with the gods.

Choosing to ignore that remark, I opened with an offer of $100 USD a day. He countered with a request for a seventh part of all gold, silver, and other plunder we might find. Having never gotten rich off being at odds with the fae and the gods, I agreed. I figured it was a hell of a deal.

Now that I had a new bodyguard and drinking buddy, I felt a bit more confident roaming around Reykjavik all by my lonesome. The troll knew his way around town, and with him watching my back, I doubted that any of the huldufólk would get the jump on me. Ásgeir found us some cheap lodging, and I took a shower before laying down for a long overdue nap.

"You aren't going to eat me in my sleep, are you?" I asked, sitting up in bed to address the troll where he stood guard next to the door.

"If you insult my honor again, I'll be tempted."

"Got it. Just making sure."

I closed my eyes, and silence fell across the room for a few brief moments before the troll cleared his throat.

"Yes, Ásgeir?"

"Er, you wouldn't happen to have a book in that bag of yours, would you?"

I stifled an annoyed sigh. No need to get off on the wrong foot with my new employee during his first day on the job. "Sure, lemme check," I said, rummaging around in the Bag. I tossed several out on the adjacent bed. "I have some Batman comics, a few Neil Gaiman novels, a Joe Nesbø book I couldn't get into—"

"Which one?"

"*Knife*, I think."

"Hand it over."

Once he began reading, the troll was quiet as a mouse, and I drifted off to sleep to the intermittent rustle of pages turning. An indeterminate amount of time later, I was awoken in a surprisingly gentle manner by Ásgeir's huge hairy hand. While still in that that state between sleeping and waking, I noted again that he didn't smell much at all, except for the faintest odor of earth and stone.

"Colin, something is at the door."

I sat up, rubbing the sleep from my eyes. "Did you ask who it is?"

"Not someone, some*thing*. A magic thing some sort of construct, I think. It's not doing anything, just waiting outside. Since you are the magician, I figured you'd want to deal with it."

"Druid, actually. Okay, keep an eye on the door while I get dressed. I have a feeling this is what I've been waiting for."

After pulling on a pair of jeans over my boxers, I stealth-shifted and summoned a fireball, which I hid behind my back. Then, I cracked the door open to find no one and nothing standing there.

"Ásgeir, there's nothing out here—"

"Ahem."

The voice was male and strange sounding, as if it were coming from far away and from underneath the floor at the same time. I looked down and nearly shat my pants.

"Gah!" I said, jumping back a step.

The troll was at my side in an instant, throwing the door open to reveal what stood behind. "It's merely a puppet," he remarked drily.

"That is a ventriloquist's dummy. Didn't you see *Goosebumps* or *Toy Story 4*? They're almost as bad as clowns." I glanced down at the dummy again, which was staring up at me with a shiver-inducing Howdy Doody smile. "Holy fuck, that's creepy."

The dummy straightened its bowtie as it cleared its throat. "My master, the great and powerful god Loki, requests your presence at his manor at 10:00 p.m. this evening. BYOB and don't be late, bitches."

Once it had delivered its message, the dummy ran off down the hallway. True to form, the damned thing ran all herky-jerky with its arms flailing in the air, laughing maniacally and bumping into shit along the way. A fat middle-aged lady wearing way too much polyester stuck her head out the door next to ours just in time to see the dummy disappear around the corner.

"Someone's kid, playing pranks," I offered lamely.

"Hmph!" she replied, slamming her door.

I retreated inside the room, closing the door and locking it behind me. After checking the lock twice, I turned to find Ásgeir sitting on the other bed, staring at me.

"You did not tell me we were working for the god of mischief," he said in a neutral voice.

"I'm not working *for* him; I'm working *with* him. Big difference."

"Regardless, it has been some time since I had dealings with the gods. Normally, I would welcome such an opportunity. But that one is hated by Aesir, Vanir, Álfar, and Jötnar alike. Even the Dökkálfar despise him, Colin, and for good reason. He cannot be trusted."

"Be that as it may, we need him to get where we're going. From what I've been told, he's the only one willing to help who knows how to get there."

"And just where is 'there'?" the troll asked.

"Er, Jotunheim."

"My fee just doubled," he said with finality. Ásgeir

stood, grabbing his book and snatching the blanket off the second bed before he headed for the bathroom. "Daylight approaches. Please keep the curtains closed until nightfall, else you may have to find another troll to employ. Good day, druid."

As we were leaving the hotel that evening, Bryn pulled up on her bike. She wore one of those dark-visored helmets that concealed your identity, like an assassin in a Korean action flick. I recognized the bike as soon as it pulled into the light due to the "Valhalla Bound!" sticker on the gas tank. After cutting the engine, the valkyrie removed her helmet and gave her scalp a brisk rub with her fingertips.

"Bryn, fancy seeing you here," I said.

"I see you've gained a companion," she replied archly.

"Got stranded, and I needed a guide. Plus, he can quote every line from *Airplane!* on cue."

"Surely you cannot be serious," Bryn replied. "He's a troll, and is as likely to eat you as to provide assistance."

"I am serious, and don't call me Shirley," Ásgeir replied flatly as he scanned the shadows for threats.

Honestly, I'd had no idea if he could actually quote from the movie. As far as I was concerned, his off-the-cuff response was worth whatever I ended up paying him. If he was a dog, I'd have given him a belly rub and a treat.

The valkyrie looked confused, and I stifled a laugh as I tried to save her further embarrassment. "I take it Click told you where to find me? He's the only one who'd know I was here. Well, him and Loki. Hell if I know how he does it, but that sneaky fucker has a knack for showing up out of nowhere, no matter where I am."

"He did. In fact, he sent me to give you a ride. We're to convene at your camp and travel to the dark god's abode from there." She looked down her nose at Ásgeir. "However, I only have room for one. The troll will need to find another way to follow us, if he so chooses."

I rubbed my forehead because her attitude was giving me a headache. "For the last time, I am not riding bitch on your bike, even if it turns into a pegasus or some shit—"

"It does," Ásgeir and Bryn replied in unison.

"—and I am not leaving Ásgeir behind. He's working for me now, so where I go, he goes."

"Whatever you say, druid," the valkyrie said. "But when he rips your arm off in your sleep, don't say I didn't warn you."

With that, Bryn slipped her helmet on, fired up her bike, and rode off into the sky. As soon as the bike's tires left the ground, I plugged my ears with my fingers. But this time, there was no flash of lightning or clap of thunder. Bryn's motorcycle merely morphed into a jet-black horse with wings.

"She's showing off, isn't she?" I said.

"Indeed she is," the troll responded.

"So, what's her deal?"

"The Valkyries work for Odin. Odin and the other Aesir hate all giantkind. It is as simple as that."

"But aren't some of the gods part giant? I mean, besides Loki. Like Thor, for instance."

"I do not bother myself by attempting to decipher the ways of the gods," he replied. "And I suggest you do not, either."

"Right. Well, we still need to meet up with Click—that's my magic teacher—"

"Your teacher is magic, or he teaches you magic?"

"Um, both, actually. Hang on, I'm about to get us a lift."

"Hang on to what, exactly?" Ásgeir said with mild amusement in his voice.

"Your socks," I said, calling on the Oak's power to transport us both to the Grove.

The troll staggered a bit as he got his bearings, then he spent several seconds staring at our new surroundings. He held out his hand, gaping at it as he turned it this way and that.

"There is... light, here. And yet, I am still flesh."

"Yeah, I brought a vampire here once, and she had the same reaction." I plucked a huge orange from a nearby tree and tossed it to him. "I hope you don't mind eating vegan, 'cause the animals are off limits."

"I, um..." the troll said, seemingly at a loss for words.

"Don't sweat it. Go frolic, find someplace to bask in the sun, take a swim, whatever you want to do. When it's time to go, I'll find you."

I left him staring at the sky overhead while I went to find Click. Truth was, I didn't really have to go anywhere to find him; I just wanted to give Ásgeir some privacy in case he wanted to take that scarf off. Obviously, he had some issues with his appearance—and why was none of my business.

A quick jog into the woods took me far enough away from the troll to break his line of sight, and I cupped my hands to my mouth as I threw my head back. "Yo, Click. Where y'at?"

"Right here, lad. No need ta' shout."

I spun around, and of course the pseudo-god was sitting on a nearby log just a few feet behind me. "Oh, good, you're here."

"Where else would I be? Playin' fidchell wit' yer new employee?"

"Hell if I know. Anyway, we need to get Bryn here and split. I portalled in using the Oak's powers—"

"I know," Click said as he trimmed his fingernails with a penknife. Each piece he cut away went up in a puff of smoke as it fell away from the blade. "Loki arranged it so the Tuath Dé will not be able ta' track ya' nor yer magic tree—least, not on the island. If ya' leave the bounds o' Loki's influence, yer' on yer' own."

"Then why did you send Bryn to fetch me?"

"I figured ya'd fancy a ride on a flyin' horse. Not often ya' get the chance ta' do such things."

"Um, no, but thanks for thinking of me."

"Suit yerself," he said, tilting his head as if he were listening to something only he could hear. "It'll only take the valkyrie thirty minutes or so ta' get here, in Earth time. That gives ya' plenty o' time ta' rest, an' I suggest ya' take it. Once yer' done, ya'd best take us Earthside ta' avoid revealing yer' Oak and Grove ta' the Aesir."

"That fast? Man, those pegasi can move."

"It's not pegasuses?" he asked, straight-faced.

"Pretty sure it's pegasi."

"Huh. Been saying it wrong fer a millennia."

On Click's advice, I ate, bathed, and then took one hell of a nap. Sleeping in the Grove always restored me more fully than sleeping Earthside—one of many reasons why it had become my preferred place to sack out. Stealing time was another, and security, a third.

I hadn't slept well at the hotel, an issue that became more pronounced the more time I spent away from Earth. It was easy to blame it on nerves, but the stronger my connection to the Grove became, the less at ease I felt sleeping elsewhere. Was I becoming addicted to its magic, or was this a natural effect of bonding with a druid oak? Yet another question I had for Finnegas once he'd recovered.

After getting dressed, I exited my Keebler cottage to find Ásgeir pacing outside. He was wringing his hands and mumbling to himself, and based on the path he'd worn into the grass, he'd been out there a while. I cleared my throat to get his attention and avoid startling him.

The troll looked up and stopped midstride, his beady dark eyes staring at me in panic from between his hat and scarf. "Oh, good, you're awake. You have to get me out of here. I can't take it any longer."

The strain in his voice was evident, so I responded in the calmest tone possible. "Ásgeir, calm down and tell me what's wrong."

"It's the light. I feel so—*exposed,* here. At first, I thought it was wonderful. But then, I couldn't get away from it. I tried to find a dark place to hide, but there weren't any to be found. It's unsettling, druid."

Damn, I should've thought of that. I may as well have thrown a scorpion in the ocean.

"I'm sorry, Ásgeir—really, I am. We're about to leave, but next time I'll make sure there's a nice, dark cave for you to rest in."

The troll shook his head furiously. "Oh no, I'm never coming back here. Not in a thousand years."

Trolls weren't meant for the light, it seemed. That made me a bit sad for Ásgeir. But if there was one thing I'd learned as a druid, it was that the natural course was almost always the best to take.

"Okay," I said, leading him by the hand toward my little cabin inside the tree trunk. "Why don't you go inside, pull the curtains, and shut the door? I'll come for you when we're ready to go."

"Th-thank you, Colin," he stammered as he eagerly squeezed his bulk through the doorway.

Well, damn, now I feel like a jerk.

As much sympathy as I felt for the troll, I didn't want to send him Earthside solo. A formidable opponent he might be, but he'd be no match for Badb or Aenghus. Not to mention, a troll appearing out of nowhere would arouse suspicion should any of their lackeys be surveilling the forest. On the odd chance they showed up, I didn't want him to face them alone.

Feeling the weight of urgency caused by Ásgeir's

nervous state, I made some hasty preparations for whatever adventures we might face. A few provisions, rearranging the gear and weapons I kept at the ready in my Bag, that sort of thing. Then, I called for the troll and took us back to the little camp we'd set up in the woods.

Oddly enough—but not unexpectedly—Click had arrived before us. He sat by the fire, kicked back against a log with a cold beer in one hand and a pair of tongs in the other. Thick, fat sausages sizzled on the grill along with kebab sticks stacked with onions, peppers, and potato halves. He might've been a pain in the ass, but he was a good cook, and the fact that he anticipated my mortal needs almost made up for the tricks and surprises he sprung on me.

It was dark out, as little time had passed while we were in the Grove. The set of Ásgeir's massive shoulders relaxed almost as soon as we found ourselves in the cool night air. Click reached into a nearby cooler, tossing the troll a cold liter of Belgian ale as he gestured at a nearby stump.

"Have a seat, troll. Ya' been wearing new holes in them shoes fer' hours. May as well sit fer' a spell whilst we wait fer' the valkyrie."

"Thank you," the troll said as he followed Click's suggestion. "How did you know that I prefer Belgian ales?"

"Um, Click has a knack for anticipating events," I said. "Call it intuition, I guess."

"Ah, you're Colin's magic teacher," Ásgeir observed as he popped the cork from his bottle. "You wouldn't happen to have a tulip snifter, would you? Seems rather barbaric to drink this out of the bottle."

Click snapped his fingers and a glass appeared in his hand. "Here ya' go."

The troll nodded his thanks. "Ah, I'd forgotten the conveniences one enjoys while in the company of wizards."

"You used to hang out with wizards?" I asked distractedly as I trimmed a nicely crisped piece of casing from a sausage on the grill. My efforts earned me a rap on the knuckles from Click's tongs, but I popped it in my mouth just the same. *Delicious.*

"Ásgeir once moved in some rather lofty circles," Bryn stated haughtily as she strolled out of the shadows. "You should ask him how he gained such status with the gods, druid."

I hadn't heard her approach, and the Oak only warned me of her presence a few seconds prior to when she made her presence known. Whatever weird form of teleportation or cloaking the Valkyries used, it was effective. I realized she'd been testing me the night previous, when we hid from Jay and Bob in that alley.

Or gauging my strengths and weaknesses. Naughty, naughty.

"Enough, Bryn," Click said abruptly, in a voice that had just enough edge to be threatening. "I'll not have ya' ruinin' my meal with yer' stories. 'Sides, we all have a few skeletons in our closets, do we not?"

The valkyrie drew her mouth into a thin line. "Indeed. Forgive my manners." She looked at the steaks sizzling over the fire, softening her expression as she licked her lips. "The ride here was long. If you have room for one more, I could stand for a bite and a drink."

"That's the spirit, lass," Click said as he tossed her a cold one from the cooler. "Hard times ahead, so ya' best tank up whilst ya' can."

The Welsh trickster's tone was way too cheerful for such an ominous remark, no matter how offhanded it might have seemed. If Click was happy, things were about to go to shit. As I met his gaze across the fire, the wink he gave me tied my stomach in knots.

Ah, fuck.

11

E xcept for Click, we enjoyed our meal in silence. The trickster was determined to entertain us with bawdy jokes, despite the mood of his audience. His earlier comment had put a damper on my enthusiasm and appetite, and our other two companions pointedly ignored each other while they ate. All in all, it looked like this was going to be one hell of a fun rescue mission.

But before we could move forward, we needed to speak with Loki. Once we'd finished our dinner, a snap of Click's fingers removed all trace of our trash, plates, and scraps. I doused the fire with some druid magic while silently instructing the Oak to return the forest to its original appearance. The fewer clues we left of our passing, the better.

Across camp, Bryn was adjusting the tack on her pegasus. As she worked, she said something to Ásgeir in Old Norse that I didn't understand. In response, he scratched his head with only his middle finger extended. The valkyrie hissed before turning back to her task. I had a feeling I would regret my choice in road companions when this whole mess was over.

"Are ya' ready?" Click asked as he appeared at my elbow. "Once we get started with Loki, there's no turnin' back."

"Why do I have a feeling I'm going to regret this?"

"Because ya' are, but there's no gettin' around it. Trust me, I've looked fer' alternatives."

"Fine. Let's get it over with," I said with finality.

Click clapped his hands and rubbed them together like a child anticipating a rather delicious treat. "Thought ya'd never ask." A portal large enough to walk a horse with wings through opened up in front of us, and the magician stepped aside, pushing me out of the way with one hand. "Ladies first, o' course. An' don'cha worry, Loki knows yer' comin'."

"Would that normally be a problem?" I whispered after Bryn had led her winged horse through.

"Possibly," Click said with a frown. "The Valkyries were the ones who ferried him ta' the island after Odin had him poisoned. So, I s'pose there might be a bit o' bad blood there."

"Great," I sighed. "Anything else I should know?"

"Invest in companies that make surgical masks an' other personal protective equipment. Ye'll make a mint. Oh, no, wait a minute," he said, tapping his finger on his chin. "Scratch that, wrong timeline."

"Why do I get the feeling I just dodged a bullet?"

"Because ya' did," Click said as he signaled that the

mountain troll should head through next. "Bad business, that."

"As bad as the Hellpocalypse?" I asked.

"Worse." He nodded at the portal. "C'mon, lad. Destiny awaits."

"One of many," I quipped.

"An' believe me, it's fer the best."

Despite my reticence I walked through the portal, leaving Click to take up the rear. We exited onto Loki's front walk behind the retaining wall. Apparently Click had the foresight to keep the valkyrie's steed away from prying eyes. I could only assume that a mortal would see her pushing a motorcycle, or see nothing at all, but those of the supernatural world might wonder.

When the portal closed, I turned to say something to Click only to be interrupted by a tug on my pant leg. I looked down, and there was the ventriloquist's dummy, staring up at me with hateful glee.

"Gah!" I screamed, jumping sideways a good five feet. "Keep your hands to yourself, alright?"

"As you wish," the dummy said, bowing deep at the waist. "My master requests your presence in the garden. Follow me."

The pint-sized mannikin did a clumsy pirouette, as if it were fighting gravity and a bad case of vertigo all at once. Then it took off toward the side of the house in a loose-limbed, awkward gait that gave me the willies. I shook my head in disgust, then I queued up an immolation spell, just to be safe.

Bryn pulled up alongside me, leading her horse like a dog at heel. "Honestly, druid. It's just a toy."

"Uh-uh, nope. What it is, is an abomination. Did you see the murder in its eyes when it startled me? The thing *enjoyed* seeing me jump."

"For once—and let me say, probably for the only time —I'm in agreement with the valkyrie," Ásgeir said. "It's harmless, if somewhat unsettling."

"Pfft, harmless to whom?" I groused. "And what the hell is animating the damned thing, anyway? It obviously has sentience, and a lot more than a golem would. I think there's something inside that little murder puppet, and it ain't good intentions."

The troll sniffled, scratching his nose through his scarf. "Well, whatever you do, don't harm it. Loki may be attached to the entity that inhabits it. The last thing you'd want to do is insult him by attacking his majordomo."

"Fine. But if it touches me again, I'm cursing it with termites," I said as I stared holes in the dummy's back.

The damned thing kept walking forward, leading us to what I assumed was Loki's backyard. But after I made that comment, its head did a one-eighty like an owl, and it winked at me. Then it laughed like a maniac in its weird, faraway voice as its head slowly spun to face front once more.

I was just about to incinerate it when Click grabbed my wrist in an iron grip. "Do not even think about it, lad. Now, chin up—our host awaits."

We followed the Howdy-Doody doll from hell around the side of the house, past a series of neatly-trimmed putting greens. The grass was real and not fake turf, and most certainly magically maintained. Just past the greens, we were led through a metal and wood origami portcullis that opened sideways by folding over on itself, instead of swinging out like a normal gate.

And beyond that, it was a bachelor's paradise.

Loki's backyard was huge by Reykjavik standards, easily the size of three tennis courts laid side-by-side. Most of the side closest to the gate consisted of a massive in-ground pool, complete with a swim-up bar, a waterslide, and a hot tub. It was obviously heated, as steam rose from the surface in wisps of moisture that rose lazily until they dissipated in the cool night air.

To our left sat another portable bar that had been set up next to a DJ's booth, the kind that you might see at a music festival rather than in someone's backyard. Scantily-clad women were everywhere, each one more beautiful than the last—some engaged in conversation, some enjoying the pool, and the rest either dancing or chasing each other around the garden.

The DJ was a familiar face, although I couldn't remember her name. As for the guests, I recognized at least three supermodels, one Hollywood actress, and a member of the Greek royal family. For grins, I scanned the yard in the magical spectrum, revealing at least three sylphs, two undines, a rusalka, and a succubi. Besides Loki and present company, there were no other men in sight.

"What. The. Fuck," I said, just before Click closed my gaping jaw with a gentle lift of his hand.

"Don't gawk, lad. Makes ya' look like a newb."

Loki sat at the edge of the pool opposite us, a drink in each hand as he held court for a bevy of young, voluptuous women. He noticed us soon after we entered, acknowledging our presence by leaping to his feet and sloshing alcohol on his nearest companions.

"Colinlingus, Clicktastic, you made it!" he exclaimed exuberantly. "Mare, grab these fellas a drink, will ya?"

I followed Loki's gaze to see who he was ordering around, since I hadn't noticed any staff when we arrived. The dummy was nowhere to be found, but a short, thin man with ginger hair and freckles now stood behind the portable bar. He wore an old-school dark-blue suit and red bowtie that matched the dummy's outfit to a T. When his eyes met mine, the little bastard winked and flashed me an evil grin.

Meanwhile, Ásgeir had faded into the background, taking up post by the caterer's table. He seemed content to avoid notice, and busied himself by sneaking food when no one was looking. Bryn stood nearby, arms crossed with a mildly annoyed look on her face, tapping her foot in time to the steady techno beat of the track the DJ laid down.

Loki's now glamoured servant shoved a couple of froufrou drinks toward Click and I, complete with fruit garnish and little umbrellas. One look into his creepy, hate-filled eyes had me setting my drink down on a nearby table in due haste. Unperturbed by the source, Click took a long pull off his and gave it a nod of approval.

"Shite, but that creature makes a bangin' piña colada," the magician said as Loki walked over to embrace him, still soaking wet. He nodded to me, and to the troll, pointedly ignoring the valkyrie.

"Ahem," Bryn said, clearing her throat loudly enough to be heard over the music.

Loki slowly turned his head, smirking as he looked the valkyrie up and down. "Oh, didn't see ya' there, Mankiller. Where's your horse?"

"Grazing on your putting greens," she replied, deadpan. "When I left him, Tordenvejr was leaving a huge shit on your lawn. Looked to be a hole in one."

The god of mischief waved the insult off with a slosh of his glass. "Meh, it needed fertilizer anyway." He turned his back on the valkyrie, throwing an arm around my neck and Click's. "Walk this way, my fellow brohemians. I'm about to introduce you to a couple of Brazilian beach volleyball players who are just dying to meet my new American friend."

I cast a sheepish backward glance at Bryn, who merely rolled her eyes in return. The valkyrie grabbed the drink I set down and parked herself on a nearby lounge chair, feet kicked up in feigned indifference. Her neutral facial expression said she couldn't care less about Loki's insults, but way she chewed the ice in her drink told me otherwise.

Personally, I was all set to meet those volleyball players, but then Click had to ruin it by slinging Loki's arm off his shoulder. "We didn't come here fer' a remake of a *National Lampoon* movie, Loki."

I raised my hand meekly. "For the record, I have no objections to meeting Brazil's finest athletes."

Loki smile broadly. "See, Clicktonator? The kid's down to party, and we have the whole night to talk business. So, why not relax and enjoy yourselves before I send your apprentice off to his doom?"

"Yeah, Click—say what?" I said as I did a double-take. "What's this about apprentices marching off to their doom?"

"Did I say doom? I meant 'room,'" Loki replied. "Mare —refill—now!" he yelled across the pool before addressing me once more. "Yeah, I most definitely meant to say room, as in the bedroom you're gonna bang those volleyball players in later. I got guest rooms out the yin-yang, so feel free to take your pick."

"Oh, I think there's a young female 'thrope who might have somethin' ta' say about that," Click said, scowling at me.

"Now, now—I was only going to chat them up," I said with a shrug. "Besides, it's been seven months since I heard from Fallyn. If she intended to continue our relationship, she'd have at least answered a text by now."

"Ghosted ya', eh?" Loki replied. "Happens to the best of us. And there's only one cure for that, Bromeslice—"

"Enough!" Click barked, snapping his fingers. Instantly, the music stopped as everything and everyone in the yard froze in place except for Click, Loki, and me.

"Loki, we don't have time fer' this shite," Click hissed, his voice cutting through the unnatural silence that had fallen all around. "The lad is on a mission, and if we don't get on with it immediately, very bad things'll happen."

"Týr's missing hand, Gwydion," Loki sulked. "When did you become such a drag?" The god of mischief whispered behind his hand to me in an aside. "I still have it— the hand, I mean. Fen barfed it up a few days later, so I kept it as a souvenir. Kids do the darnedest things, ya' know?"

I gave Loki a polite smile and nod before I addressed Click. "What 'very bad things' are we talking about here? And why didn't you mention this to me earlier?"

Click had the grace to at least look flustered. "It's best that ya' not know yer' own future, lad. Knowin'll cause ya' all sorts o' trouble. Ye'll go tryin' ta' change things, an' if yer' not careful, ye'll create more problems than ya' solve."

"He's right, kid," Loki said. "I've always told the Gwydster he was nuts for messing around with time magic, but he wouldn't listen. Powerful mages are *always* like that. Tell 'em not to mess with necromancy because they might start a zombie apocalypse, and they'll say something like, 'Oh, but think of the problems we could solve,' or 'And what's so bad about that?' More hubris than scientists, and way more dangerous."

Despite the nagging curiosity at the back of my mind, I didn't want to ask the obvious question. Click was right; it was best if I didn't know. But fuck destiny—I'd cheated death enough times to know that you make your own fate. Sure, there were millions of alternate outcomes to every decision a person made, but the only one that mattered was the path you chose. If life was a sea voyage, then choice was your rudder—no matter what the gods tried to make people think.

Click crossed his arms as he stared down his nose at the pale deity. "Speaking o' which, I seem ta' remember that a certain god was supposed ta' cast an augury fer us."

"And I did!" Loki exclaimed as he raised a finger skyward. "I know exactly where that Diane Keck chick is being held, too. Thing is, I can't send you there myself— I'm too weak. But I know some dudes who can show you the way."

"Great, then introduce us and we'll be off," I said.

Loki frowned and scratched the back of his head. "Yeah, about that—"

"Loki..." Click said in a warning tone.

"Don't get all pissy with me, Brodhisattva," Loki objected. "It's not like I was the one who cursed them and turned the whole clan into draugar. That's was Odin's deal, man. I had nothing to do with it."

"Feckin' shite," Click said, hanging his head and covering his eyes with one hand. "I knew this was goin' ta' be a dog's breakfast."

"'Draugr'—as in undead?" I asked. "What's the big deal about a bunch of zombies? We just go in, kick their asses, and make them show us the way to Jotunheim."

"Eh, not quite," Loki replied. "Our undead are a bit more, shall we say, *complex*, than what you've seen in the States."

"How so?"

"Hmm, let's see. They retain all the skills they had in life, so if they were a warrior, they'll fight just as well dead as they did alive. They also have giant-like strength, they can shape-shift, and the really nasty ones can do magic. Weather control, dream-walking, altering their size and mass, and the like." He snapped his fingers as if remembering something important. "Oh, and they're resistant to most weapons. Iron will ding 'em up a bit, but it won't kill them. You pretty much have to drag them back into their graves to defeat them. Yeah, I think that's it."

"One draugr can be a handful fer' a single hero," Click added. "An' if a whole clan were cursed—"

"It won't be a cakewalk, that's for sure," the god of mischief said. "The good news is, all you gotta' do is beat their leader, Jerrik. Once you kick his ass, the rest will fall in line."

"Oh, joy," I replied. "Anything else I should know?"

The Norse god nodded. "Beating Jerrik probably won't convince them to help you. All that'll do is settle them down."

"So, how do you suggest that we get them to show us the way to Jotunheim?" I asked.

Loki looked around, framing a nearby model's ass with his hands. "I dunno. Lift their curse, maybe? That'd probably work. Pretty sure they're tired of being undead by now." He glanced at Click. "Mind lifting this stasis field? I have a party to get back to."

"Uh-uh, nope," Click replied. "This is yer' plan, so yer' comin' with us."

12

Needless to say, Loki wasn't too keen on accompanying us to the draugars' location. At first, he refused to help us at all—until Click reminded him of our deal.

"No trip to Jotunheimr, no trip ta' Vegas," the magician had stated with finality.

After Loki pissed and moaned for several minutes, Click promised he wouldn't have to do anything other than advise. That seemed to mollify the immortal fuckboi, and Loki finally agreed to tag along in an advisory capacity. The god was still hacked at having to leave his own party, though.

Our destination was a small, bowl-shaped barrow, hidden in a craggy valley high in the mountains of the central Highlands. Click portalled us there, and I led the way into the depression with Bryn at my side and Ásgeir on rear guard. Loki sulked above us, leaning against a large boulder at the edge of the barrow, wrapped in a fur blanket with a bottle of Brennivín in hand.

Click appeared at my side as we neared the entrance, resting a hand on my arm to halt me before I walked in.

"I'll scout ahead," Ásgeir said as he brushed past. It took a pointed look from Click before Bryn also took the hint. "Fine, I'll help him. The troll shouldn't be left alone, anyway. He's sure to betray us at the first opportunity."

I rubbed a hand across my face as Bryn entered the tomb. "I can already tell that this is going to be a hell of a fun time." Loki looked to be asleep above us, so I leaned in to whisper in Click's ear. "Hey, I meant to ask you—"

"Loki's not using magic ta' seduce women, lad," Click said, cutting me off. "I'd not be friends with him if he were. 'Sides, it's against the trickster's code. We're not a bunch of bloody fookin' rapists, like that prick Diarmuid."

"That's cool. I'd be damned disappointed if he did. Loki might be annoying, but I can't help but like the guy." I nodded at the crypt. "So, what can we expect in there?"

"That's what I was goin' ta' tell ya'. Loki spoke true with regards ta' the powers o' the draugar. Ye'll hafta' best their chieftain, and quickly, if ya' wish ta' barter favors with 'em. Yer' other half'll likely want to scrap with the lot o' them, so resist the urge. Even that one can't fight off a couple dozen draugar. Jest' focus on wrestling their leader back to his grave pit, and that'll give ya' time ta' bargain."

"Anything else I should know?"

"Hmm. If ya' get into a bind, fire might hold 'em off. They're basically creatures o' cold, and as old as they are, some'll go up like a wick under the right conditions." He clapped me on the shoulder like a little league coach sending his star player off to win the game. "Now, go get 'em, lad. And remember, Finn's fate and the fate o' the world depends on ya'."

"What? Hey, wait—" I said, but Click had already disappeared. "Ah, fuck."

With nothing left but to enter the crypt, I started shifting. I was tempted to change into my full Fomorian form, but I decided that the element of surprise might gain me some small advantage. It was a sure bet that the draugar would recognize Bryn for what she was, and they'd likely focus on her and Ásgeir. If those two could keep the clan occupied, I might be able to sneak up on Jerrik and drag him back to his grave.

The whole plan sounded like a lot of "ifs" and "mights" to me, but it was the best I could come up with on short notice. You'd think with a couple of legendary tricksters on my side, they'd have concocted a better plan than, "The bad guys are that way—have at it." Somehow, this whole thing felt like a setup, but that was a given where Click was involved. I simply had to trust that whatever scheme he was working on was ultimately to my benefit.

Yeah, right.

I'd nearly completed the process of stealth-shifting when Bryn stuck her head around the corner of the entrance. "First few chambers are clear, but the place is a maze." She glanced over her shoulder and shook her head. "I don't like this plan, druid. The fearsome reputation of the draugar is well-deserved. And Odin had a very good reason for cursing Jerrik's clan."

"Don't tell me," I said. "They were working for the giants."

"How did you know? Theirs is not a tale written in the sagas."

"Lucky guess. Listen, you and Ásgeir will have to keep them distracted while I take out Jerrik. Can you do that?"

She rubbed her chin for a few seconds before responding. "Perhaps, with the troll's help. Facing the entire clan in battle would be a death sentence, but we might be able to draw most of them away. I prefer large battlefields and open skies, so skulking through tunnels is not my strong suit. However, the mountain troll will be at home under earth and rock. He should be able to keep us ahead of the draugar for a time, if he does not betray us."

I threw my head back and let my mouth hang agape. "Fuck's sakes, would you give it a rest? I don't care what your beef is with trolls, or Ásgeir in particular. I just need you to help me rescue Dian Cécht."

She gave me a heavy-lidded sneer. "Fine. But don't say I didn't warn you, about the troll and the trickster both."

Bryn turned on heel and anger-strutted back into the barrow. When she was gone, Loki's voice echoed from above me.

"Valkyries. Can't fuck 'em, and you sure can't kill 'em."

"Why not?"

"Why can't you fuck 'em, or why can't you kill them?" he responded.

"Yes."

Loki chuckled. "Daddy issues."

Seeing in starlight and moonlight wasn't a problem when I stealth-shifted, but total darkness was another matter. Just to be safe, I cast a spell that would allow me to see in total darkness. The last thing I needed was to be caught blind when one of these draugr things attacked.

Ásgeir stood to my left, in front of the lone exit from the tomb's antechamber. The troll sniffed the air, then he laid a hand on the rock wall that framed the arched doorway.

"The draugar stir, druid."

"So much for the element of surprise," I replied. "Ásgeir, I want you and Bryn to take them on a wild goose chase. No need to fight unless it's absolutely necessary. Just distract them while I find their leader and bring him to heel. And if things get hairy, I want you two to split for the surface. I'll find my own way out."

Bryn hissed softly. "I do not think that's wise—"

"Then it's a good thing you're not in charge."

The valkyrie bristled. "Might I remind you that I do not work for you, druid? I am here on a voluntary basis, and I'm under no compulsion to take orders from you."

I knuckled my forehead before responding. "True, but there's a reason you volunteered to help me. I haven't figured out what it is yet, but I suspect you're under orders to either keep me alive, keep me under tabs, or both. Regardless, it'd make things a lot easier on everyone if you quit bitching and started acting like a team player."

"Fine, I will do as you ask," she said through gritted teeth. "And when the draugar are tearing the flesh from your bones, I will stay safely outside the barrow and listen as your screams fade away to nothing. Come, troll, it is time for us to do as the druid asks."

She took off at a jog, past Ásgeir and into the darkness. The troll merely chuckled.

"What?"

"It's just that what the magician told me about you is true," he said in an amused voice.

"And what is that?"

"He said, ah, that you certainly have a way with women."

"What's that supposed to mean?"

"As he put it, 'That lad could chase off a sex-starved spinster after slipping her a love potion an' giving her first mention in his will.'"

"Hold up—you think Bryn has the hots for me?"

"I believe she admires you, for reasons unknown," he replied. "Whether she wishes to breed with you remains to be seen."

"Er, right." I chewed my lip for a few seconds. "You think I was too hard on her?"

"You are a stranger in a strange land, on a quest to rescue a god from a jötnar chieftain who has hundreds of his brethren under his command. From what I've seen, your list of allies is rather short. I do not think you can afford to alienate those you have."

"I'll take that under consideration. You'd better catch up to her before she leaves you behind."

"The valkyrie could no more lose me in these tunnels than she could out-swim a seal in the sea," he said matter-of-factly. "But I will do as you ask. Do not tarry on your way to finding Jerrik, druid. Despite my talents, we will only be able to evade them in their own territory for so long."

The troll gave me a nod, then he was gone, moving more swiftly than I'd have thought possible on his spindly Herman Munster legs.

"And now that we all know where we stand," I muttered. "Time to get this show on the road."

I pulled Gunnarson's cloak of invisibility out of my Craneskin Bag, draping it across my shoulders as I prepared to wage a war of wills with the item. The cloak was semi-sentient and still pissed at me for killing its former master, the last of his line. Thus, I usually had to persuade it to work for me.

Surprisingly, for the first time ever, the cloak triggered as soon as I put it on. I still didn't trust it, though. For insurance, I cast a chameleon spell on myself in case the damned thing decided to go on the fritz at the worst possible time. It had happened before, after all.

Once I knew I wouldn't be seen, I took off at a slow, measured pace into the bowels of the tunnels. As I moved further into the darkness, it occurred to me that I was basically doing a dungeon run. Hell, I may as well have been playing an MMO or an open-world RPG; I was headed into a system of ancient catacombs, which were inhabited by draugar, on a mission to subdue their skeleton king.

All-in-all, it was a pretty wicked scenario. It'd be even better if I didn't get killed in the process. To avoid such a disaster, I'd need to keep my head in the game. Since I had no real-world experience raiding draugar dungeons, I thought back to the years I'd spent gaming when I was a kid, long before my first brush with The World Beneath.

So, what's the first thing you usually run into on a typical dungeon dive?

Spider webs?

Check.

Spooky runes and creepy faces carved into the walls?

Double check.

Traps?

Click.

"Aw, son of a b—!"

I fell about twenty feet, landing on a heap of bones with a loud crunch. Thankfully, the pile was large enough to keep me from being impaled on the rusty iron spikes that lined the bottom of the pit. Based on the height of the stack, dozens of grave robbers and other dungeon delvers had died here. Some had fallen prey to the spikes, while others appeared to have perished from injuries suffered on impact.

Lucky for me, Fomorian bones didn't break easily. I stood unsteadily, bones crunching underfoot as I scanned

the chamber for an escape route. The stone trapdoor I'd
fallen through revolved on a hinge in the center of the slab.
As it tilted back into place above, I heard something click,
then a tiny pulse of magic flowed through the trapdoor.

So, the trigger was magical as well as physical. Interesting.

It made sense, considering it would be impossible to
get a giant stone slab so perfectly balanced that it would
swing open at the slightest pressure. Magic would be
required to make the trap work, either to reduce friction
between the stone and hinge or to overcome inertia and
get the trapdoor moving—or both. Using a pressure plate
to trigger the spell was a simple, yet elegant solution. No
need for complicated spell weaves, just a few carved runes
that would complete a circuit when the plate was
depressed.

Slick.

It was ingenious enough to impress me, and I knew a
lot about creating wards and magic traps. Yet the sapper's
ingenuity also meant I couldn't easily trigger the latch
from underneath, even if I could reach the door above.

Piss.

"Well, it could be worse," I muttered to myself.
"Imagine if some of these skeletons were alive."

At that precise moment, a thin, bony hand latched
around my ankle.

"What the—?"

The hand was definitely not disembodied, although
that was the first thing that came to mind when I looked
down. Instead, it was attached to a gray leathery arm, one
with ancient Nordic runes tattooed into its flesh. Its grip

was supernaturally strong, enough to cause me pain even in my stealth-shifted form. I suspected that if I had been in my fully human form, it would have snapped my ankle.

As if being grabbed by an obviously undead creature while stuck in a pit full of human bones wasn't bad enough, the thing shrieked beneath me. The creature's howl was a cross between a moan and a roar, and it echoed with the sort of frustrated rage that only the undead can manage. In the Hellpocalpyse, I'd heard similar cries on a nightly basis. I'd spent most of my evenings there hiding on rooftops and in attics, drifting off to sleep while the living dead wailed their never-ending lament below.

It still gave me nightmares.

On instinct, I released a very weak lightning bolt spell that struck the creature on the back of the forearm. The shock did very little to harm it, but that wasn't the point. As the electrical charge hit the nerves and muscles I targeted, the hand slightly flexed open for a brief instant. That opening was enough for me to yank my leg free so I could gain a few feet of distance between me and my assailant.

There are things they never teach you in magic school that every magic user learns on the fly. One of them is that it's very hard to safely dry your own clothes with magical heat while you're still in them. An afternoon spent smelling of burned pubes is usually enough to cure a magician of that notion forever.

Similarly, attempting to fly by way of wind power almost always ends in disaster, you can't charge a phone with a lightning bolt spell, trapping spiritual entities inside mundane objects is a lot scarier and more dangerous than cartoons would have you believe—and, oh yeah, never cast a fireball spell in an enclosed space.

Of course, anyone who has ever played D&D could tell you that. But people from all walks end up studying the magical arts, and many of them have never even heard of tabletop roleplaying games. So, every year, some dumbass apprentice blows himself up by casting a fireball inside his house. Such events are always reported as natural gas explosions, but those of us who are clued in know what really happened.

Anyone who makes it past their first year studying magic learns these things, usually the hard way while their tutor laughs at them from a very long distance away. I knew them, and I'd most definitely learned those lessons through trial and error while Finnegas had his share of laughs at my expense. Thus, casting a fireball inside that pit of horrors wasn't the first tactical option that came to mind.

But when every last skeleton and cadaver in that place began to stir, I very nearly lost my shit. And when they all came crawling at me like a pile of angry, dusty, click-clacking ants, I got over my fear of self-immolation faster than you could say "Fire Marshal Bill." Before I knew what I was doing, I'd summoned a fireball in each hand while backing up into the farthest corner of the pit.

I had one last thought before I unleashed hell's fury on the roomful of skeletal warriors.

Hopefully my eyebrows will grow back.

13

I knew that if I just blasted the center of the room, I'd get tossed back into the wall and be caught in the expanding flame-ball of death that I was about to release. So, I decided to get creative. Having near-vampire speed and werewolf strength came with a few advantages, chief among them being capable of superhuman feats of agility.

At Click's behest, I'd recently spent a great deal of time experimenting with said skills. In addition to practicing magic spells old and new, I'd put in endless hours pushing the limits of my shifted physical abilities in the relatively safe confines of the Grove. As I'd previously discovered, each form had its own unique benefits and drawbacks—but now I knew how to take advantage of them.

My full Fomorian form was stronger, more durable, and it healed a heck of a lot faster, but its bulk made it difficult to do maneuvers that required rapid changes in direction and speed. On the other hand, my stealth-shifted form was quicker and lighter, although it lacked the sheer toughness and hard-hitting mass of my other form. Still, all that speed and agility had its advantages, and I was practically the king of parkour in this form.

Figuring that I could kill two birds with one stone, I tic-tacced up the corner of the pit, kicking off one wall and then the other. Within two strides I'd covered fifteen feet of vert, at which point I twisted in midair so I faced the ground with my back to the trapdoor above. Then, I released my fireball spells, aiming them at the writhing pyramid of desiccated corpses and skeletons in the center of the room.

One decent fireball spell can do a lot of damage. Two was probably overkill in a space that small, but I was going for more than just incineration. The fireballs converged just as they hit the mass of bones and dried flesh, releasing all that pent-up heat in one massive conflagration of fiery magic. I closed my eyes just as the skeletal warriors were engulfed, covering my face before the explosive gases expanded to include me as well.

I had yet to reach the apex of my upward trajectory, so I was moving with the pressure wave when it hit. As the rapidly-expanding ball of heat and gas struck, it propelled me into the underside of the trap door. I hit the stony surface hard as I performed a simple judo break fall, a maneuver designed to protect the vulnerable parts of the body upon being thrown to the ground.

Having never done the move upside down, my timing was a bit off, and I accidentally shattered my elbow on impact. The good news was that the pressure wave hit the trap door harder than it hit me, breaking the latch and swinging it open as all those gases released into the tunnel above. With expert timing—and a little luck—I kicked off the door, landing lightly in the corridor where I'd started moments before.

My clothes and hair were nearly burned off, my skin was blackened and blistered in several places, and I had a broken arm—but I was alive and had escaped the pit of doom. The only items on me that weren't damaged were my Craneskin Bag and the invisibility cloak, both having been imbued with resistances to elemental and physical damage by their makers. Despite the broken arm and the second and third-degree burns I'd suffered, I thanked my lucky stars that I hadn't suffered worse.

Moreover, the noise from the explosion seemed to have attracted a number of the barrow's other denizens. As the trap door slammed back into place with a sort of booming crunch, I noticed a handful of human figures running up the tunnel in my direction. The smoke and dust from the explosion made it difficult to make out many details, but it was clear they were different from the animated skeletons I'd just incinerated.

Deciding it was best to hide and heal until I knew what I was up against, I ducked into an alcove to wait for them to pass. As they emerged from the rapidly dissipating plume of dust and smoke, my enhanced vision revealed their strange features in the near dark of the tomb.

Rather than being made of dried up bones and flesh, the figures that ran up the tunnel were completely whole, and their flesh was entirely intact. However, their skin had taken on a sickly, blue-green hue, like that of a nasty bruise the day after an injury. In addition, their bodies were bloated and deformed, like corpses left in the sun to rot. Ugh, and the smell—it was the decaying stench of putrefied human flesh, a scent I'd become intimately familiar with in the Hellpocalypse.

So, these must be the draugar.

I'd expected them to be wearing armor and clothing appropriate for ancient Viking warriors, but instead they were mostly naked, save for the odd loincloth or leather skirt. Presumably, their bloated, malformed condition made it impossible to don such attire, but they did carry weapons of all kinds—axes, swords, maces, and the like. And based on the way they cast their hazy, bloodshot eyes this way and that, they intended to use them.

The five of them had nearly passed when the last in line paused to sniff the air. Without warning, his hand shot out with superhuman speed, grabbing me around the neck to lift me off the floor. As the draugr's hand closed like a vise, I felt tendons and ligaments pop in my neck, and the edges of my vision began to dim.

The suddenness of the attack and the surprising strength of the draugr threw me for a loop. The last thing I'd expected was to be found out so quickly. I'd personally had a hell of a time locating Gunnarson when he wore this cloak, so I knew from personal experience that it was a bitch to detect someone wearing the thing.

"Smoke gave ya' away, drood." the thing hissed in

thickly-accented English, its breath a fog of putrid gases. "They told us ya'd come."

I wanted to ask him *who* said I'd be coming—really, I did. But he was choking the shit out of me, making it kind of difficult to speak. My first order of business was getting free, as his buddies had taken notice and were headed back our way. Since I was hanging from the draugr's grasp, my feet were free to attack, so I gave him the mother of all drop kicks—both barrels, straight in the chest.

The impact loosened his grip slightly, allowing me to gasp a single breath. However, the undead warrior wasn't giving up that easily. Instead of running me through with the chipped, rusty sword he bore, he dropped it and clamped both hands around my neck. Then, he *grew*, expanding like the Hulk until he was half again his original size. No way was I getting out of his grip now.

I don't have time for this shit.

My hand was already gripping Dyrnwyn's hilt inside my Bag. As I slid it out, the blade blazed so hot it nearly burned off the rest of my hair. I whipped the sword around in a quick arc, landing a blow just above the draugr's left elbow. But rather than the satisfying *snikt* of Tylwyth Teg steel separating flesh and bone, the blade struck the thing's arm with a resounding *thunk*, bouncing off as if it had hit stone.

The draugr chuckled. "Immune to weapons, drood. Benefits of Odin's black curse."

He held me in one massive hand like a child, batting the sword from my grasp with the other. Then he shook me like you'd shake a dog, if you were a total asshole and thought it a deterrent to bad behavior. Laughing at my sword was one thing, but that really pissed me off.

Let's see if you're immune to this, dick.

"What'cha got there, Njal?" one of his companions said as they approached.

"Got the drood," my captor replied. "Tried cuttin' me with his magic toothpick. Tickled."

They all had a good laugh at that. Meanwhile, I started prepping a spell inside my head. I worked through the finger forms and arcane gestures openly, since I knew he couldn't see me. When it was ready, I began to grunt and struggle in earnest.

"Aw, that's cute," one of the draugr exclaimed. "He's makin' puppy noises."

"I think he wants ta' say somethin'," another said.

"Should I let 'em?" Njal asked.

"Why not?" one of his companions said. "Jerrik's going to hand him over anyway. May as well have some sport while he's here."

"Oh, alright," Njal replied, loosening his grip. "What say you, drood?"

"Grrmrrph," I croaked.

"What's he sayin'? I can't make it out," one of the draugr complained.

"Hang on," Njal responded, loosening his grip more. "Come again now, little one? What's yer' complaint?"

Finally able to take a breathe, I inhaled the foul, stale air that had been even further tainted while they spoke. Despite how nasty it smelled, it was the sweetest breath I'd ever taken. Extending my hands and spreading my fingers wide toward Njal and his buddies, I spoke.

"I said, *gearradh*," I growled as I unleashed Mogh's Scythe.

When Click and I first arrived on Icelandic soil, I'd struggled to cast the spell with any level of consistency. But after months spent here and the equivalent of years spent inside the Grove in practice, it was now one of my most potent weapons. The spell triggered instantly, sending a molecule-thin sheet of super-compressed air hurtling through the five draugr.

Since he was supporting my weight, Njal fell first, his arms, shoulders, and head tilting off his torso and sliding to the stone below as my feet hit the floor. A millisecond later, his friends suffered a similar fate, each of them bisected horizontally by my spell at the shoulders or neck, depending on how tall they were. Heads literally rolled, yet their bodies remained upright, as did Njal's legs and lower abdomen, which had been neatly sliced just above his nipple line.

The most disgusting smell was released from inside Njal's body, easily ten times as gut-churning as his breath. I gagged and dry-heaved as I peeled his hands from my throat. He was still animated, however, as were his companions, who were now bumping into each other as they stumbled around in an attempt to find their heads.

Not wasting any time, I grabbed Dyrnwyn and backed away quickly, leaping over the trap door to land on the other side. Allowing myself a brief backward glance to enjoy the scene I'd left behind, I snuck off down the corridor with Njal rasping curses behind me.

"Ya'll pay for that, drood. Just as soon as I get my body back together, I'm gonna find ya' and rip ya' limb from limb!"

"Get in line," I muttered as I headed deeper into the darkness.

———

By the time I found the chieftain's burial chamber, Ásgeir and Bryn were already there. But instead of being locked in a heated battle with Jerrik, they sat on upturned barrels around a stone sarcophagus, using the tomb as a table for a game of cards. My companions sat on one side, and a tall, gaunt draugr sat on the other. Based on the piles of gold, gems, and jewelry each player had in front of them, the troll was ahead by a vast margin.

Jerrik—or the draugr I assumed to be Jerrik, due to the gold jewelry he wore—had a huge stogie in his mouth that he puffed on as he looked at his hand. Ásgeir took a long drink from a silver mug, again somehow managing to do so despite the scarf covering his face. Meanwhile Bryn also puffed away on a cigar, flicking ash on the floor as she reached for a half-full bottle of vodka.

Needless to say, I was a little pissed that my companions were sitting around drinking and gambling while I was fighting draugars. I walked into the chamber, pulling off the invisibility cloak and stuffing it in my Bag. When no one noticed, I cleared my throat loudly.

"Druid, glad to see you made it," Ásgeir said as he gave me a sideways glance. "You look like hell."

"What the fuck are you two doing here, playing cards and shit while I was falling into pits and fighting the undead?"

Bryn examined her cards, scowling before she set them down on the makeshift table. "After the commotion you caused, we assumed that you'd taken on the task of distracting Jerrik's guards. We likewise assumed that you wished for us to approach the chieftain to negotiate his assistance in getting us to Jotunheimr."

"Brilliant idea, that explosion," Ásgeir added. "That really got their attention. Left us a clear path to Jerrik's tomb."

"Speaking of which," Bryn said, "allow me to introduce you to Jerrik the Betrayer, formerly king of the Norwegian Westland, now banished to the cold reaches of Iceland for complicit acts of treachery against Odin One-Eye." She turned to face the draugr before continuing. "Jerrik, meet Colin McCool, itinerant druid, descendant of Fionn mac Cumhaill, justiciar, giant-killer, god-slayer, fae-deceiver, ruler of the Junkyard Realms, and last of his line."

"Yeah, yeah," Jerrik rumbled in a deep, dry voice as he turned his cloudy gaze on me. "Enough with the horse shit introductions—I already know who he is. The Hidden Folk told us all about you, drood. Asked us to kill you. Lucky for you, they offered little in return."

"Little enough for Jerrik to entertain the proposition I presented," Bryn said. "And he has agreed to our—rather, your—terms."

I stood there for several moments, digesting the info while I tried to pretend I wasn't confused as all hell. "Um, great. So, you'll get us to Jotunheim?"

"He will assist us in finding the portal door to the realm of the jötnar, yes," Bryn replied. "On condition that you lift the curse Odin has placed on them, so they might find rest in death until Ragnorak comes."

"I—say what?" Flustered, I walked up to the table, snagging the vodka and taking a long slug. "You want me to lift a curse that was placed by a god—and not just any god, but Odin himself?"

Jerrik threw a card in the discard pile, drawing another card from the deck as he spoke. "The valkyrie has confidence you can complete this task. You don't look like much, but magicians never do. I have chosen to put faith in her judgement. Complete this task, and we will show you the doorway that leads to Býleistr's lands in Jotunheimr."

Oh, what the hell. The old man's life depends on it.

"I can try," I said. "That's the best I can promise."

About that time, Njal and his cronies ran into the burial chamber. Except for a thin scar across his chest, Njal looked none the worse for the wear, but two of his buddies held their heads under their arms. When he spotted me, he roared in anger at the top of his lungs. Spittle flew everywhere as his jaws stretched unnaturally wide, as if he meant to consume me whole where I stood.

"I will fucking kill you, Drooood!"

"Friends of yours?" Ásgeir asked as he plucked a card from the deck.

"I ran into them on my way here," I replied.

"Prepare to meet your gods," Njal said as he stormed across the chamber at me.

"No one will be meeting any gods today," Jerrik said, glancing at his cards and tossing them on the sarcophagus in disgust. "Cool your heels, Njal. If the drood bested you, that merely serves as proof that he's the man we need."

Njal skidded to a stop, his chest heaving as he glared at me. "What do you mean, Jerrik? He trespassed here, so his life is forfeit. That is our way."

Jerrik stood to his full height, leaning forward with his knuckles on his makeshift card table. He was considerably tall, seven feet if I guessed right, although I wasn't certain if that was due to his ability to alter his size or just his natural stature. He gave his underling a put-upon look, as if Njal was too stupid to comprehend what Jerrik was about to say.

"How long have we lived under the All-Father's curse, Njal? A thousand years or more. All because we chose to help one of the jötnar, who happened to be a chieftain among their people. For this we were branded traitors, cast out and cursed with the 'gift' of undeath."

"It was Odin's will, Jerrik," Njal said. "We got the fate we deserved."

"Bullshit," I said. "So you helped a giant. Big deal. Does that mean you deserve to suffer for a thousand years? Look, I've had plenty of dealings with the gods, and from what I've seen, the only thing that separates them from us is the power they wield. They use that power to make us suffer for their own amusement and whims, and frankly, I am fucking tired of it."

"What do you know of suffering, whelp?" Njal asked.

"The aetheling has good reason to hate the gods," Bryn said. "As do all who are present."

Njal crossed his arms over his chest. "I fail to see what this has to do with our clan, Jerrik."

"The arseling needs our help. In exchange, he has promised to lift Odin's curse from the clan."

"If I can," I interjected. "Lifting a god's curse is no easy task, so no promises. But if I do, then Jerrik has agreed to help us get to Jotunheim."

Njal looked back and forth between his chieftain and me, a smile slowly forming on his lips that turned into a full-blown belly laugh. "So, he helps us, and then we help him commit suicide?"

"Yes," Jerrik said.

Njal chuckled as he looked at the large pile of money in front of the troll, and the comparably minuscule piles that sat before Jerrik and Bryn. "You might be shit at games of chance, Jerrik, but this time I think you got the better deal."

14

Truth be told, I had no idea how to lift Odin's curse. When I asked Loki and Click for their assistance, they both claimed they couldn't help me. Loki said it was due to his current diminished state. Click simply stated that he was already being hunted by a powerful god, and he didn't need to piss off another.

I didn't bother pursuing that line of questioning further. I'd already tried to get Click to divulge his reasons for hiding out in Maeve's demesne—but, strangely, the quasi-god was atypically mum on that topic. Instead, I focused on the problem at hand, which was lifting the curse Odin placed on Jerrik and his clan.

"Are you sure they're the only ones who can get us to Jotunheim?" I asked.

"For the hundredth time, Bro Diddly, yes," Loki said. He lay prone on his kitchen island, covering his eyes with one arm while he treated his hangover with a bottle of Screaming Eagle '92. "No giant will take a mortal there—

willingly—and that's if you can find one to do so. Jerrik and his clan are the only mortals left who know how to navigate the paths that lead to Jotunheimr."

"Wait a minute," I said. "I thought we just had to find the portal and then, boom, we're there."

Bryn stuck her head out of Loki's fridge, where she'd been busy scrounging for food. "The gateways merely guard the way to the paths beyond—the pathways being the *real* Yggdrasil," she said as she took a bite of cold pizza. "We'll need to traverse the paths to get to Jotunheimr. The gods did this so that the jötnar, álfar, and duergar could not easily invade the other realms."

I walked around the kitchen island, snagging a slice from the pizza box Bryn had set on the counter. "Explain to me again what's so hard about finding a way through these magic paths?"

"They're a maze to those who don't know the way," Loki replied. "Not only that, but take one wrong turn and you'll end up in Álfheim or Svartálfheim—or even worse, Niflheim or Muspelheim." Loki gave an involuntary shiver. "Hard pass on that one, broski."

"Loki, aren't you one of them? I mean, why can't you take us there?" A collective gasp rose from the others in the room, and Click, Bryn, and Ásgeir suddenly averted their eyes. "What?"

Loki sat up, swinging his legs off the side of the counter. He paused to massage his left temple, shutting his eyes tightly against the bright lights overhead. "It's alright. I'm a lot less sensitive about the topic since dear old dad disowned me." He turned to me, fixing me with a squinty-eyed, bloodshot stare. "I used to know the way, but that's one of the things they took from me when Odin had Váli punish me for Baldur's death. I guess those douchebags didn't want me rallying my kin and starting Ragnarok early."

"Which begs the question," Ásgeir said, "what will the god of mischief do, should he be reunited with his jötnar brethren?"

Loki waved off the troll's question with a belch. "Believe it or not, I like this new, modern Earth too much to go starting an apocalypse. But a little good old-fashioned vengeance is never out of the question, eh?"

Click set aside the newspaper comics he'd been reading, folding them neatly and placing them on the dining room table. "So, lad, what's yer plan? How do ya' intend ta' lift the curse?"

"First off, what type of curse is it, anyway?" I asked.

"Dark magic," Loki replied. "Odin loves to dabble in those arts he forbids others to practice. That's how he maintains his position of power."

"He means necromancy," Bryn said between bites of pizza.

"Hmm," I said, rubbing my stubble with my knuckles. "If anyone knows anything about that topic, it's Crowley."

Click scowled. "I'd prefer it if ya' didn't involve that one," he said. "He's no friend o' yers, lad."

"True, but he's no enemy, either. And he hates the gods as much as any of us." I pushed off the counter, addressing Bryn and Ásgeir. "Pack your bags, you two. We're going to Texas."

"Seriously?" Bryn said as her eyes lit up. "I've always wanted to meet a real cowboy."

"Um, not to disappoint you, but good luck finding one of those in Austin," I said. "Besides, we won't have time for sightseeing. I'm being hunted, remember?"

"You're no fun at all," the valkyrie said, glowering once more as she took a bite of pizza.

"If yer askin' me, I believe 'tis a mistake," Click said.

"Thankfully, I wasn't asking you," I replied, only half meaning it. The immortal magician might've been a pain in the ass, but he meant well. "Relax, Click. I have everything under control. Trust me, we'll be there and back before Badb has a clue."

As Badb and Aenghus were tracking my use of the Oak's magic, and since Loki could only mask that while I remained in Iceland, I had Click cast a portal that would take us just outside of Crowley's farm. The shadow wizard's wards prevented us from taking the direct route, but close enough was good enough as far as I was concerned. I figured he'd detect the portal, spot us via whatever scrying methods he used to surveil his property, and let us in.

For Ásgeir's sake, Click waited until night had fallen in Texas before he cast the portal. After I stepped through, I closed my eyes and took a long, deep breath of the relatively warm evening air. It smelled like home. Springtime in Austin was always a great time to be alive, and I wanted nothing more than to head to Zilker for a swim and a long day spent laying in the sun. But duty called, so I opened my eyes and turned toward Crowley's front gate.

Only to find that it wasn't there.

"Hey, look, a cow," Ásgeir said, pointing across the county road at a couple of Brahmas grazing behind a barbed wire fence. He pointed further down the road, where more livestock milled around in an open field. "And goats."

"We have cows and goats in Iceland, troll," Bryn said with a shrug.

The troll raised a thick, hairy, calloused finger. "Ah, but these are Texas cows and goats. I wonder, are there any Texas cowboys nearby?"

Bryn perked up. "Where?"

"Sorry you two, but the closest you'll find out here will likely be some thirty-something hipsters running an organic produce farm," I said as I tapped my foot, staring at the spot where Crowley's farmstead used to be. "If you want real cowboys, you have to go to South Texas for that. The King Ranch down in Kingsville would be the best bet."

Ásgeir walked over to the cows, holding his hand out and making cooing noises in an attempt to pet one. They weren't having it, and they startled and galloped away as soon as they caught his scent. Cows were dumb, but they weren't stupid. They knew a predator when they smelled one.

"Something wrong, druid?" Bryn asked.

"Well, I—" A sound in the distance gave me pause.

That sound was unmistakable—a late-model Harley V-Rod with custom pipes. "Aw, shit."

A few seconds later, the motorcycle and rider came into view as they crested a low hill fifty yards down the road. The bike was flat black with minimal chrome, and the rider wore jeans, modern black tactical boots, and a black leather motorcycle jacket. She also wore an identity-concealing brain bucket like the one Bryn favored, but the long, dark hair billowing out over her shoulders gave her identity away instantly.

Belladonna pulled into Crowley's driveway, kicking up gravel and dust as she skidded to a halt. She slipped off her helmet, setting it on the tank as she kicked the stand and hopped off her bike.

"Looking for Crowley?" she asked, not even bothering with a greeting. "He keeps the place locked down all the time now. If he's in his lab, you could be waiting a week or a month out here before he notices you."

"Hi, Bells. Good to see you too," I said.

She ignored my jab, instead glancing at Ásgeir and then looking Bryn up and down. "Man—you move fast, Loverboy. I'd expected you to go for a blonde this time, though, considering you've already gone the brunette and redhead route."

"Nice bike," Bryn said, unconcerned with Belladonna's assumption.

"Thanks," Bells said, holding out her hand. "Belladonna Becerra."

The valkyrie tilted her head as she gave Belladonna a curious look, then she shook her hand. "Bryn. The ugly one is Ásgeir, and you already seem to know the stupid one."

"She'll do," Bells said with a smirk.

"Hey!" I protested. "We're not involved. Bryn's just helping me sort some stuff out."

"'Sort some stuff out...' where?" Belladonna asked.

"Nowhere," I said.

"Iceland," Ásgeir and Bryn said at the same time.

"Damn it, that's supposed to be a secret."

"Please, like I'm going to tell anyone where you're hiding," Belladonna replied with a roll of her dark, exotic eyes. She turned to Bryn, giving her one of those looks girls give each other that carries multiple layers of meaning. "Don't let his babe in the woods act fool you, *mija*. He might be a dork, but he's a womanizer through and through."

"Ouch," I muttered.

"Oh, I figured him out about five minutes after we met," Bryn said. "The whole, 'I'm attractive but I don't know it' thing is pretty easy to see through, and he's way too charming to be harmless."

"Oh-kay," I said, interrupting them with my outdoor voice. "About getting into Crowley's?"

"Keep your Jockeys on, *tramposo*—I have a key." Bells pulled a leather thong necklace with a black onyx raven charm from inside her t-shirt, dangling it for all to see. She called across the street to Ásgeir, who was trying to get the cows to come back by waving handfuls of grass at them. "¡*Oye, gordo!* This is Texas—they shoot cattle rustlers here."

"I wasn't going to eat it," he replied in an abashed tone. "I merely wanted to see if its fur was as soft as it looked."

"Crowley has a cow skin rug in his living room," Bells said. "I'm sure he'll let you pet it. Now, gather round. Unless you want to get fried by my partner's wards, we'll need to be in contact to enter the premises."

"Partner?" I said, arching an eyebrow at her choice of words.

"Did I say 'partner'? I meant to say, 'friend,'" Bells replied in the most unconvincing voice ever. "Now, everyone put a hand on me and don't let go until we cross the barrier."

As we complied, Bryn leaned over to whisper in my ear. "I can see why you're still jealous. Your ex would make an excellent valkyrie."

One thing about Crowley's missing farm that stumped me was how I couldn't see it in the magical spectrum. It wasn't an illusion, because I'd have detected the magic. And it wasn't an invisibility spell, either; my other senses would've picked up on telltale signs that would reveal the presence of a habitation. Cooking smells, sounds of livestock, and the like, or just bits of trash and leaves floating beyond the boundaries of the spell.

No, this was something different. As we all walked hand-in-hand through whatever magical barrier separated Crowley's property from the surrounding countryside, I paid close attention to every magical detail. First, there was nothing. Then, we walked into a dense, black fog. When we emerged a few steps later, his farm, tower, and outbuildings stood before us.

"Son of a bitch, he's keeping it out of phase," I said, mouth agape.

Bells nodded. "Yeah, he stole *una cosa mágica* from some local magician—a book, I think. Said that's what allows him to keep his tower hidden so well. I don't know the details. That stuff doesn't really interest me."

I shook my head in disbelief. Magical tomes that were that powerful didn't just grow on trees. "Doesn't the guy want his grimoire back?"

"How do you know it wasn't a her?" she replied. "Anyway, no. He's too dead to care anymore."

She cleared her throat, giving me a coy smile as she looked down. My eyes followed her gaze, all the way to our still-locked hands. Feeling my face flush, I removed mine from hers with an awkward, apologetic laugh.

"Uh, sorry. Old habits die hard."

"Oh, for Odin's sakes," Bryn said, brushing past us on her way to Crowley's tower. "Come on, troll. Let's go find this wizard before the druid embarrasses himself any further."

"I don't recommend walking into his tower alone," I said, changing the subject. "He might not recognize you, and he's not the type to ask questions."

Belladonna turned toward the tower, but not before I saw the self-satisfied smirk on her face. "This way, everyone, and mind the magic traps."

Moments later, we waited downstairs on the first floor

of Crowley's tower while Bells went to retrieve him. The "tower" was actually a converted grain silo, and the bottom level served as his kitchen and living room. The wizard had a farmhouse on the property, but he preferred living close to his work. I doubted that he even slept, so focused was he on magical experimentation.

To what end, I'd never asked, as I simply assumed it was something dark wizards did in their spare time. But after hearing about that mysterious grimoire, I thought I might want to invest in a little inquiry after things settled down with the Celtic gods. In the meantime, I'd have to be content with knowing that Bells was keeping an eye on him. And, despite our history, I trusted her to let me know if Crowley was up to no good.

"Nice place," Ásgeir said, sitting on the couch closest to the cowhide rug that sat beneath an industrial steel and glass coffee table. He reached down to stroke the white and auburn fur, muttering to himself. "It is soft—very soft. I should like very much to sleep in such warmth and comfort."

"I'll see if I can get you one, after we get Dian Cécht back from that dick Býleistr," I said. "But no promises."

"Pfah," Bryn exclaimed. "He's as likely to eat it as to sleep in it."

"I don't know if you've noticed, but Ásgeir seems awfully gentle and refined for a troll," I remarked. "I really can't picture him being as bloodthirsty as you make him out to be."

"Thank you, druid," the troll said. He was now sitting on the floor with his back propped up against the couch, running his rough hands back and forth over the rug beneath him.

"Hah! You just wait until you see him in battle, McCool. Then you'll know why the Norse mountain trolls have such a fearsome and hated reputation."

"From what I understand, some of them were known to be wise, and helpful even," I countered.

"Only to the highest bidder," Bryn said under her breath. "And you'd best hope he doesn't get another, better offer."

That line of conversation was interrupted when Crowley and Bells came walking down the stairwell that encircled the tower. I gave Bryn a disapproving glance, then I pasted a smile across my face as I greeted my old frenemy.

"Crowley, you look good," I said, meaning it. His scars had almost faded completely, although you could still see some light discoloration against his olive skin. I extended my hand, and he shook it as if he were picking up a dead fish. "These are my current companions, Bryn the valkyrie and Ásgeir the troll. Bryn, Ásgeir, this is my, er, associate, Crowley."

"Charmed, I'm sure," the tall, athletically-thin wizard said, tossing a lock of his dark, curly hair out of his face as he clasped his hands behind his back. "To what do I owe the honor?"

"Well, we sort of need your help. You see, there's this necromantic curse that was placed on some Vikings about a thousand years ago by Odin, and we need you to break it."

"I'm rather in the middle of something right now," he said, furrowing his brow. "Besides, my foster mother has been most persistent in her search for me recently. If I were to leave these confines, the act might betray my home's location."

I opened my mouth to respond when he raised a hand in a shushing motion, cocking his ear as if listening to something in the distance.

"Nameless, attend to that disturbance and report back," Crowley said, speaking at the ceiling. A floor or two above, we heard the flapping of feathered wings trailing off into the night.

"Trouble?" Bells asked.

"Hmm," Crowley replied, pursing his lips. "Druid, just how *did* you arrive at my doorstep?"

"Um, we were coming from Iceland, so Click portalled us in."

We heard a raven's shrill alarm call in the distance, and Crowley hung his head as he gave me a put-upon look. "Well, what's done is done. Mother and her minions are here. I suggest that you and your companions prepare to either flee, or fight."

15

Ásgeir stood with an index finger extended in the air. "If you don't mind my asking, who exactly is his mother?"

"He smells of Irish fae and does dark magic," Bryn said in a not-quite caustic tone. "He's obviously a changeling, so I would assume his mother was *aes sídhe* royalty."

Crowley and Bells had already bustled back up the stairs, to what end I hadn't a clue. "Ah, Fuamnach, actually. I, uh, stole the Stone of Fál from her a while back, so she's probably still pissed at me for that. Crowley helped, and his foster mom's been trying to kill him ever since."

"Wonderful," Bryn said, narrowing her eyes at me. "You weren't kidding when you said you'd pissed off the Celtic pantheon."

"Thankfully, it sounds like she came alone," I offered. "Badb and Aenghus both want a piece of me too."

Bryn hissed. "The Morrígna are known to the Valkyries. As is the fop."

Ásgeir walked over to slap me on the shoulder. "Well done. Only the mightiest of heroes garner such attention from the gods."

"So..." I said, stalling as I found the right words. "I can't abandon Crowley and Bells in their time of need, especially since I led his evil foster-monster right to his doorstep. That said, you two don't need to stick around as far as I'm concerned. I can send you back to Iceland right now, no hard feelings."

What I didn't mention was that I'd have to act as a decoy to keep the Celtic gods from tracking them back to Iceland. Meaning, I'd have to make my presence known, confronting Fuamnach face-to-face. Badb and Aengus would likely show up soon after, but fuck it—I wasn't about to force Bryn and Ásgeir to fight my losing battles.

Bryn frowned. "And miss a good tussle? No valkyrie in her right mind would do so."

Ásgeir shrugged. "I am unafraid of witches, even when they are deities in their own right. Besides, I would be breaking our contract if I were to flee now. No, I think I shall stay and help your friend defend his home."

"Looks like it's unanimous," Bryn added with a twinkle-eyed wink. "Gird your loins, druid. Tonight, you head into battle next to a valkyrie and the Godspear."

"Alrighty, then." I leaned into the stairwell to holler at the shadow wizard. "Yo, Crowley, looks like we're sticking around to help. What do you want us to do?"

A shadowy appendage floated into view above, similar to an octopus tentacle but made from oily black smoke. Soon a head formed at the tip, bearing a near-facsimile of the shadow wizard's face. As if that wasn't creepy enough, the damned thing blinked at me and spoke.

"The perimeter of the farm is filled with magical traps, so I advise that you do not wander past the gravel lot in front of the house and tower. However, I expect Mother's forces to eventually break through. She'll likely trigger all my wards and traps using masses of undead, and then send in her assassins and shock troops after that."

"I'm familiar with how fae assassins operate—but shock troops?"

I wasn't certain, but I thought the face might've rolled its eyes. "Giants, druid. We dealt with the same in Underhill, remember? You should expect a small number of unseelie fae as well."

"Great. So, you want us to set up an ambush?" I asked.

"In so many words, yes. I'll need Belladonna's assistance in triggering the last of my defenses, so you'll be on your own. Defend the tower while I finish my preparations, then I'll deal with my mother."

"Got it," I said. "By the way, how can your foster-monster access this place if it's out of phase with reality?"

"She's a three-thousand-year-old sorceress, Colin. She has her ways. If you'd taken your magical studies seriously, you would know such things." At that, the tentacle withdrew quickly, disappearing upstairs.

"Smartass," I said under my breath as I headed for Crowley's front door.

Explosions and flashes of light in the distance shattered the relative peace and calm of the farm. Apparently, the wizard's assessment of his foster mom's capabilities was accurate, and timely. If we were going to set up an ambush, we'd need to do it fast.

"Quickly, you two—do you prefer to fight at a distance or up close?"

"I can do either," Bryn said. "But I prefer to be in the thick of battle."

I nodded. "Ásgeir?"

"The same." He tugged at his scarf nervously. "And I fight alone."

"Understood." I wondered what he hid under that scarf, but now was not the time to ask. Besides, I had a feeling I'd know soon enough. "And how good are you guys at hiding?"

"Pfft. I am a valkyrie. We traverse battlefields unharmed at will."

"I can move unnoticed in nature, if I wish," Ásgeir said.

"Okay, great. Then, here's what we're going to do..."

I hid behind an old rusted-out tractor, fully transformed with Orna in hand. Of course, as soon as I drew the sword from my Bag, it began reciting more of Tethra's deeds, so I had to cast a silence spell on the damned thing. Ásgeir lurked somewhere behind the farmhouse across the way. He'd torn up a piece of farm equipment and had left piles of plow discs in strategic places all over the yard.

Meanwhile, Bryn had posted high above us in the clouds, mounted on Tordenvejr. I hadn't seen her bring the pegasus through the portal, and how it had gotten here, I hadn't a clue. No matter. All I cared about was that we had artillery if and when we needed it. I just hoped her lightning was as badass as her thunder.

The first signs of Fuamnach's forces showed up just seconds after we got situated, an unorganized line of ghouls and zombies that staggered across an empty pasture. I counted a dozen or so, barely a nuisance except for the fact that they might force us to give away our positions. I suddenly wished I'd stealth-shifted. I could've picked them off with my suppressed Glock 19 if I had smaller hands.

No matter. As they neared the gravel lot that demarcated the main compound, the ground beneath their feet turned into a bog and they were sucked down beneath the ground's surface. As the last ghoul's head sunk into the muck, the earth solidified once more, transforming into terra firma and leaving no trace of the undead.

"Nice," I said to no one in particular.

That's when the assassins showed up. At first, I didn't see them, so stealthily did they move through the tall grass and weeds. Crowley didn't seem to care if his fields were overgrown, and unfortunately that made it easier for the fae to hide. No magical traps were triggered as they closed in on the farmhouse and tower, and I feared I'd be forced to deal with them myself.

Just before I leapt out from cover, lightning struck the ground in multiple places from the clouds above. Each strike landed on or near one of Fuamnach's troops, churning the earth and exploding the sneaky little bastards into chum. The three that were left abandoned all stealth, zig-zagging with supernatural speed toward the tower. Each of them was kitted out much like other fae assassins I'd faced, in tight-fitting leathers with various knives, swords, and darts strapped to their bodies.

Before I could react, a trio of two-foot-wide rusted metal discs shot out from somewhere near the farmhouse, each finding a target despite how quickly the fae moved. One severed a leg, another, an arm, and the third cleaved the last assassin in two. Lightning strikes from above finished off the two that weren't insta-killed by Ásgeir's makeshift missiles, leaving me with nothing to do but wait my turn.

I didn't have to wait long. Soon the ground shook with the thunderous footsteps of six giants as they came loping across the field. They varied in size between nine and twelve feet tall and bore the twisted, deformed features of ettins—dim-witted, in-bred giants that once roamed the lands bordering northern England and Scotland. Each wore crude leather armor and held maces and clubs made from tree trunks shod with blackened metal cuffs and spikes.

Again, lightning struck them as they lumbered forward, but the ettins either had magical protection or they were immune, shrugging off Bryn's strikes like rain. However, no magician or sorceress could defend against every elemental attack at once. Leaning out from cover, I tossed a couple of fireballs at the two in the lead.

Over the last several months—years inside the Grove —I'd learned to concentrate my magic to yield the greatest effect possible. Thus, the fireballs I threw were more like fire baseballs, but they made up in potential energy and density what they lacked in size. Each of my spells struck true, one hitting a giant in the chest, the other in the face, exploding with fiery *whoomps* on impact.

The giant I struck in the torso was blown off his feet, his chest a huge, charred cavity. He landed on his back, unmoving, and my expert opinion was that it was unlikely he'd recover. The other giant continued to march forward, at least for a few awkward steps. When its body realized it no longer had a head, it fell in a boneless heap to the ground.

I rose to confront the remaining four giants just as two more metal discs whizzed by my head. The projectiles were deflected by the ettins, pinging off their clubs and ricocheting into the distance. Ásgeir ran by me with long, even strides, yelling over his shoulder as he passed.

"I'll deal with the giants," he roared. "Your skills are needed for what comes next."

The troll pointed across the field at a figure that strode almost lazily toward us, although the way he walked was as alien as his appearance. He was perhaps six feet tall, with a bare, muscular, red-skinned torso. He had a goat's black-furred hips, legs, and cloven feet from the waist down. His face was a caricature of a human's features, with an exaggerated brow, nose, and chin that each jutted out like craggy hills on a flat plain.

In keeping with the general theme, he had two short, pointed horns poking out from his thick, curly black hair on either side of his head. Over his shoulder he wore a thick leather baldric, and a long, thin scabbard dangled from it on his right side. At his waist he wore a wide leather belt that bore a sheathed dagger and, rather unfortunately, nothing more beneath that.

Yellow eyes with red pupils stared across the field at me from beneath that prominent brow, and a long, forked tongue snaked out from the creature's lips, which were bordered by a thick, pointed beard and mustache. He smiled in a way that was most unkind, leering as he displayed a mouth full of razor-sharp teeth. In short, the damned thing looked like the textbook description of a devil. All he lacked was a pitchfork.

"Ásgeir, what in the actual fuck is that?" I asked, dropping my chameleon spell since it was nearly useless once I'd revealed myself.

"I have no idea, druid," he yelled. "But I'm certain that the creature falls within your area of expertise."

The troll whipped off his hat and scarf as he ran at the first giant, discarding them so they floated off on the breeze to land in the grass and weeds. He wasn't facing me, so I couldn't get a good look at his features. But I was fairly certain that he had a horn sticking out of the top of his head, and that a large hissing snake whipped around in the vicinity of his mouth.

I had no time to process what I'd just seen, because the devil-creature had closed the distance toward me, loping to a stop at the edge of the gravel lot. Keeping his eyes on me, he bowed at the waist, in the manner a courtier might bow to some medieval duke or duchess. When he stood, he flashed me a toothy, evil grin.

"Allow me ta' introduce ma'self," he said in a thick

Scottish accent. "I am Owd Hob, hired in the service o' the Black Sorceress. Ya' currently stand between me and my prey, ogre. So, if ya' don't mind, I'd kindly ask ya' ta' step aside."

In the background, Ásgeir fought all four giants with a grace and precision that I'd not have expected from someone of his bulk. He'd pulled a tall, thick fence post up from the ground and swung the heavy, concrete-encased end around in dizzying patterns, striking his opponents at will while simultaneously dodging their clumsier, slower attacks.

That was, until they managed to flank him. I was about to toss a couple of spells that way to help him out, but then Bryn landed on a giant's head with a flash of lightning and ear-shattering thunderclap. When the smoke cleared, the valkyrie stood where the giant had a second before. She jumped into the fray without delay, in full armor with sword and shield in hand, harrying the giants from behind while Ásgeir tore into them with his makeshift mace.

Assured that they had the situation in hand, I turned my attention back to the devil that called himself Owd Hob.

"Yeah, that is a problem," I rumbled in my deep, Fomorian voice. "He's a pain in the ass, but I need him."

"Ah, love," Owb Hob said. "The second-oldest motivation."

"What? Um, no."

Hob looked confused. "But ya' spoke o' how he hurt your ass, and your need for the changeling. Ya' mean ta' say ya' two aren't lovers?"

"Uh-uh, no way. What I meant was, I need his help. And 'pain in the ass' is just a saying. Like, 'thorn in my side' or 'stick in the mud.'"

"If ya' say so," he replied, obviously unconvinced.

"Anyway, you're not getting past me. Like I said, I need him alive."

"Oh, I'm not goin' ta' kill him. My job's merely ta' bring him ta' his mam, so she can do the honors."

"That's splitting hairs, don't you think?"

Hob's brow furrowed. "'Splitting hairs'? Sounds like one o' those impossible an' futile tasks, o' the kind ya' give ta' summoned spirits ta' keep 'em occupied so they don't kill ya'. Well, I won't fall for it."

"No, it's—oh, never mind. Fight me already, because I'm getting tired of this conversation."

The creature nodded, sizing me up. "A monster fightin' a goblin ta' protect a hound. There's a certain twisted poetry ta' the situation, don't ya' think?"

I had no idea what he meant, calling Crowley a hound, but I was more intrigued by how he described himself. "I've mixed it up with plenty of goblins. You look more— er, devilish to me. Not very gobliny at all."

"Oh, but I am a goblin," he said. "In fact, the king of all goblins. An' I did not come by that position easily."

"Huh. You wouldn't happen to worship an evil clown god, would you? Because if that's the case, I have some really bad news for you."

"The Usurper, ya' mean," he said, stroking his beard in a very devilish manner. "He's caused me a great deal o' trouble. No, I do not worship him, and if I ever find him, I intend ta' run my blade through his heart."

"Best of luck with that. Now, skin that smoke wagon and let's see what happens."

Hob looked down at his gross goat junk, and then back up at me. "Pardon?"

"It's a line from a movie." The confusion on his face told me that he had no idea what a movie was. "You don't get out much, do you?"

He gave me an apologetic look. "I spent the last two centuries trapped inside a summoning circle, in a dungeon buried deep beneath a Scottish castle. In fact, that's how I entered the sorceress' service. She found an' freed me. And for that, I agreed ta' help capture her whelp."

"Sucks for you, then, because you're not getting inside that tower."

"You say ya' want ta' what?" The devilish goblin king shook his head as he rested his hands on the hilts of his sword and dagger. "Every other word out o' your mouth seems ta' have dual meanin'. Ta' be honest, I'm not sure whether ya' wish ta' fight me or bed me."

"Fuck's sakes, draw steel already!" I roared.

"Ah, now that I understand," he said with an evil grin. He drew his sword and parrying dagger in a flash of steel, and before I knew it, we were crossing blades.

16

H ob was no slouch when it came to swordplay, that was for certain. He was quick, easily as quick as one of the high fae, and perhaps even a match for a vampire. And strong, too, as the first beat of his thin blade nearly knocked Orna out of my hands.

This posed a problem for me, because despite the size advantage and longer reach, I couldn't harm the goat man if I couldn't touch him. And while I was fast in my full Fomorian form, I was fast like a freight train—speed that was generally only good in one direction. Quick turns and stopping on a dime were damn near impossible feats when you weighed almost half a ton.

Had I chosen my stealth-shifted form, this guy wouldn't have been a problem, because I could've easily matched him move for move with Dyrnwyn in hand. Yet as I swung and spun Orna around in an attempt to decapitate or otherwise incapacitate Owd Hob, he danced in and out of range with the grace of a bullfighter, slashing and stabbing me with his pig sticker almost at will. Thirty seconds into the fight, I was bleeding in half a dozen places while Hob looked fresh as the morning dew.

"That's the problem wit' size an' strength," he taunted as he ducked under a swipe of my sword, dancing just out of reach. "Doesn't matter how big your sword is if ya' can't hit your target."

"Now who's speaking in double entendres?" I asked as I lunged forward, thrusting Orna at the creature's chest.

Seemingly to emphasize his previous point, the goblin king pivoted, leaning just slightly out of the way as he stung my hands with lightning quick jabs of his rapier. I turned the thrust into a horizontal slash, but too late—he'd already spun away, strutting like a two-dicked rooster in a yard full of hens. He had me outclassed and he knew it, and honestly, it was really starting to piss me off.

Could I have cheated with magic? Maybe, but I was fairly certain that while I was busy casting a spell, he'd skewer me through the eye—a quick glance through the immediate time streams showed me that. As for my chances of beating him with swordplay, there were few options available. Eager to get this fight over, I mentally searched the most likely pathways branching off the present, and only one strategy proved to be reliable enough to give it a shot.

The thing about fighting with a rapier was that it was purely a thrusting weapon. Some had rudimentary cutting edges, but they lacked the heft necessary to truly be used for slashing in combat. In order to kill someone quickly with such a thin blade, you had to run them through the heart or the eye. Not that it didn't happen, as historical accounts of 16th and 17th century duels were full of such deaths.

But to a Fomorian, getting run through with a rapier was about as scary as being stuck in the finger with a sewing needle. I suspected Hob was used to fighting conventional giants, like the ettins that were currently having their asses handed to them by Bryn and Ásgeir. So, maybe Hob didn't know how quickly I healed. Meaning, he'd assume that running me through was a sure way to win this duel.

On our next exchange, I left an opening in my guard on my left side, leaving myself vulnerable for a thrust to the abdomen. Hob wasted no time in taking advantage of my mistake, easily sidestepping my own thrust and skewering me through my side. Which, of course, brought him into clinch range. Immediately, I dropped Orna and grabbed Hob around the neck with my left hand, and around his upper left arm with my right.

The goblin king's eyes widened in shock for a split second, narrowing as his mouth split into a self-satisfied grin. Before I even knew what had happened, the bastard blinked away, leaving me grasping at black wisps of smoke and ash. He didn't make a "bamf" sound, but his ability to teleport definitely reminded me of a certain superhero to whom Hob bore a resemblance.

Well, fuck.

"So sorry to disappoint ya', laddie," he gloated as he reappeared about a dozen feet away. "The talent's instinctual, an' it teleports me away in random patterns when I'm in danger. So, don't think ya'll be aimin' that great cleaver o' yours where I'll show up next, because it's impossible ta' predict where I'll be after I 'port."

That was why I didn't see Hob using his talent when I looked through the time streams. When a chronourgist followed an individual's life thread, they could only see branches caused by voluntary decisions and acts. Every decision that person made caused a split in the time stream, forcing it to branch off into multiple different realities. I'd once asked Click if all those realities existed. His answer was that theoretically they did, but they only became extant if someone actually experienced them.

"That's why ya' don't want ta' be traipsin' through the Twisted Paths fer' fun," he'd said. "Each trip brings a new reality in ta' existence. That makes ya' responsible fer' everything that happens in that new time stream—an' every single sufferin' that results. It's a terrible burden, lad, believe me."

I'd taken his warning to heart, resolving that, if I ever learned to walk the Twisted Paths, I'd use the talent sparingly. The last thing I wanted was for my life to become like some horrible, made-for-television comic book adaptation. I couldn't imagine what it would be like, resetting the time streams over and over again just to correct the consequences of fucking it up the first time.

Which was all fine and dandy, but knowing the dangers of chronomancy and chronourgy didn't do a damned thing to help me beat Owd Hob.

As I bent to grab Orna from the ground, my blood fell in thick droplets, spattering the gravel as my fingers wrapped around the sword's hilt. I was in a really shit situation, no doubt about it. Physically, Hob had the advantage over me while I was in this form, because he was quicker and the better swordsman to boot. And I couldn't even the odds by cheating with time magic, either.

Basically, I was fucked.

"Well, laddie, here's the score," he said as he strutted around me on his weird goat legs, whipping his rapier through the air in lazy patterns. "I kin pick ya' apart, bit by bit, takin' a piece here and a piece there, until yer' left bleedin' out on this damnable plot o' land—all because ya' were loyal ta' yer' friend. Who, incidentally, is a heartless bastard that'd as soon sell your soul as serve ya' a cup o' tea."

"Or..." I said, stalling for time with one hand clamped around my wound, and the other holding Orna in a fencer's third position.

I wasn't waiting for the wound to heal—Hob could spit me a dozen times before my Fomorian healing factor patched this wound up. Nor was I stalling for a moment of rescue by my companions. Bryn and Ásgeir were acquitting themselves well, having taken down two more ettins. Unfortunately, more fae had shown up to help the two remaining giants, so they weren't going to bail me out of my predicament any time soon.

No, I was angling for more time because the loud explosions and flashes in the distance were getting closer, which meant Fuamnach would be here shortly. And if that was the case, I'd need to get everyone out of here in a jiffy. But I'd have to keep Hob from running that needle of a sword through my eye before I could do anything of the kind. Unfortunately, he was fast enough and sneaky enough that a momentary lapse of concentration to communicate with the Oak could spell my doom.

My only chance was to cast a spell that would catch Hob off guard and give Ásgeir and Bryn a chance to retreat to the tower. I thought about casting the stasis shield spell I'd discovered in that alien wasteland Click had stranded me in days ago. After a moment's consideration I discarded the idea, as it would tip Fuamnach off that I knew time magic. Once word of that got out, no telling how many gods would be after me.

A different spell was required for this situation, and I was fairly certain I had just the thing. Hopefully, Crowley was done cooking up whatever magical surprise he had for his step-monster by now. If so, then I could get the Oak to portal us all back to Iceland. And, if I was lucky, Loki's magic would keep Fuamnach from following us there.

Let's hope all that practice inside the Grove pays off.

Hob spoke, snapping my thoughts back to my present and most pressing concern. "Or ya' could concede, an' give the sorcerer up. Let his mam take him, an' wash yer' hands o' the whole affair. You live, I don't have ta' kill ya', an' the rest o' yer' friends walk away."

I thrust the point of my blade into the ground, leaning on it heavily as if I were more wounded than I was. In reality, I wasn't that badly injured, but a half-dozen more thrusts like that and I'd be a goner. Even so, I'd need both hands for the spell I was about to cast. I just prayed I could pull it off before Hob caught on.

"That sounds tempting," I said, laying both hands on Orna's pommel so I could rest my forehead on top, to hide the intricate finger positions and gestures I was working through. "But there's just one problem with that plan."

"An' what would that be, laddie?"

"You see," I said, lifting my head as I made circular motions with both of my hands, "I don't think you'll be around to follow through on your end. *Hairicín!*"

Cathbad's Planetary Maelstrom was a very advanced spell, and perhaps the pinnacle of battle druid magic. In fact, it was the spell Finnegas had cast when he had his stroke, but whether his illness was caused by magical strain or by Badb's meddling, I couldn't say. Regardless, it was a spell that could only be cast properly by a master druid. I wasn't quite there yet—no way could I manage to levitate hundreds of stones and boulders in the air at once like the old man did—but I was good enough now to fuck someone's day up royal.

Crowley's parking lot was full of gravel, including some golf ball- to fist-sized stones that made perfect missiles. When I uttered the trigger word, a dozen or so of those rocks flew into the air, immediately spinning into seemingly random orbits around my person. Some flew around me at a range of just a few feet, while others orbited at ten, fifteen, and twenty feet out. They picked up speed rather quickly because my control over the spell was limited, and casting it was an all or nothing affair.

Thankfully, I caught Hob by surprise. Maybe Fuamnach hadn't told him about what he'd be facing going up against me, or perhaps she didn't know I'd be here. Either way, the self-described goblin king found himself standing in a literal whirlwind of flying debris, and soon he began teleporting from place to place in order to avoid the effects of my spell.

Interestingly, it seemed that his "talent" could only teleport him a short distance, maybe ten feet max in one jump. So, each time he disappeared in a cloud of smoke, I took a step forward to keep him inside the spell. This had the effect of forcing him to teleport almost non-stop, and that gave me an idea.

With a supreme act of will, I channeled more energy into the spell until the stones surrounding me were nothing more than a blur. Meanwhile Hob kept 'porting here, there, and everywhere, and I kept advancing to keep him doing so. Before long, he wasn't even materializing anymore, not really—and based on what I knew about magic, he couldn't keep that up forever.

Wait for it...

Finally, Hob's magical reserves petered out and his talent initiated a teleport just a second too late. Before he could dematerialize, my stones hit him in multiple places, punching holes through him until he looked like one big bloody piece of Swiss cheese. I kept the spell going, increasing the radius of the orbit while decreasing the speed slightly, as it was easier to keep the spell going that way.

Sword in hand, with just a trickle of blood coming from that hole in my side, I approached Hob's mutilated body. He lay mostly still, quivering now and again as his wounds leaked black blood all over the tan-colored gravel below. I stopped beside him, waiting for him to turn his single remaining red and yellow eye on me before I spoke.

"Word of advice, Hob," I said as I raised Orna over his chest, point down. "Next time you face a Fomorian, don't offer parley. We don't negotiate for surrender."

Once I'd dispatched Hob, I widened the orbit of the stones I controlled further, dealing with the single remaining giant and a dozen fae assassins all in one fell swoop. Exhausted and near the end of my own magical reserves, I let the spell go, sending stones flying in every direction, including Crowley's house, garage, and tower. The sound of glass shattering, wood smashing, and galvanized steel being punctured echoed all around us, but I barely noticed as I shifted into my half-human form.

As soon as her foes fell, Bryn spun around to face me, sword raised high with blood spattered all over her face. Her expression was somewhere between extreme rage and unbridled glee. Her eyes were wide and wild, her nostrils flared, and her mouth was spread in a rictus of laughter that seemed to have frozen on her lips. I thought she might charge me, but instead she shivered slightly and lowered her sword. Finally, the crazed aspect faded from her face to be replaced with a disappointed, sneering frown.

"We'd have had them," she said, slinging blood from her blade.

"Yeah, well—shit, where's Ásgeir?" I panted as I slipped Orna back into my Bag.

The troll grunted as he pushed out from beneath a pile of corpses, sitting up where he'd been buried beneath them a few feet away. Interestingly, his scarf and hat were already back in place. The guy was serious about hiding his face, that was for certain.

"Speak for yourself, valkyrie," Ásgeir said. "Once you entered your blood fury, I was left to deal with their leader and a half-dozen fae alone."

"You're still alive," she replied in a neutral voice. "Be thankful I was here at all."

Ásgeir was about to say something else, but I cut them both off, pointing into the distance with a shaky, human-looking hand. "I don't mean to break up your lover's spat before the make-up sex, but we need to get the fuck out of here, pronto."

They each turned their heads to follow my gaze. A quarter-mile away or so, Fuamnach floated in the air, gliding toward us from the far edge of Crowley's fields. She wore fitted, wide-leg black slacks, strappy heels, and a white silk blouse. Combined with the string of pearls around her neck, she might've been headed to a high society dinner party or a formal work function.

That was, except for the fact that she looked like a demoness on a mission from hell. Her long, black hair twisted and snapped around her head in a Medusa-like fashion, and crackles of ghostly yellow energy shot from her extended hands. Her eyes were aglow with a sickly, yellowish light, and the vegetation beneath her withered and browned in her wake.

"Death magic," Bryn hissed.

"Impressive," Ásgeir added.

"Run," I shouted, "to the tower, now!"

They were in better shape than I was, so I was the last to duck inside the front door, slamming it and locking it tight. As I'd suspected, I felt the whoomp of powerful magic wards snapping into place as I set the deadbolt. Just as I did, something struck the door from the other side, shaking it in its frame and sending shock waves through the entire structure.

"Crowley!" I shouted up the stairs. "Whatever you're doing, I hope you're nearly finished, because your foster-monster is pissed."

"Did you lock the front door?" he yelled back.

"Yes," I said.

"That'll only hold her for a short while," he replied.

"Ya' think?" I hollered back in a slightly high-pitched voice as another attack shook the tower. "Let's go, man, before she busts through."

"Just a moment," he said as Bells came bouncing down the stairs.

"And where was she while we were fighting all of Underhill?" Bryn asked.

Belladonna tossed her hair over her shoulder as she gave Bryn a bored look. "Crowley needed someone to hold his grimoires for him," she replied in a flat, unconcerned voice.

"Crowley, we gotta' go, dude," I shouted again as the

tower shook for a third time. This time, cracks began to show in the walls, and drywall dust fell all around our heads.

"Ready," he said as he strolled down the stairs with a single, expensive-looking briefcase in hand.

"What happened to the night raven?"

"I sent him to tidy up my new place. Hopefully he won't steal any children along the way."

"I seriously hope you're kidding about that," I said, pointing at his satchel. "Is that all you're taking?"

"Yes, it is," he replied while examining his fingernails. "I've been planning for this moment for a long, long time. Now, if you'll be so kind as to portal us out of here, I'll trigger my doomsday spells."

"Doomsday spells?" I asked. "Will there be anything left of Austin after you're done?"

"Stop playing the faux-naif, druid," he said. "I wouldn't want to anger Maeve, after all, as I do intend to return to this city once Mother leaves."

"Oh, right—we wouldn't want that," I said in a mocking tone. "Hang on to your panties, everyone, 'cause we're about to go for a ride."

17

When we landed in Iceland at Jerrik's barrow, everyone took a moment to recover from the battle. Well, almost everyone. Crowley marched right over while I was still catching my breath. He tossed me a quart-sized mason jar that was nearly filled to the brim with a dark, viscous substance that quivered as if it were alive.

"Put that in your magical bag, and do not lose it," he said. "Someone's life may depend on it."

"Crowley, this stuff isn't going to leak out and release a shadow demon inside the Bag's pocket dimension, is it?"

"Unlikely, but not out of the realm of possibility," he deadpanned. "I suggest you place it somewhere safe."

Reluctantly, I did as Crowley asked, wondering how I got myself into these situations. Once his goop was safely stored away, I did a quick head count to make sure everyone had made it back alive. Bryn tended to a few minor battle wounds, while Ásgeir stood near the barrow entrance, scanning for enemies, without and within.

Nearby, Bells rubbed her arms and stamped her feet, cursing up a storm in Spanish. "*¡Me cago en tus muertos, Colin!*" she said, glaring at me from a few feet away. "I'm not exactly dressed for this weather. Couldn't you have dropped me off at my apartment, *tonto*?"

"Sorry, Bells—couldn't risk it. If I sent you anywhere else, Fuamnach would've tracked you down and held you ransom to get at me or Crowley."

"*¡Pendejo!* I can take care of myself," she replied. "But what I can't do is warm myself up with magic like you and *el otro tonto*."

"Sorry," I said, rummaging around in my Bag. I found an old winter coat and tossed it to her. "Here."

She snatched it out of the air, sniffing it suspiciously. "Great. It smells like werewolf."

"Um, yeah—Fallyn might've been the last one to wear it."

"*¡Carajo!*" she muttered, slipping the coat on as she stormed off.

"Wow, you're like the woman whisperer or something," the valkyrie teased from where she sat on a boulder a few feet away.

"Oh, shit, Bryn," I said, smacking my forehead. "I forgot about your horse."

"He'll be fine," she replied. "I sent Tordenvejr home shortly after I entered the battle."

"Phew, good to know."

"I do appreciate the concern." The valkyrie tilted her head at the barrow entrance. "We'd better get moving. I'll take the troll into the tomb to let Jerrik know we're here."

"Good call. I wouldn't want them to mistake Crowley and Bells for grave robbers."

"That could be awkward," she said. "And messy."

"You have no idea," I muttered.

As Bryn headed to the barrow, I sent a message to the Oak, thanking it and asking if there was any sign of Fuamnach or the other Celtic gods. According to the Oak, it appeared we'd escaped scot-free. Sooner or later, however, the huldufólk would rat us out.

They didn't know our exact location, but it was a small island and they had eyes everywhere. Eventually they'd find us, and then we'd be royally screwed. That's why I'd had the Oak take us directly back to the tomb. Considering recent events, there was no better time than the present to fulfill my promise to Jerrik and get on the road to Jotunheim.

While I pondered our current situation, Crowley was examining a line of runes carved around the entrance to the tomb.

"Interesting," he said, rubbing his chin.

"Does it say anything about how to break the curse?" I asked.

"No, but it does include a rather promising recipe for bear stew."

"Holy shit, Crowley has a sense of humor." His expression remained somewhere between polite disinterest and go fuck yourself, so I decided I'd better see if we were cool. "Sure you're not pissed at me for leading Fuamnach to your doorstep?"

He gave me a resigned, slightly annoyed look. "It was

only a matter of time before she located that hideout. Although I took pains to avoid revealing where I lived, it became common knowledge among the Cold Iron Circle after your alter-ego leveled my tower. Mother or one of her lackeys would've figured it out eventually, and in this case, your presence afforded me time to leave her a parting gift."

"It almost sounds like you're thanking me," I said.

"Hardly," he scoffed. "And you will owe me for helping you lift this curse. Speaking of which, the sooner you lead me to these draugar, the better. I'd like to return to my new lair to continue my research."

"'Lair'? Cliché much?"

"You should talk, McCool. When it comes to wizard-detective clichés, the only thing you lack is a trench coat and a magic staff."

"Hey, now—"

Just then, Bryn's alarmed voice drew my attention. "Druid, I hate to interrupt your male bonding moment, but there's something you should see."

———

Inside, the place was a slaughterhouse. Only, the ones who'd been slaughtered were the former undead inhabitants of the crypt. Some were nothing more than ash and a few bone fragments, while others had been hacked up so thoroughly as to be unrecognizable.

"Bryn, who could've done this?" I asked.

She knelt next to a pile of ash, rubbing a bit between her fingers as she took a sniff. "This wasn't the work of the gods—at least, not any I'd know. My best guess is that a band of fire giants came through and cleared the place out, not long after we'd left."

"Yeah, but how'd they wipe Jerrik and his clan out so easily? Jerrik's draugar clan seemed to be fairly formidable."

She wiped her hand on her jeans and stood. "I suspect they were caught unawares. Jerrik's people once had a friendly relationship with the jötnar—it was the reason they were punished by Odin, in fact. Perhaps they arrived under false pretenses and attacked when the draugar least expected it."

"Great." Ásgeir jogged into the chamber just then. "Any sign of Jerrik?"

"None, druid," the troll said. All I found in his tomb was ash and gold slag."

"Damn it," I said to no one in particular. "How'd they know we were here?"

Bryn gave Ásgeir an accusing look. "I'd say we have a traitor in our midst."

Ásgeir ignored her, but I stepped between them just the same. "Hang on. Before we start leveling accusations, let's think about who knew we were headed here."

"We three, obviously," Ásgeir said.

"Plus Click and Loki," I added, looking at Bryn, who suddenly grew silent. "Bryn?"

"Look to the troll for your traitor, druid, not to my sisters. Valkyries do not betray one another, for any reason."

"That's not exactly a straight answer," I replied. "Don't you have to report to Gwen?"

"She works for Odin, and none other," Ásgeir said. "Although their relationship has been strained for some time."

"Hold that snake tongue of yours, troll," she hissed, "or I'll cut it from your mouth."

"I'm pretty sure all the Valkyries answer to Odin," I said. "And I doubt Odin is working with the giants. So, that just leaves the huldufólk. Question is, how'd they know we were here?"

"This one would do almost anything to get back in The All-Father's good graces," Ásgeir said, his voice taking on an edge for the first time since I'd met him. "Perhaps she curries favor with the Hidden People as a way of pleasing her god."

"Liar!" Bryn exclaimed, leaping at the troll and knocking me on my ass to do it.

The valkyrie caught me by surprise, otherwise I'd have stopped her. Still, I needn't have worried. Ásgeir extended an arm, palm-outward, stiff-arming her in the chest while she was in mid-leap. Bryn went flying across the chamber, bouncing off a wall and falling awkwardly to the floor.

"That'll be the last time you lay hands on me, troll," the valkyrie spat as she slowly pushed herself back to her feet. When she reached behind her back to draw steel, I knew I had to act before I had a full-on brawl on my hands.

"*Claochlaigh*," I said, gesturing at the cavern floor beneath Bryn's feet. Instantly, the solid stone surface turned into a sort of muddy quicksand. When the valkyrie had been swallowed up to her waist, I caused the stone to harden again, trapping her in place.

"Ásgeir, if you could give us a moment," I said.

"Certainly," he replied. "I'll be outside."

I walked over to Bryn, squatting down just out of her reach. "I think it's time you and I had a talk."

Bryn slammed her fists down on the now solid surface of the floor while cursing in old Norse. "Druid, if you don't release me immediately, I swear—"

"Stop," I said, letting a bit of my Fomorian side into my voice. "Threaten me all you want, but I'm going to leave you right where you are until you settle down. I've had a really shitty year, my mentor is about to die, and I need to get to Jotunheim to rescue the only guy who can save him. So, I really don't have time to referee your squabbles with Ásgeir."

"You don't know him, or what he's capable of," she said. "His kind cannot be trusted."

"That's what you keep saying, but thus far, he's been nothing but polite and cooperative." I pointed a finger at her accusingly. "You, on the other hand, have done nothing but stir up shit with him at every opportunity. And, frankly, I don't see the need to keep you around. I thought you were sent here to assist me, but it's quickly becoming clear that you're a liability."

"I'm not a liability," she said, lowering her eyes.

"Okay, so answer me this. Why are you really here? Why did the Valkyries send one of their own to help me? And don't tell me it's because I impressed Gwen, because I don't buy that bullshit."

Bryn kept her eyes downcast as she spoke. "I'm supposed to let the others know if Badb or the other Morrígna set foot on Norse soil. In ages past, they kept us from retrieving the souls of Viking warriors who died in *Irland*. We have long memories and seek revenge. That is all."

I scratched the side of my head as I rocked back on my heels. "Shit, why didn't you tell me that? Did you think I'd object to seeing a bunch of Valkyries put the hurt on that bitch? She wants me dead, after all—not to mention she's the reason why Finnegas is dying."

"We didn't know if we could trust you," she said. "We'd heard rumors that the Celtic gods were hunting the last remaining druids, but few of us believed it until you showed up in Iceland. And even then, we were skeptical."

"I see," I replied, chewing my thumbnail. "Obviously this is shit detail, helping me rescue a Celtic god from the jötnar. So, tell me—why send *you*?"

"Because, among all the Valkyries I am the one Odin cares for least. And due to past transgressions, my sisters consider me without honor. If I were lost, no one would come for me. If I fell in battle, none would avenge me. I am expendable—it is as simple as that."

"An outcast, eh? It makes sense," I said, cradling my chin in my hand. "So you're here to get off Odin's shit list and to get some respect from your fellow Valkyries. Sticking it to old Badb would probably go a long way toward making you one of the popular girls again, eh?"

"Do not mock me, druid," she said sullenly.

"I'm not." I exhaled heavily, because I didn't know if I

was making the right decision. Still, I needed allies if I was going to pull this thing off. Besides, it felt right. "Be honest do you still want a shot at Badb?"

She locked eyes with me, glaring fiercely. "I hate her, more than I hate the troll."

"Okay, then here's what I'm offering. Bury the hatchet with Ásgeir until this thing is done, and I'll make sure you get a chance to face that bitch down. Maybe not soon, but certainly at a future date. Deal?"

She set her mouth in a grim line and nodded. "Deal. But if you ever trap me like this again, I will castrate you and feed your oysters to Tordenvejr."

I was about to pull Bryn out of the floor when Crowley strolled in holding a charred and blackened skull in his hands. He'd come from the direction of the main burial crypt, where Bryn and Ásgeir had been playing cards with Jerrik. I didn't know much about necromancy, but I figured the shadow wizard carried that skull for good reason. Still, it wouldn't do to pass up a prime opportunity to give him shit.

"Found a new friend?" I asked. "Or are you just gathering decorations for your new pad?"

He glanced at me with detached indifference. "I didn't know you were into bondage, druid. Moreover, I'd most certainly have pegged you for a submissive."

"Valkyries do make very good doms," Bryn remarked

drily. "Although I doubt the druid would survive such an encounter."

"Hey, lady—one heckler in the crowd is enough," I said, yanking Bryn out of the floor and back on solid ground. "Speaking of hecklers—two jokes in one day, Crowley? Are you feeling well?"

"It's Belladonna's idea," he replied, staring at the skull again. "She suggested that I learn to use humor to put people at ease."

With a gesture, I solidified the floor before turning to address him. "I have to admit, it does make you seem less like an android and more like a human being. It'd probably work better if you weren't carrying around that skull, though."

The shadow wizard continued to examine the thing, turning it this way and that. "Ah, yes—the skull. I believe I've found your draugar chieftain. Or, at least, what's left of him."

"Huh. Ásgeir said he was nothing but ash and melted jewelry," I remarked.

"For the most part he was, but thankfully someone beheaded him before they burned him to cinders. I found this skull behind his sarcophagus, where it must've rolled when they cast the fireball spell." Crowley pulled a silk scarf from his satchel, wrapping the skull in it as he continued. "Obviously, whoever attacked Jerrik intended to deny you of his assistance. Sloppy of them to leave bones intact. Then again, I suppose they didn't expect you to return in the company of a master necromancer."

"Since when are you a master necromancer?" I asked.

"Since I was raised by the greatest necromancer in Underhill," he replied.

"Master necromancer or no, I want nothing to do with such unnatural magic," Bryn said. "I will await you outside."

"Bryn," I called after her as she was leaving the chamber. "Play nice."

"You have my word, druid," she replied as she walked down the corridor. "At least, until you deliver on your promise."

"And what promise would that be?" Crowley asked. "That she be allowed to call you 'daddy' whilst in the throes of passion?"

"Damn, Crowster. You are on a roll."

"Hmm, yes. I shall tone it down. Belladonna hates it when men try too hard."

"That she does," I said with the slightest smirk. "Are you two dating again?"

"I have no idea what you're talking about," he snapped.

"Hah!" I replied, stabbing a finger at him. "I knew that once we broke up, you'd be all over her like glitter in a strip club."

"Are you jealous, McCool? Then you should not have discarded her."

"Naw, I'm not jealous." I clapped a hand on his shoulder, which made him jump a bit—Crowley wasn't used to casual physical contact. "If you can make her happy, more power to you."

"No one can make anyone else happy, Colin. People make their own contentment. Even I know that."

"True. That said, if you two end up together, I hope Bells finds happiness with you. Heaven knows I couldn't give it to her."

"I—thank you, druid."

"Don't mention it," I said, pointing at the skull. "Now, can you make that thing talk?"

He gave an annoyed, imperious look that would've made Vincent Price proud. "As if it were ever in question. Come along, and you shall have the information you seek."

I followed Crowley back to Jerrik's burial chamber, where he set the skull down in the center of the sarcophagus lid. He pulled a length of white chalk from a pouch at his waist, using it to draw a necromantic circle around the skull. Being naturally curious, I watched for a time, but soon the symbols and runes he etched began to wriggle and swim in a way that made my head hurt.

Necromancy was simply not compatible with druidry, something I'd learned in my dealings with the Fear Doirich. To avoid making my headache worse, I averted my eyes while Crowley worked, busying myself by examining Jerrik's tomb. Most of his belongings had been trashed, but I did find a huge lump of slagged gold on the floor. On a whim, I tossed it in my Bag, figuring that he didn't need it anymore.

"What was the jarl's full name and title again?" Crowley asked.

"Jerrik the Betrayer," I replied, turning to see the results of his labors. "Former king of the Norwegian Westland, according to Bryn."

The lines he'd drawn in the stone surface of the coffin

now glowed with a sickly yellow light, and Jerrik's head floated in the middle of the circle. The runes and symbols no longer wriggled with a life of their own, but I got a metallic tang in my mouth when I looked at the circle, and my nose filled with the smell of burning offal and decay. I swallowed bile, forcing myself to watch despite the discomfort his magic caused me.

Crowley's eyes were locked on the skull, his face lit up with strange shadows by the flickering magic of his rune work. "Jerrik the Betrayer, I summon you from your eternal unrest, so that you may fulfill your vow to the druid named Colin McCool."

The skull's jaw worked back and forth a few times, then it spoke in a hoarse, faraway voice. "I will, if the druid promises to uphold his end of our bargain."

Uncertain regarding where we stood on that front, I looked at Crowley. "Can you do it?"

"Certainly. Odin's curse has weakened over the years, and he never bothered to renew the magic. Typical of a god," he said disdainfully.

"Then, yes, Jerrik, I'll uphold the bargain as we agreed, so long as you tell us how to get to Jotunheim."

"Look below for the answer you seek," Jerrik's skull croaked.

I arched an eyebrow. "Could you be more specific?"

"I think he means to look inside his crypt," Crowley suggested.

"At least one of you has some brains," the skull added as it gently floated to rest on the sarcophagus.

The glow slowly faded from Crowley's runes, leaving

us in near darkness. I snapped my fingers, lighting the torches on the walls. Then, I stealth-shifted and slid the lid from Jerrik's coffin. Inside his crypt was a portal, one that opened up on an elevated stone pathway that stretched away into utter darkness.

18

"Huh. You think the giants knew that was there?"

Crowley shook his head slowly. "I do not. I think Jerrik was the doorway. Or, rather, he was the key. The giants must have known this, having given him the ability to travel to their realm in times past. By obliterating his presence, they likely meant to ensure that he could not open a gateway to their realm."

I rocked my hand back and forth as I looked through the portal. "Er, sort of to their realm. From the looks of it, we'll still have to traverse Yggdrasil."

"Ah, yes—the pathways. Mother always thought it was a silly precaution for the Norse gods to take." The corners of his mouth turned up slightly as he gave me a sideways glance. "Perhaps she thought better of that notion, after the stunt we pulled."

"Couldn't have done it without you," I replied.

"As I'm aware," he said. "Now that my work is done, I'll

gladly accept a portal back to Austin, where I intend to warm up with a hot cup of tea and a good grimoire."

"Do you need your goop back?"

"Yes, I do. It's food I make for Nameless, a mixture of hell hound dung, night hag entrails, and ectoplasm from the shadow plane. Keeps him from eating the locals, you see."

"Gross," I said, reaching in my Bag for the jar. "And just how many locals has that little shit eaten?"

"No one who would be missed," he said with utter seriousness.

I was about to press Crowley on the topic when Ásgeir ran in with Belladonna on his heels. "Druid, we have guests—of the divine kind."

"Is it Badb or Aengus?" I asked, abandoning my search for the jar so I could grab Dyrnwyn.

"Some big blond guy," Belladonna said. "He's cute, and very pissed."

Ásgeir shook his head. "This is not just 'some guy.' The god Váli has arrived, with two great beasts." He paused, clenching and unclenching his fists, a nervous tell if I ever saw one. "I believe he has summoned two of the *landvættir* against you."

"The land what?" I said in an incredulous tone.

Crowley scowled. "Do you not research the lands to which you travel? The four *landvættir* are great beasts that defend Iceland in times of need. Supposedly they were sent by the gods to protect the people from invasion by the Danes."

"Colin's not much for reading up on history," Bells said.

"If it doesn't involve geek culture, cars, or the opposite sex, he's not interested."

"Sheesh, is it gang up on Colin day?" I protested before tilting my head in acquiescence. "Okay, so maybe I've never heard of these 'land vaders,' but I know who Váli is, for sure."

"How can you not know about these creatures?" Crowley chided. "They are on Iceland's national coat of arms, and their coins as well."

"I might be a geek, but I'm not geeky enough to take up vexillology and numismatics." I turned to the troll. "Ásgeir, has Váli said what he wants?"

The troll cocked his head before responding. "He is saying that you are implicated in the disappearance of his son."

"Well, that's not good," I muttered.

Crowley cradled his chin and chuckled. "So that's what happened to the demigod who ran that bar. I should have known."

"You're the reason The Hammer and Anvil closed?" Belladonna's voice grew wistful. "*Carajo*—I liked that place, and the bartender was hot."

"Druid, what do you intend to do?" Ásgeir said, his voice growing higher in pitch as he spoke.

I'd never seen the troll rattled, and that had me worried. But if I was going to be hunted by another god, I wanted to know what I was up against. "I need to see this guy with my own eyes before I decide. And those land thingies."

"Wights, in your tongue," the troll said. "As for the god,

I'll tell you all you need to know. As for power, he is the equal of his brother Thor. Also consider that he was born solely for the purpose of avenging Baldur's murder, which says much about his temperament. He's perhaps a bit less rash than his brother, and more just, but Váli is also self-righteous and vain. It would be wise of you to avoid him, especially if you were responsible for the death of his son."

"Noted." I cast a chameleon spell on myself and headed for the entrance to the barrow. "Be right back."

Ásgeir sighed and followed, while Crowley and Bells remained behind. Crowley likely wanted to ensure that he and Belladonna could escape easily in case of emergency. The wizard was good in a scrape, but when it came down to it, the guy looked out for number one. I didn't hate him for it, but he wouldn't be my first choice for back-up against the gods, either.

When I peeked out of the tomb's entrance, Bryn was confronting a tall blond guy who was dressed like a lumberjack—beard, watch cap, felling axe and all. And by tall, I mean NBA tall, but built like an inside linebacker with lots of functional muscle and nothing soft about him. A quick peek in the magical spectrum revealed he was definitely a full-on deity, and his axe bled magic like a sieve.

Besides the god, we had other concerns. Something large flew in circles high above, but I couldn't tell what because all I could see was its shadow. And behind Váli stood the biggest fucking minotaur I'd ever seen. Granted, he was the only minotaur I'd ever seen, as we didn't have any back in Austin. Still, this fucker was huge, maybe seven feet tall with the muscularity of a 'roided up body-builder.

Otherwise, he looked just like I would've expected—short brown fur, bull's head, big horns, and no armor or clothing except for a black, kilt-like skirt and a ridiculously large pair of Crocs. No shit, the minotaur wore lime-green Crocs. It was the weirdest damned thing I'd seen since I landed in Iceland.

Behind them lurked Máni, Rós, and Sigi, the three huldufólk who likely sent the giants to torch my tree. Just the sight of those assholes had me reaching for Dyrnwyn, but Ásgeir laid a hand on my arm to stop me. He was as well-hidden as I was, blending into the shadowed walls of the tomb using his innate glamour.

"Wait, druid," he said in an almost imperceptibly soft voice. "Let us listen to what the valkyrie says."

"Stand aside, wench," Váli said as he stared her down with cold blue eyes. The god stood with relaxed calm, unlike the valkyrie, who balanced on the balls of her feet, ready to fight or flee. "The Hidden Folk have told me of your pact with the American, and I know he is nearby, which is why I choose to speak to you in this detestable language."

"Just kill her, Váli," the minotaur said. "Odin will not mourn her loss."

"Father no longer favors her, true," Váli replied,

keeping his eyes on Bryn. "But his judgement is swift for any who would harm his handmaidens. Tell me, Urion—if I should slay her, will you take the blame and suffer his wrath?"

"I still say we should kill her and be done with it," Urion muttered. He had a Greek accent, which seemed fitting, if confusing.

"Thankfully, you appear to have no say in the matter," Bryn replied. "And you'd find the task to be much more of a challenge than you might think. Besides, the druid is not here."

"She lies, great prince," Máni said as he peered around the minotaur's huge shoulders. Rós and Sigi merely nodded in agreement. Apparently, they weren't dumb enough to butt into this conversation.

"I know this," Váli said in an annoyed tone. "And when I want your opinion, worm, I shall ask for it."

Máni hung his head, clearly knowing that discretion was the better part of being a snitch. I'd deal with him later. Currently, my main concern was getting Bryn away from Váli so we could make a hasty retreat to Jotunheim.

Váli swung his axe off his shoulder, planting the axe head in the ground so he could rest his hands on the handle. "I will not ask again, Brynhildr—stand aside so I may confront the druid."

"Are Odin's warriors not the domain of the Valkyries?" she asked. "Should I allow you to trespass in a tomb of the fallen, defiling their graves for the sake of this wild goose chase? What would Odin say, if I ignored my duties simply so you can pursue your whims?"

"The tomb of treasonous swine, you mean," Váli sneered. "The draugar are no concern of mine, and they will not object to my presence. I do not intend to disturb them."

"Indeed, you are too late for that," Bryn replied solemnly. "Someone recently delivered the second death to those your father condemned to eternal unrest." She paused to stroke her chin. "In fact, the manner in which they were slain leads me to believe that it was the work of a god. I wonder, will your presence here implicate you in the act?"

"Choose your words with care," Váli growled. "You know I would never undermine my father's authority."

"I can only report what I see—no more, no less. Thus far, I can honestly say I never saw you set foot inside the tomb." She let her statement of fact hang in the air. "And if you do not enter the crypt, that is what I will tell Odin when he asks me what happened to Jerrik and his clan."

Váli's face turned beet red, and a blood vessel popped out on his forehead. His hands gripped the butt of his axe so hard I thought it would splinter, and for a moment I was sure he was going to take Bryn's head off. Then, he closed his eyes and took a deep breath, opening them only to glower at the valkyrie.

"This is not over, Brynhildr. I will catch up with the druid at some point, and then there will be a reckoning." He turned and addressed the minotaur. "Come, Urion. We shall dine and drink at my home until this human shows his face again."

"I still say this is bullshit," Urion complained unironically. "Should've just killed her and been done with it."

Ignoring the minotaur's mutterings, Váli swung his axe over his shoulder with one hand while using the fingers of his other to whistle loudly. I heard the sound of huge feathered wings beating overhead, then the biggest fucking griffin I'd ever seen landed outside the tomb. It was easily the size of an elephant, with a lion's rear legs and hindquarters and an eagle's forelegs, chest, wings, and head. The god and the minotaur leapt on its back, and then they flew off into the sky, leaving the three huldufólk standing there looking like idiots.

"Wait a minute," I said to Ásgeir. "I thought minotaurs were a Greek thing."

"I believe he was a gift from Zeus to Odin," the troll said. "The All-Father didn't know what to do with him, so he placed him in charge of guarding the northwestern regions of the island."

"Makes sense," I replied, observing the three huldufólk, who were looking around nervously. "Back me up here, will you?"

Váli, Urion, and the griffin were just a speck in the distance, so I ran out of the tunnel using my Fomorian speed, snagging Máni by the scruff of the neck. I threw him on the ground, pinning him with my cold iron hunting knife at his throat. Rós and Sigi both drew wicked-looking bone daggers in response, but then Ásgeir appeared in front of them, causing them to back down.

"Alright, Máni—it's time to share what you've been up

to lately. Who killed Jerrik and his clan, and how'd they know we came here?"

Máni began to stutter and stammer, pleading for mercy. Before I got any intelligible info out of him, Bryn tapped me on the arm. "Druid, I believe Váli is coming back. We should flee while we can."

The speck in the sky was now the size of a fly and growing larger by the second. "Ah, shit."

"Should I kill them?" Ásgeir asked, as if he were asking about the weather.

"No, not yet. As much as I'd like to cross these idiots off my list, I don't want to start a war with the whole huldufólk nation." I bitch-slapped Máni hard enough to split his lip, then I whispered in his ear. "I've had about enough of you, *elf.* I strongly suggest you let me finish my business here in peace, before I lose my shit and kill you and your uptight, privileged sidekicks."

Then, I set him down rather roughly, taking time to straighten the collar on his very expensive-looking gray-flannel suit. I glanced skyward again, noting that Váli was closer now, close enough for me to see his axe's gleam in the moonlight. It was definitely time to go.

"Come on, everyone," I said, mostly for the snitches' sakes. "Jerrik had an escape route in the back of the tomb."

When we ducked inside the tunnels, I hooked a thumb at the entrance. "Ásgeir, can you do something about that?"

"Yes," he replied. "But collapsing a cave is easier than

clearing it. If there is no other way out, we will be trapped here once the entrance is sealed."

"Do it, then meet us in Jerrik's burial vault." I took off down the tunnel with Bryn hot on my heels. "I'm curious, could you have taken Váli?"

She chuckled. "With all my sisters at my back, certainly. But alone? No. Odin made us powerful, but he did not make us gods."

"So, why'd you stand up to him?"

"I might be despised by my kind, but I am not without honor. We made a deal, and I want vengeance—and vindication." There was an explosive boom behind us, followed by a long rumbling noise. Bryn looked back over her shoulder before continuing. "That will not hold Odin's son for long, and he will be eager to pay me back for my deception. I only hope it was worth it."

"Oh, don't worry about that. Stick around long enough and eventually one of the Celtic gods will show up to kill me. Right now, you have a one-in-three chance it'll be Badb, but I intend to increase those odds very, very soon. You'll get your opportunity, believe me."

"We shall see," she said, just as we entered the jarl's burial chamber.

"So, does another god want to kill you or not?" Bells asked as we jogged into view.

"I believe that Váli is undecided, but in my estimation, he is leaning toward murder," Bryn said.

"Great," my ex replied. "Can you send us back to Austin, then? Because as much as I enjoy a good scrape, gods are out of my league, and I have a case to solve."

"A case?" I asked.

"We've, er, started an agency," Crowley said in a quiet voice as he rifled through Jerrik's tomb. Every so often, he'd slip something in his satchel. I didn't say anything, because I figured it was payment for helping me out. And it wasn't like Jerrik needed it anymore.

"In fact, we're partners now," Bells added, slinging an arm over Crowley's shoulders. I noted that he did not object. "And I have a client waiting for me back in Round Rock, so if you could zap us back to my apartment—"

"Um, I have some bad news," I said, squinting one eye shut in a lopsided, apologetic grin. "If I send you back to Austin, there's a good chance Váli will follow you there looking for me. Or, even worse, Badb or Aengus will show up, and then you'll really be fucked."

"Which means?" Bells asked, leaning in menacingly.

"It means we're accompanying the druid on the next leg of his journey," Crowley said in an annoyed tone. "To Jotunheim."

Belladonna's eyes tightened as she curled her fists into tight balls at her sides. Her pupils transformed from neat, round circles to vertical slits, and silvery scales began to pop out on her forehead. Then, she took a deep breath, closing her eyes for several seconds. I began to open my mouth to speak, but Crowley urged me to hold my tongue with a surreptitious wave of his hand.

Finally, the scales receded, and she opened her eyes. "Fine. But if I lose this client, you're reimbursing me for the loss out of that fat justiciar money you've been getting."

"Deal," I said as Ásgeir sprinted into the room on his weird stick-like legs. "Time to go?"

He nodded. "Váli and the bull man will dig through the rubble in minutes."

My gaze swept across the room, and then down at the portal inside Jerrik's coffin. "Alrighty, then—let's go rescue Dian Cécht."

19

Ásgeir insisted on taking the lead, and I let him since we didn't have time to argue. After he squeezed his massive shoulders through the tunnel, I hopped down behind him, followed by Belladonna, Bryn, and, finally, Crowley. Rather than climbing down, the shadow wizard descended on dark tendrils of oily smoke, careful not to snag his tailored black slacks and expensive gray cable-knit sweater.

"Um, Crowley—the curse?"

"Yes, yes—I took care of that while you were spying on the latest god who wants to murder you," he said as he knelt down to examine the path beneath our feet. He rapped his knuckles on the stones. "Eldritch magic. Odin dabbles in forbidden arts, it would seem."

"What about the doorway?" I asked, pointing to the portal above us.

"Give it a minute."

Crowley crossed his arms over his chest, tapping his

foot impatiently as he watched the portal. Soon, the mino-taur's head popped into view above us. As Urion reached a hand through the portal to follow, it snapped shut, severing his hand at the wrist. The hand dropped to the stone pathway at the shadow wizard's feet with a soft thump. Crowley picked it up and wrapped it in yet another silk kerchief before slipping it inside his satchel.

"Took them long enough," Crowley said.

"Was that really necessary?" I asked.

"Oh, he'll grow another," he replied. "You're a shifter. You know better than I how animal-human hybrids heal."

"And they accuse me of making friends everywhere I go," I said as I drew Dyrnwyn from my Bag.

It failed to light, although it did flicker a bit when I accidentally pointed it in Crowley's direction. No surprise there, but at least there weren't any immediate threats around other than my best frenemy. Satisfied that we were more or less safe for the moment, I did a visual scan of our surroundings—a task that didn't take long at all.

The pathway we stood on was roughly ten feet wide, without a guardrail or even a small lip to prevent a person from falling into the great dark void of Yggdrasil beyond. It was made of gray stone blocks, each carved with a single rune—and from what I could tell, nothing appeared to support it underneath.

As for visibility, the path glowed with a pale golden light, yet it was darker than pitch everywhere else. In fact, the only thing I could see was the walkway we stood upon, winding away into the vast blackness that stretched out in every other direction.

The place reminded me a lot of the pocket dimension inside my Bag, except it was a lot less crowded. Based on my past experience with pocket dimensions and the Void, I knew that *things* lurked out there in the dark. It was best that we found our way to Jotunheim as quickly as possible, before some ancient evil found us first.

"Alright, so who knows the way to Jotunheim?" I asked.

"There's only one path, *pendejo*," Belladonna said. "Seems like it's obvious which way we should go."

"Actually, it's not that simple," Bryn replied. "The paths of Yggdrasil are many, and they twist and turn back on each other. This is merely an entry branch, and as we travel, we'll come to forks and junctions along the way."

"Do you know which way to go?" I asked.

"No, but I have a feeling that the wizard might," she said.

"If you're inquiring as to whether or not I kept the skull, of course I did," Crowley said. "The first thing you learn in necromancy is to never release a captive soul until their task is done."

"Druid," Ásgeir said, "I think it is best we do not tarry."

"Agreed," I replied. "It goes without saying, but I'll say it anyway—don't step off the path."

"Why, what's down there?" Bells asked, looking over the edge.

"Nothing," Crowley said, gently grabbing her by the arm to pull her toward the center of the path. "Nothing at all."

"*¡Claro que sí!*" Belladonna snarked. "Colin always did take me to the nicest places."

That elicited a snort from Bryn, as well as a muffled chuckle from the pathway behind us. "You may as well show yourselves," I said to the darkness.

"Oh, you're no fun," Loki replied as he and Click slowly shimmered into view. "I was going to startle the troll to see if I could get him to leap off the path."

"Which is exactly why I want you and Click in plain sight," I replied, acknowledging my substitute magic teacher with a nod. "Speaking of, glad to see you made it."

"Oh, ya' know me, lad. I'm ne'er one ta' pass up a jaunt through a pocket dimension." Click snapped his fingers, and a lit cigarette appeared in his hand. "'Sides, I'm itchin' ta' see what happens when ya' go up against that tosser, Býleistr."

Bryn gave the quasi-god an amused frown. "Are you really that eager to see your pupil torn limb from limb?"

"Oh, don't worry about that *cabrón*, chica," Bells said as she shouldered past the troll to head down the path. "He could fall face-first in a pile of ghoul shit and still come up smelling like roses."

———————

Shortly thereafter, we came to the first junction just as Bryn said we would. The path came to a crossroads of sorts, where another path crossed the one we were on at an oblique angle. Several other paths hung above and below us, winding off into the distance like gold and gray lengths of rope against the black void beyond.

"Which way, Crowley?" I asked.

He held the skull up to his ear. "Straight ahead."

"Well, that's damned convenient," Click observed. "Mayhaps I should pick up a bit o' necromancy and take a floatin', talkin' skull with me everywhere I go. Give 'em flames fer' eyes, and such."

"I believe one empty talking head is enough," Crowley remarked in a flat voice.

"Watch'er tone, youngling," Click said with a smile that didn't meet his eyes. "Ya' might think Fuamnach's the deadliest magician the Fair Folk e'er issued forth, but ye'd be mistaken."

"Enough, you two," I warned. "Save it for the jötnar."

As we continued on, the two of them continued to bicker back and forth over the relative merits of aes sídhe magic versus that of the Tylwyth Teg. In my opinion it was a moot point, because the two were essentially one and the same—if not in geography, than in nature, at least. Crowley didn't seem to know what to make of Click, and I got the feeling he didn't trust him, which was funny because the feeling was mutual. Their arguing was giving me a headache, and I was about to intervene before it got out of hand. Thankfully, Bryn beat me to it.

"Odin's left eye—would you two give it a rest?" the valkyrie said in a peeved tone. "You've been at it since the last intersection."

"Thank you," Bells said. "It's bad enough that I have to hear him arguing with his bird back home."

"Oh, an' I should jest let this upstart mage tell me how ta' animate a magical construct?" Click huffed. "As if. I created ma' first golem while this twit were still shittin' his drawers."

"In truth, I have no idea how old I am," Crowley replied, drawing himself up to his full height so he could look down his nose at Click. "Although I don't think age has anything to do with the relative skill of a practitioner of the dark arts."

"Ah, look what you've done," Loki said, belching as he took a swig from a bottle of wine. "You've gotten Snape here all riled up. Now, he'll never shut up."

I was about to step in and referee before things got out of hand when I noticed Ásgeir looking in the distance behind us. "Trouble?"

The troll threw his hands up in the air. "Perhaps, but it's hard to tell with this incessant chatter."

"Hey, guys—cut it out for a second," I said, holding my hands over my head to get their attention. Crowley and Click continued to bicker in the background, oblivious to my request.

"I don't think they heard you," Belladonna said as she blew a strand of hair out of her eyes.

"Guys—aw, fuck it." I put a little Fomorian in my voice. "Quiet!"

My voice boomed across the stone pathway, reverberating off the walkways above and below until the echo got lost in the void. Crowley and Click both turned to look at me as if I'd gone mad, while the others did the whole, "this is awkward, averting my eyes now" thing. I stood there feeling kind of stupid, but I kept the stern look on my face as I returned their stares.

"An' who put the bee in his bonnet?" Click asked.

"Oh, he's terribly excitable," Crowley replied. "It doesn't take much to upset him."

"Ssshh," Ásgeir said. "There it is again."

A hush fell across our group, and all remained silent as we strained to hear whatever had the troll riled. The only noise I heard was Ásgeir's stomach rumbling, so I cast a cantrip to enhance my senses.

"I don't hear anything," Bryn said. "The troll merely jumps at shadows."

Then, I heard it—a cry in the distance, kind of a cross between a lion's roar and the cry of an eagle. I'd heard a noise like that twice before, once in a cave in Kingsland, Texas, and again in Mag Mell. It was the hunting call of a—

"Dragon," Loki said with drunken indifference. "Looks like my brother roused the other two *landvættir*."

"Meh, could be anything," Click said. "Ya' know how things get in the Void, what wit' the Byakhees an' Huntin' Horrors flyin' 'round."

"Hunting whats?" Belladonna asked.

"Hunting Horrors," Crowley said, eager for the opportunity to recite a bit of arcane knowledge. "A predatory airborne creature existing on two planes at once, mostly made up of dark matter and shadow, roughly the size of a young dragon. Nyarlathotep uses them to track down his enemies on the mortal planes."

We heard the screeching noise again, this time even closer.

"That's not anything from the Void," Loki said,

finishing his bottle and tossing it off the walkway. "In Yggdrasil, sound only travels along and between the paths. If it was out there, we couldn't hear it, because there's no atmosphere. It's definitely a dragon."

I poured every bit of magic I could into my sensory enhancement cantrip, straining my eyes as I looked back in the direction we'd come. Off in the very far distance, I could barely make out a flying creature with a rider on its back. I'd spent some time studying dragons after my last brush with Caoranach, and based on what I knew of dragon anatomy, only adult dragons were strong enough to carry riders. Meaning, that rider was almost as tall as a fully-grown dragon.

"We need to get moving," I said, looking back and forth at my companions. When they didn't budge, I made a shooing motion with my hands, letting the Fomorian side of me slip back into my voice as I spoke. "That's a giant riding a fucking dragon—run, you morons!"

"I still don't see why we can't just stand and fight," Bells said as she huffed along beside me. "We have a wizard, a valkyrie, a troll, another wizard that's almost a god, an actual god, a druid who can turn into a troll-looking thing, and me. I like those odds."

"I beg to differ," Crowley said from above us. He was doing his Doctor Octopus thing, strolling along on shadowy tentacles that carried him several feet above the pathway. "To battle a dragon requires room to maneuver, in order to avoid being immolated by their fiery breath. While we might win the battle, we'd likely lose several members of our party in the process."

"Not to mention, Loki and Click disappeared on us," I said as I glanced back to check on Bryn and Ásgeir.

The troll had taken a rear-guard position by default. Not to be outdone, the valkyrie had opted to do the same, but what they intended to do against a giant on a dragon was beyond me. Bryn didn't have her pegasus, and the troll had no weapons. And the dragon was getting closer.

"And why can't you teleport us out of here again?" Crowley asked.

"I told you, it's because they'll use it to track us."

"Down here?" Crowley said, clearly puzzled. "In the Void?"

"I know, I know," I said. "But I'm not taking any chances."

Crowley frowned, because he knew there was something more to it. And he was right. What I kept to myself was that my connection to the Oak was very faint here in the pathways of Yggdrasil. I didn't want to risk leaving one of them behind due to a miscommunication with the tree.

"*Joder*," Bells growled. "These *pinche* boots are rubbing blisters on my heels."

"You're a shifter, right? Just heal them on the fly," I replied.

"That's not how it works, Colin," she hissed. "I'm a serpenthrope—I turn into a naga."

"So?" I said. "What's the big deal?"

"Naga don't have feet," Crowley said. "So she has to completely transform to heal her lower body."

"Seriously? Weird. Sorry, Bells."

"I'll kill you later," she said. "Right now, I just want to know how far it is to the exit."

"Not far, according to Jerrik," the shadow wizard replied. "Maybe a mile or so."

I looked over my shoulder again. "That's too far— they'll be on us before we get there. You guys go on ahead and secure the exit. I'm going to shift and buy us some time."

Belladonna looked at me like I was nuts. "You can't fight a dragon by yourself, Colin."

"I don't plan to," I muttered. "Crowley, make sure you give us something to follow."

"Indeed," he said, spinning off a strand of shadow that attached itself to the pathway like a length of thin black spider silk. "Don't get killed, druid."

"Ditto that sentiment," Bells said.

"Um, thanks," I replied as I pulled up short, tearing out of my clothes so I could start to shift. I watched the two run off into the distance then focused on my change, completing the transformation just as Bryn and Ásgeir pulled up alongside me.

"You would make an excellent troll," the troll said with complete seriousness. "Any female of our kind would be keen to mate with you."

"Um, no thanks. I have some troll friends back at home, and—" I stopped myself before I said something that would offend him. "What I mean to say is, I'm taken."

Bryn snickered. "That's no obstacle for a troll wench. Their men are polygamous. Why, I bet Ásgeir here has a dozen wives, at least."

"Only seven," he said. "But I will have more soon, once I return with my pockets full of gold from this adventure."

"That's if we don't get eaten by a dragon first," I said, looking back down the pathway. "Speaking of which, you two should get going and follow the others to the exit. I'll be along in a minute."

"Nonsense," Bryn said. "It's been ages since I hunted dragon."

"If she stays, I stay," the troll added, pushing his hat firmly down on his head.

"Fine, but stand behind me," I said, shoving the last of my clothes inside my Craneskin Bag.

"As if," Bryn said, pulling a highly polished metal shield and a brace of throwing spears from behind her back.

"Never mind me, I'm just the one in charge," I sighed. "So, you used to hunt dragons?"

"Indeed," Ásgeir replied. "The Valkyries' enthusiasm for hunting wyrms was only exceeded by their lust for hunting my kind."

"That was long ago, troll," the valkyrie replied. "And we only hunted those who were stupid enough to attack human settlements."

"Why?" I asked. "I thought the gods didn't care what happened to humans."

Bryn answered while keeping her eyes focused on the rapidly-approaching dragon and rider. "The trolls steal children—male children. Odin needs warriors to fight for him at Ragnarok, and he grew tired of losing his future army to the ravenous appetites of trolls."

"Touching," I said.

"Imagine if all of trollkind had banded together to hunt vapid, self-involved Valkyries," Ásgeir mused. "Why, there'd be none left."

"I don't get it," I said. "She seems more tom-boyish to me. No offense, Bryn."

"None taken, as I am the exception to the rule," she replied. "Many of my sisters now make their living as social media influencers."

"No shit?" I remarked, rummaging around in my Bag for weapons. "Guess I shouldn't be surprised. Gwen sure looked the type."

"Perhaps we should continue this conversation at a later time," Ásgeir said, interrupting us. "The dragon comes."

20

The thing was massive, bigger than even Caoranach. The dragon's body was the size of an average two-story house, with a wingspan that had to stretch fifty feet or more. It was almost pure white, with scales that glimmered like icicles under the soft light of the walkway and bright blue eyes that shone in the dark. Yet it still breathed smoke, and when it opened its jaws to roar at us, I saw just the faintest glow of heat within its throat.

Its size actually worked in our favor, because the dragon was too big to land on the walkway. Instead, it hovered directly over the path about fifty yards away or so, holding position until its rider jumped off its back, at which point it flew off. When the giant hit the ground, the impact sent a shockwave through the stones, which rocked and reeled under our feet for several seconds until they became still.

The giant was among the largest I'd seen, perhaps twenty-five feet tall or more. He dressed like a Viking of old, in a sleeveless bright-red tunic that looked to be made of sailcloth and leather pants that had been sewn from dozens of cattle hides. He wore sandals with thick rubber soles that must've been cut from semi-truck tires. Instead of leather straps, the shoes were tied around his ankles with thick lengths of nylon rope.

Regarding his features, he looked like a very ugly man with a round, bearded face, a bald head, and a bulbous nose with a wart on the end. His beard was clean and well-kempt, however, as were his clothes and the rope belt and leather purse at his waist. As for weapons, he carried none. I guess when you were over two stories tall, you didn't need any.

Deciding that I didn't want to give the guy a chance to get close, I plucked a spear from the pile at my feet and chambered it to throw. The spears I'd found were man-sized, so I'd need to hit him with a couple dozen to do any real damage. Even so, I figured if I hit him in the eye it might give us time to run.

"Wait," Ásgeir said, placing a hand on my arm. "Let me handle this."

"You sure?" I asked, because the giant was striding toward us, and he looked even bigger up close.

"I think so," he said under his breath. "But if he throws me from the walkway, I expect you to avenge my death."

The troll took off before I could object to his spur-of-the-moment plan. "Damn it," I swore. "He's going to get himself killed."

"I don't know why you care what happens to a troll,"

Bryn said. "He probably ate one of your ancestors. They used to go on raids to Irland with Vikings, you know."

"He reminds me of someone," I said, thinking of Elmo, the world's gentlest ogre. "Now, hush. I want to hear what they say."

Ásgeir and the giant stopped about ten yards apart, sizing each other up. The troll looked a lot more relaxed than I'd have been, facing a behemoth like that. After several seconds, he nodded to the much larger creature who stood before him.

"Halvor, it has been a long time."

The giant squinted, then he held up a hand. "Hold on, I need my glasses," he said in a booming voice with a faint Scandinavian accent. He reached into the leather bag that hung from his rope belt and pulled out the biggest pair of bifocals I'd ever seen. After adjusting them, he looked through the top half of the lenses at the troll. "Ah, Ásgeir. They didn't tell me you'd be here."

"If you're speaking of the other *landvættir*, they never saw me," the troll replied. "I remained hidden in the tunnels when they arrived."

"Yes, that prick Urion, and Havardr. They sent me to pursue you into Yggdrasil, to stop you from reaching Jotunheimr."

"You mean they didn't want you to catch us?" I broke in. "Because Váli acted like he really wanted to speak with me."

Halvor adjusted his glasses again, squinting to make me out where I stood. "And who is this? Your son, Ásgeir?"

"No, he is my current employer," the troll said. "Halvor, meet Colin McCool. Colin, meet Halvor."

"Ahem," Bryn added.

Ásgeir ignored her. "Colin is a druid from America, in search of one of the Celtic gods, Dian Cécht. We hear he's been abducted and taken to Jotunheimr by Býleistr."

"McCool, McCool," the giant muttered. "Isn't he the fellow who ran from Benandonner?"

"His ancestor, many generations removed," the troll replied.

"Well, he seems ready to do battle now," Halvor said. "And that's good enough for me. Well met, McCool. And, no, they did not request that I capture you. Although the other landvættir travel with the god Váli, they do the bidding of the huldufólk and Býleistr."

"Hah!" I said, smacking my fist in my palm. "I knew those bastards were working together."

The giant pulled his glasses off, cleaning them with the hem of his tunic. "They know you come for the Physician. While I have no idea how Býleistr could abduct a god, I do know that he intends to keep you from finding him."

"Yeah, he wants revenge," I said. "The question is, are you going to help him?"

"I'm Bryn, by the way," the valkyrie said as she fumed beside me.

Halvor put his glasses on again. "Oh, I didn't even see your *kertilsveinr* there. Does she belong to McCool, or you, Ásgeir?"

The troll laughed out loud at Halvor's innocent question, while Bryn's face turned beet red. "Neither," I said. "*She* is a valkyrie."

The giant nodded sagely. "Ah. No offense meant, shield-maiden. I am losing my eyesight in my old age."

I was afraid to ask what a "kertilsveinr" was, so I kept my mouth shut on that topic. "So, Halvor? Are you helping them or not?"

"Well, I am duty-bound to defend *Eylenda* from any foe who seeks to invade her shores." He stroked his beard for a moment. "But you're obviously fleeing the island, not invading it. So, I'll stand here to make sure you don't turn around, but I'll not keep you from your destination."

"Thank you, Halvor," Ásgeir said, bowing slightly at the waist.

"Oh, don't mention it. I never liked that Greek bastard anyway, nor the huldufólk since they took on modern ways." He held a hand up to his mouth, speaking in a softer voice as if sharing a secret. "And when all this is over, come visit me at Fjallabak nature reserve. There's a hot spring close to my cave where we can soak our feet and talk about the old times."

"Well, he seemed nice," I said as we followed the shadow strand Crowley had left for us. "Not at all like the other giants I've met here."

"Don't expect all the jötnar to be so kind," Bryn said. "That one has gone soft with old age."

"Halvor was always all bark and no bite—mostly,"

Ásgeir said. "His size is why he was chosen to guard the island. By stature alone, he is a deterrent to most invaders."

Since I was in my Fomorian form, we made good time to the exit. When we arrived, Crowley and Belladonna were nowhere to be found, but Crowley's shadow silk strand led straight through the portal. I saw no one on the other side. I'd been fooled before, so I decided to remain in my Fomorian form—just in case.

Thankfully the portal was giant-sized, so I had no problem making my way through with Bryn and Ásgeir close on my heels. We stepped out into the bottom of a rocky canyon, with walls of gray rock stretching up a hundred feet or more. There was a ledge that followed the canyon wall about thirty feet above us, but the coast was clear from what I could see. However, Belladonna and Crowley were nowhere to be found.

"Yo, anyone home?" I said, hoping they were hiding nearby.

Ásgeir tapped my arm. "Druid, look."

He pointed at the ground where Crowley's thread lay. As I watched, the thread writhed in the dirt, twisting in on itself until it spelled a single word in cursive.

TRAP

"Aw, shit."

I turned to shove Bryn back through the portal, but it had already closed. Now, there was only a flat blank wall of gray rock where the entrance to Yggdrasil had been moments before. Above us, all along the ledge, dozens upon dozens of giants shimmered into view, much the same way that Loki and Click had earlier.

Fighting was futile, but the Fomorian side of me didn't care. I reached into my Craneskin Bag to draw Orna with killing on my mind. Before I could draw her out, a voice boomed from overhead.

"Wouldn't do that if'n I was you, drood."

The speaker's accent was familiar and unmistakable. When I finally located the source among the sea of jötnar above us, I instantly knew who I faced. He was taller than his son by five feet or more, but the resemblance between the two was uncanny. The blue beady eyes, the blond hair, the underbite—this was Snorri's dad, Býleistr, or I was a monkey's uncle.

He had one of his enormous hands around Belladonna's neck, dangling her over the cliff's edge. She'd shifted to protect herself, and she squirmed and twisted in his grip as she fought to get free. Bells scratched at his arm like a cat at a screen door, wrapping her tail around his forearm for leverage, but Býleistr's grip would not be broken.

Crowley knelt nearby, tied hand and foot in thick leather straps with two giant spearmen standing ready to run him through. I had no doubt they'd laced his fingers tightly to prevent him from casting any magic, a fat lot of good that would do. Based on the look in his eyes, he was ready to do murder if they actually harmed Bells.

"Let her go, Býleistr," I said, my voice echoing through the canyon. "This is between you and me."

"Oh, but I beg ta' differ," he replied. "Ya' killed my son in cold blood, and he weren't doin' nothin' but followin' our ways."

"I was acting as justiciar under authority of Queen Maeve—"

"Lies!" Býleistr roared. Spittle flew out of his mouth, and his face twisted into a mask of rage. He squeezed Belladonna's neck tighter until she started to turn blue. "You'll surrender ta' stand trial afore all of Utgard, or I'll pinch this shifter's pretty little head off, like a flower from its stem."

"You can't fight them all, druid," Ásgeir said in a low voice. "And he will kill her."

"The troll speaks true, Colin," Bryn added. "They will riddle us with spears and smash our heads in with boulders before we ever reach the cleft on which they stand. If you value your friend's life, you will give yourself over to the jötnar. I will do what I can to see that you get a fair trial."

"Listen ta' the valkyrie an' the half-breed, boy," Býleistr said as he pointed a finger at me in warning.

The Fomorian in me wanted to go apeshit and slay some giants, but my human side suppressed those urges. "Swear you'll not harm my friends, and that you'll let them go if I give myself up peacefully."

Loki's brother gave a short nod. "Aye. Surrender, and yer' companions kin go free, all of them. Ya' have my word, drood."

I slowly withdrew my hand from my Bag, then I raised my hands over my head. "Fine, I surrender to stand trial according to jötnar customs. You can let them go."

Býleistr chortled with malice. "An' I will—after ya' stand trial and I have justice fer' me boy's life." He gestured to his subordinates while still holding Bells over the ledge. "Seize the valkyrie and the troll, but do 'em no harm. When the drood shifts back to his true form, tie him up an' toss 'im in the pit."

The pit was a smooth-walled hole cut in the limestone floor of the canyon, approximately ten feet in diameter and thirty feet deep. It was obviously designed as a punishment for giants, as it would barely give the average jötunn enough space to lay down. It lacked a privy hole, so the floor was covered with a thick layer of muck. While they'd thrown some moldy straw down, the place absolutely reeked of giant piss and shit.

Býleistr's troops had tied me up securely after I shifted back to human size, binding my fingers in fine strands of sinew before dropping me into the pit. I was no fool, though—I'd stealth-shifted rather than turning back into my human form. A good thing, too, as that long drop would've broken some bones had I not retained my Fomorian resilience. The giants watched me for a time, so I feigned an injury until they laughed and left me to wallow in jötunn shit and regret.

When they were gone, I tried to contact the Oak. Whether it was due to distance or some spell that blocked Jotunheim off from other worlds, I couldn't even manage the faintest whisper of communication. Feeling defeated and alone, I found a relatively muck-free spot and made myself as comfortable as possible.

Some rescue mission. Sorry, Finnegas.

Soon, Býleistr came along to gloat, as I knew he would. He leaned over the hole, hands on his knees, peering at me through the thick iron bars that capped my prison high overhead. I remained silent, waiting for him to speak. No way would I give him the satisfaction of thinking I'd beg for clemency.

"How do ya' like your quarters, drood?" the giant asked.

"It lacks a certain ambience, I'll say that. Please inform your housecarl that I take my tea at dawn, and I expect hot towels and an even hotter bath a quarter-hour after."

He spat a big gob of phlegm into the hole, narrowly missing my leg. "Joke all ya' want, human. Tomorrow morn' we'll hold yer' trial, and then ya'll not be laughin' no more."

"Tell me something, Býleistr," I said, feigning a calm I didn't feel. "I've heard that the jötnar live by a warrior's code, much like the Vikings did in years gone by. So how is it that your people are letting you railroad me with a fake trial, when I killed your son in fair and mutual combat?"

The giant snarled his reply, low and dangerous from between clenched teeth. "When that damned fae queen sent his body ta' us, the boy's hands an' feet was blistered an' charred by magic. Ya' cheated, drood, an' there'd be no way ya'd best ma' son otherwise. Tweren't no fair battle."

"Nah, I didn't cheat. He attacked me when I was still human-sized, so I did what I had to do to survive. After I shifted it was hand-to-hand, and I ripped his femoral artery out with my own teeth." I paused for a moment, letting the jötunn king seethe. "Then, I watched him bleed out in the river. I'll say this much—he fought well, and he died with honor. Quite unlike his father."

"I know wha'cher doin'," he replied. "Ya' think ya' kin goad me inta' jumpin' in that pit an' tryin' ta' throttle ya' ma'self. Well, it won't work. Clan's gonna see yer head on the block, an' I intend ta' chop it off with ma' own hands. Enjoy yer' last night on the planes, drood."

Having said his peace, the bastard whipped his dick out to piss on me through the iron grate. It was impossible to avoid the downpour, and I was drenched in the foulest-smelling liquid imaginable within seconds. The laughter of several giants echoed nearby, and all I could do was fume as Býleistr's voice joined them when he walked away.

Eventually I was forced to shift back to my human form, which left me at the mercy of the elements. Still, I wasn't completely helpless in my current state, and I was able to cast a cantrip to warm myself as I sat shivering in the pit. Jotunheim was cold, and my Bag had been taken from me, so I covered myself as best I could with rank straw, settling in for a long night.

At some point I drifted off, only to be awakened hours later by someone whispering overhead.

"Psst. Hey, lad, how're ya' doin' down there?"

"Click, is that you?" I asked, feeling a bit of hope creeping into me. "Get me out of here already. I'm fucking freezing."

"No can do, boyo. Hole's magicked, an' there's too many o' those tossers hangin' round up here ta' bust ya' out. But don'cha worry yerself none, cause me an' Loki have a plan." He went silent for a moment. "Oops, someone's comin'. See ya' tomorrow at the trial."

"Click?" I whispered, getting only silence in return. "Click, you crazy Welsh bastard, come back and get me the fuck out of here."

There was only more silence, then footsteps. Moments later, Váli's face appeared above the hole.

I stood and scowled. "Ah, hell—are you coming to piss on me too?"

He watched me for a moment, firelight flickering off his face in the dark. "No. I'm not some honor-less knave like your captor." He went silent again, and since my teeth were starting to chatter, I waited for him to continue. "Tell me, druid, how did my son die?"

"You too, eh?" The god made a sound halfway between a snarl and a hiss. I couldn't blame him—I'd want to know what happened to my son, too. "Alright, I'll tell you. He was your son, after all."

"In truth, I have no shortage of offspring. However, Calder and I parted poorly when last I saw him. Thus, it weighs heavily on me that we did not reconcile before his passing."

"Calder? Really?"

"What of it?" he asked. "Calder is a fine name."

"No, I mean it's a cool name and all, it's just—oh, never mind. I'm a little tired right now, so I hope you don't mind if I give you the *Reader's Digest* version."

"Go on."

"Cade was working for this witch in exchange for help

controlling his berserker nature. She was a *soucouyant*—you know what that is?"

"I've been around a very long time, druid," he replied, crossing his arms over his chest. "Yes, I know of the species."

"Right. So, her master was killing humans in my city. I killed her to get to him, and Cade took umbrage at that. So, he showed up at my junkyard, he went berserk, and then I killed him."

The god cradled his chin in his hand. "You bested a half-god berserker warrior in his were-form? Was he armed?"

"Yes, and yes. It wasn't easy, let me tell you." I paused, wondering if I should go on. I didn't want to piss him off more, but I said I'd tell him what happened, so I continued. "He died ugly, but it was quick, if that's any comfort to you."

Váli grunted softly. "It is. We are warriors, and warriors fall in battle. To know he died with his weapon in hand means much to me."

He started walking away, and I suddenly sensed an opportunity slipping through my hands. "I still have it, by the way." I blurted. "Didn't seem right to use it, and hammers aren't my style. So, I tucked it away someplace safe."

"I would bury him with his weapon, if possible," the god said. "Could you return his remains and hammer to me if you survived this place?"

"I could, yes." *If only he knew.* Cade's remains were inside a couple of junked cars that had been crushed into a four by four cube, buried in deep beneath the junkyard stack. No need to tell his dad that, though.

"I cannot risk angering the jötnar by helping you escape. Father would not be pleased if I started a war." Váli remained silent for the better part of a minute. "When you go to trial tomorrow, ask for the rite of *hólmganga*, as is your due. That is the best I can offer."

He walked away quickly, leaving me to whisper in vain to the empty sky above. "Wait—what the hell is a home gang?"

21

The next morning, they hauled me out of the pit by a rope—wet, shivering, and smelling like I'd been dunked in a latrine hole. The guards checked my bonds, then they dragged me to an icy stream where they dunked me over and over until I was relatively clean. Unlike the guards who tossed me in the pit the night previous, these giants seemed to take little pleasure in their duties. And while they weren't gentle, they didn't go out of their way to do me harm.

So, not everyone in Utgard is a complete dick. Good to know.

After I'd been forcefully bathed, the guards tied a thick rope around my neck. Then they led me deeper into the canyon, until we came to a huge wall and gate that were approximately five stories high and spanned the width of the ravine. The guards yelled above and the gate opened, at which point we entered their city.

I hadn't seen much of Jotunheim the night previous, since they'd tossed me into the pit with little fanfare. Now that I had a chance to look around, I had to admit that I was impressed by what I saw. The jötnar lived in homes that had been carved from the canyon walls—reminiscent of photos I'd seen of Petra, but on a much larger scale. From top to bottom on either side, terraces and giant-sized stairs had been cut from the rock, dividing their city into several levels.

The higher up the cliff face, the more opulent the carved dwellings became, and larger as well. In fact, the dwellings at the top were adorned with bright tapestries, precious metals, and gems that had been set into the stone around the doors. But down below at ground level, the homes were little more than caves in the wall. There, the people wore simple clothing and the women toiled at menial tasks, pausing to watch and comment as we walked past.

I didn't bother asking where we were headed, because I'd seen this movie before and knew how it ended. As we continued through town, a crowd gathered behind us, and giants lined the central road that bisected the canyon and their city. The crowd began to hiss and boo, some spat on me, and I was pelted more than once with rotten fruit and fish guts as we passed.

Thankfully my sinner's march was brief, and we arrived at our destination within a few minutes. Here, the valley widened, opening up into a series of foothills above a broad rocky plain. When the crowd parted before us and I was able to see in all directions, I realized that the valley was nothing more than a cleft in the vast, never-ending mountain range that stretched from horizon to horizon.

This part of Jotunheim wasn't much for vegetation, that was for certain, although herds of oversized sheep grazed here and there on the slopes. Off in the distance, I noted that the lower mountainsides were covered in greenery, presumably tall conifers of the kind that favored such climates. The sun shone bright above in the hazy gray-blue sky, but it did nothing to warm the chill I felt deep down to my bones.

A hundred yards ahead, on the crest of a broad hill, stood a sort of outdoor amphitheater, easily the size of four high school football stadiums. It was constructed from stone blocks that had obviously been cut from the canyon, perhaps back when they'd first built Utgard. People filed into the structure from the city and foothills in droves. Some were common folk, but most were wealthy carls, thegns, reeves, and ealdormen—if their bright clothing, jewelry, armor, and weapons were any indication.

We walked through a wide opening that led to the coliseum floor, and I was tied to an upright stone pillar in the center of the stadium. Giants continued to shuffle in, finding seats while those in the stands mingled, talked, and laughed amongst themselves. Knowing I was pretty much fucked in the most royal manner imaginable, I still took the time to conduct a mental inventory, just in case I saw an opportunity to escape.

Escape? Right. Not while they have Bells and my friends.

I couldn't exactly call Bryn a friend, yet she wasn't an enemy either. And Crowley—he was just Crowley, but hell if I was going to be responsible for his death. I'd grown fond of Ásgeir over the last few days, so I certainly didn't want any harm coming to him. As for Click and Loki, those two could go fuck themselves unless they hatched a plan to get me out of this mess.

Ultimately, however, I was most concerned for Finnegas. Dian Cécht was being held captive in that city back there; I was certain of it. And if I didn't manage to get myself free to rescue him, my old mentor would die a long, slow death inside the Grove. Fucking hell, but I couldn't allow that.

The question was, could I sacrifice one for the others, or vice versa? For several minutes, I pondered that conundrum. If I stealth-shifted and tore free, I might be able to flee the coliseum and find Dian Cécht. Then, I could fight my way to the portal...

Which was closed, and I had no idea how to open it. Belladonna and all the rest would be dead as soon as I escaped, although I know they'd go down swinging. Then I'd be stuck here in Jotunheim to fend for myself, fighting a one-Fomorian guerrilla war for vengeance until they tracked me down and slaughtered me.

Yeah, I'm fucked. Let's just hope that Váli's "home gang" is enough to get me out of this mess.

Býleistr strode into the stadium about an hour later, dressed in fine furs and a shiny mail shirt, with gold bands on his arms and thick gold chains around his neck. He had a short sword at his waist, nothing fancy—a killing weapon. His face bore a grim smile, as if he were about to take care of a distasteful but necessary chore, but that look was purely for the audience. His eyes told the tale of how he really felt, and they were bright and focused on me from the moment he walked into view.

The jarl was followed by a sizable retinue of jötnar warriors, all armed to the teeth. The last carried a huge two-handed sword over his shoulder, and although it looked ceremonial, the nicks in the blade and the sheen on the edge told me it had seen recent use. Another carried a large wooden block on his back, followed by a young boy with an equally large wicker basket in hands. When the giant laid the block on the stone floor of the coliseum, deep cut marks and bloodstains were revealed on its topmost surface.

An executioner's block. Great.

The guy with the greatsword stood at parade rest next to the block, and the warriors lined up in a wide circle around the jarl and me. That's when I noticed that several of the more brightly-clothed giants sat in their own section, nearest to the coliseum floor. There were two-dozen of them, and all but three were male. Each watched their king silently—some with grim stares, others bored, the rest leaning forward in eager anticipation of the proceedings.

Býleistr strutted to the center of the floor and began speaking in old Norse. That pissed me off, because if I was going to be on trial, I wanted to hear what was being said. I started to raise my hand, then a familiar voice whispered in my ear.

"Relax, kid. I'll spell you up so you can understand

what my pissant of a brother is saying. The magic should allow you to answer in *dönsk tungu* as well."

"Loki—"

"Shhh, I gotta go. Stay frosty, Colinatrix. Gwyd and I are rooting for you."

"Hey, don't leave me," I whispered, only to get silence in return. "Great, just great."

Temporarily at a loss, I turned my attention to Býleistr as his foreign words morphed into English. Oddly, it seemed that the jarl was much more eloquent in his native language. The backward bumpkin was gone, replaced by a sleazy, utterly persuasive speaker—the kind who grows up to become a televangelist, or a politician, or an infomercial host.

"Noble citizens of Utgard," the jarl boomed. "We bring before you one who has committed the crime of regicide, having killed your noble prince, Snorri Býleistr's son, in cold blood."

The crowd booed in response, throwing more rotten fruit and veg my way, although none managed to touch me. I glanced over at the jurors to find several glaring at me with contempt. Things did not look good.

"As you might imagine, I am still heartbroken at the loss of my eldest, yet I stand here as your jarl to do my duty as our law demands." Býleistr wiped an imaginary tear as he continued his diatribe, gesturing and grandstanding for all he was worth. "Thus, we gather today so that this criminal's foul deeds may be recounted to the council of ealdormen and ealdorwomen. I pray they deliver justice for poor Snorri, as they sit in judgement over the foul knave who brought a beloved son of Utgard low."

The crowd hissed and booed in response, and they threw more trash at me. No doubt, the guy was a fucking expert at stirring up a crowd with fancy words and appeals to emotion. If I let this continue, my severed head would be looking up at that ugly sky above from the bottom of a wicker basket. It was now or never.

"*Hólmganga!*" I shouted at the top of my lungs. "I demand the rite of *hólmganga*."

A hush fell over the crowd, followed by murmuring amongst the members of the jury. For a moment, Býleistr's face contorted in a rictus of rage, and his fist gripped the collar of his fine fur robe tight enough to rip hair from the edge. Then, his expression relaxed, replaced by one of cool, detached calm. He stood tall as he spoke, addressing me as if he were addressing a flea.

"Hold your tongue, human," he said. "You cannot demand *hólmganga*, as you have no standing in jötnar society."

"Actually, he does," Váli said, walking out of the stands and onto the stadium concourse. "He has Fomorian blood, a fact witnessed by a good number of jötnar warriors when he first arrived here from Yggdrasil. If memory serves, several millennia ago, the jötnar and the Fomorians entered into a treaty that provides certain diplomatic privileges to visiting parties. Not the least of which is the right to resolve disputes via a fair and honorable duel."

"Walk away, Odin's son," the jarl hissed, just loud

enough for those on the stadium floor to hear. "You have no right to speak in this forum."

"Oh, I have every right," Váli replied. "I represent the will of the All-Father here in Jotunheim."

At that very moment, a pair of voices started a chant in the stands—voices that sounded suspiciously like Click and Loki's. "Holmgang, holmgang, holmGANG, HOLMGANG!"

Soon, most of the giants in the stands had joined in the chant. In all likelihood, this was not because they desired any clemency for me, but because they were jötnar and they liked a good scrape. Sure, a public trial and execution was cool and all, but a duel to resolve a blood feud—now, *that* was entertainment.

Váli leaned against the wall of the stadium, arms crossed and looking like the cat who ate the canary. "It seems your people have spoken, jarl. What say you—will the druid get the fair trial he demands? Or will you be shown craven before all of Utgard?"

Býleistr's face turned beet red as he stared daggers at the Norse god. The two locked eyes for several seconds, then the giant raised his hands to calm the crowd. "Loyal subjects, your jarl has heard your cries. The human and I will settle this matter through trial by combat."

The crowd roared, many jumping to their feet or stamping noisily where they sat. The ealdormen and ealdorwomen were silent, some nodding in approval, while others frowned at the irregularity of the proceedings. As for me, well—I was already busy figuring out how to kill their king.

The sun was high overhead when Býleistr's men finished setting up the stadium for a trial by combat. The chopping block was taken away, and a hundred-yard-wide circular ring was laid out in the center of the coliseum floor using man-sized stone blocks. The blocks were high enough to demarcate the fighting area, but not so high as to block the crowd's view. Finally, the floor inside the arena was covered in red clay dirt, which was then groomed and compacted until it became a single smooth, uniform surface.

Somehow, Váli had been designated as the officiator for our duel, being a neutral third party and a god to boot. He called us both to the center of the ring, speaking loudly enough so everyone in the stadium could hear his instructions. The god gave Býleistr a questioning look, and the giant spat off to the side.

"Get on wit' it, Aesir," Býleistr grumbled.

Váli turned to me. "You are the challenger, druid. Therefore, you get to decide the rules and weapons."

"Oh, you don't say?" I'd hoped that would be the case, although I had a plan if it went the other way, which was pretty much *don't die*. "We'll face each other giant to giant in a battle of magic—no weapons of any kind allowed, and empty-handed combat is off-limits."

Býleistr's eyes lit up for a moment, then his expression settled into a bored poker face. "I agree to those terms," was his only reply.

"Then it is settled," Váli said. "If the challenger falls, then his accuser will be deemed to have received the justice he sought. If the accuser falls, then the challenger will pay half a weregild for both prince and jarl. Is this agreed by both parties?"

"What's a weregild?" I asked.

"It's the man price," Váli said. "Just recompense for taking the life of one who provides protection, service, or livelihood."

"Oh, I'll gladly pay a fair price to kick this fool's ass," I said, meaning it. "But Býleistr must also agree that my companions will be released, no matter the outcome of the duel. And you have to bring me Dian Cécht."

The god glanced at the giant. "What does the jarl say to those terms?"

Býleistr grunted. "Aye. Fair 'nuff terms, they are."

Váli's gaze turned back to me.

"Agreed," I growled.

The god grunted. "Then retreat to opposite sides of the ring to prepare. You have five minutes. When the war horn sounds, the battle begins."

I walked back to my side of the ring, stripping down to my lycra skivvies so I could shift. Sure, I'd set the terms so we wouldn't be engaging in physical combat, but I was counting on my Fomorian healing factor to get me through this battle. I'd make a smaller target if I stealth-shifted, but I just wasn't as tough in that form. More agile, sure, but my human exterior afforded me little in the way of protection from elemental damage.

As I shifted, I wondered if I'd made the right decision. Back when I fought Snorri, I'd managed to fully transform during the final part of our battle. Although Snorri was smaller than his dad, he'd still nearly beaten me, and not just by way of brawn. That bastard knew how to wrestle, and he'd been damned good at it. I figured that Býleistr would be twice the combatant his son was, so I'd decided to avoid physical combat altogether.

The only problem was, the jarl had seemed to like that idea, and that gave me pause. He was Loki's brother, after all. And while Loki might've been weakened by what Váli and Odin did to him, he was still a formidable magician. I had to assume that Loki had inherited some of his powers from his jötnar parents, and that his brother shared the same.

Yet all I'd seen Býleistr use thus far were powers of illusion. He'd concealed an entire battalion of giants from us when we arrived through the portal, after all. So, maybe I'd lucked out and tipped the scales in my favor by opting for an all-magic battle. Who could say?

Then again, I wasn't feeling all that lucky. Since I wasn't connected to the Oak at the moment, my greatest source of magical energy was gone. Sure, I could still emulate all the spells I'd previously performed using the Oak's power, plus everything I'd learned from Finnegas and Click. Unfortunately, I'd be powering them with my innate magical energy only, which meant I might run out of juice long before Býleistr.

Fuck.

At least my Craneskin Bag had turned up. I'd asked for it after Býleistr agreed to the holmgang, but of course no one could find the damned thing. That was to be expected because it was semi-sentient. The Bag had bonded with my family ages ago, and anytime someone took it from me, it had a way of reappearing when I most needed it.

It had been nowhere to be found when I walked over here—of that I was certain. But when I looked for a place to stash my clothing, there it was, sitting on one of the boundary blocks. Too bad it was only good for storing weapons and valuables, and hiding evidence from the cops. Even so, I grabbed a few things from it while I was storing my clothes, figuring even a small advantage was better than none.

Váli's voice echoed across the floor of the stadium. "Are the combatants ready?"

By then I'd spooled up a couple of spells, and I'd fully shifted into my Fomorian form—nine-feet-plus of twisted steel and sex appeal. Okay, maybe not that last part, unless someone was into the Quasimodo look. But I was ready as I'd ever be.

"Aye," Býleistr said as he gave me the figurative evil eye.

"Then bring it, you cross-eyed, mangy, genital-wart-infested goat fucker," I said. It wasn't my best work, but it was an extemporaneous performance. "Ready!"

Váli chuckled as he deftly leapt atop the centermost demarcation block. "Let the duel begin!"

22

I thought Býleistr might open with something brash and flashy, but I was wrong. As soon as the horn sounded, the fucker went invisible. Since illusory magic seemed to be his bread and butter, I'd figured that would happen at some point. And I had a plan. While I might have insisted that there'd be no weapons, I hadn't said a word about clothing.

Draping Gunnarson's cloak over my shoulders, I side-stepped left and said a silent prayer that the damned thing would cooperate. Again, the cloak's magic fell over me immediately. I thanked my lucky stars just as a fireball exploded on the boundary blocks, right where I'd been standing a split-second before.

So, he does have some elemental magic. Shit.

For some reason, I'd thought Loki's siblings were frost giants, a notion likely derived from popular media. After all, most of my knowledge of the Norse pantheon came from comic books and movies. And, in hindsight, ignoring such a gap in knowledge had likely been a major tactical error.

Oops. Should've boned up on some actual Norse mythology before I came here. Oh well.

Nevertheless, I couldn't see him and he couldn't see me, which left us at a sort of stalemate. I was pretty sure I had the superior invisibility magic, though, as Gunnarson's cloak erased all trace of the wearer's passing. The only thing it couldn't do was remove your presence from your current plane of existence, which was how I'd located the former owner to kill him. I was betting that Býleistr's magic was sloppier, and that it'd leave some trace of his passing that I could detect.

So, I scanned the ground for scuff marks on the previously pristine clay, waiting to see if he'd reveal himself by casting another spell. Then, I could blast an area of effect spell in that direction. Lighting him on fire would be ideal —you could use magic to make yourself invisible, but there was little you could do to conceal smoke from your own burning clothing.

Soon I saw the tiniest mark appear on the clay surface of the ring, an almost imperceptible impression in the shape of a huge-ass foot. You'd think a giant would leave deeper footprints, but the jötnar were known for the ability to manipulate their own size. Maybe Býleistr had altered his mass instead, to ensure he didn't give himself away in said manner.

Regardless, I figured I had him, so I blasted two fireballs back at him as I ran an evasive pattern to my right. The idea was that I wouldn't be where the fireballs had come from when my opponent countered. Hopefully, that was.

My second fireball hit something solid while I was still on the move. I skidded to a stop, thankful for the cloak's magic, which covered up my footprints as I passed. Then, I waited for something to happen—smoke, flames, whatever. All I got for my efforts was bupkis, zip, nothing.

Damn.

Býleistr's voice came from somewhere nearby, causing me to jump in response. "Were you expectin' flames, drood?" he taunted, as his voice shifted to another location. "I were born o' fire—cain't nuthin' burn me, not natural heat nor magic."

Ah, he's throwing his voice. Clever.

"Why don't we drop cover an' fight like warriors, eh, drood?" he continued as his voice came from yet another direction. "Settle this fist ta' fist. I know ya' want ta', so jest say the word an' we kin have at it."

Fuck that.

Býleistr seemed a little too eager to engage in hand-to-hand combat. Earlier, it was clear he wanted this exchange. I strongly suspected he wanted me to believe his magic was limited, perhaps not in power, but in scope. And if that was the case, he was a much more powerful magician than I'd guessed earlier.

"Siegfried's cloak, eh?" Býleistr said, throwing his voice all over the ring so it came from several places at once. "I thought it were lost. Such a treasure oughta' remain with its own kind. I'll gladly rip it from yar' corpse after yer' dead."

By this time, the crowd was getting restless, since the big fight they'd been expecting had turned out to be a dud. Soon, shouts of, "Kill someone, already!" and "Stop talking, and start magicking!" could be heard above the din of hundreds of jötnar fidgeting in the stands. Giants started booing in the cheap seats on high, and they began throwing rotten food in our general direction. Where the jötnar got such an endless supply of spoiled meat and produce was beyond me, but I made a note to avoid eating at any giant's house in the future.

As for me, I was really getting tired of Býleistr's yapping. Since we were more or less evenly matched on the invisibility front, I had to force a mistake. I reached inside the waistband of my Jockeys, grabbing a small object I'd taken from my Bag earlier. With the noise of the crowd providing some cover, I whispered a trigger word then tossed the thing across the ring.

The magically-enhanced M80 firecracker exploded with a loud boom. As I'd hoped, the giant reacted by sending another fireball hurtling at the spot where the explosion occurred. But I wasn't looking there; instead, I watched carefully for the origin point of Býleistr's spell.

Bingo.

His fireballs had popped into view at a spot near the edge of the ring, about fifty feet away from where I stood. I estimated his approximate location based on the trajectory, then I cut loose with the mother of all lightning bolt spells. My lightning bolt crashed into the wall beyond and detonated with a tremendous thunderclap. Much to my surprise, it appeared to have completely missed my intended target.

"Gotcha," a voice said to my left, just as I was struck by a lightning spell even more potent than my own.

The force of the blast knocked me across the ring. I landed on my back, temporarily stunned by the impact and effects of the spell. I'd actually never been hit by a lightning spell of that magnitude, and to be honest, it took me by surprise. The wind had been knocked clean out of me, and while I wanted to move, my muscles refused to obey my brain's commands.

Somehow I managed to sit up, only to see that my flesh had charred and blackened around the fist-sized entrance wound in my stomach. Additionally, half my left foot had been vaporized where the charge had exited into the ground below. Even worse, the wounds trailed vaporous streams of smoke, just enough to betray my presence to my foe.

Ah, shit—time to move.

With a supreme effort of will, I rolled to the right just as another lightning bolt struck the earth beside me. Although the spell had missed, I was close enough to catch the ground current, which sent my body into convulsions where I lay. Another bolt struck me in the leg, then the fourth volley hit me in the chest. While I could see where they were coming from, I was temporarily helpless to respond in kind.

All the while, the giant's disembodied voice taunted me from all directions at once, as the crowd cheered his imminent victory. "Thought ya' was smart, choosin' a magic duel. Tweren't quite what ya' were expectin', eh, drood? Turns out, ol' Býleistr knows a thing or two 'bout magic, he does. So much fer' the luck o' Irlanders."

My thoughts were fuzzy, and my body didn't want to respond—never mind the extreme pain I was in due to the extensive damage multiple 100,000-volt strikes had caused internally. And while my Fomorian healing factor was already repairing my injuries, I needed time to recover if I was to survive this battle.

Think, Colin, think.

The cloak was still intact, because I could sense its magic still working to conceal me. That meant Býleistr was locating me due to the wisps of smoke coming off my burned flesh. All he had to do was keep clobbering me with lightning and the odd fireball, and I'd be a sitting duck for his attacks.

A half-dozen more of those and I'd be toast, Fomorian form or no. That simply would not do, because I had plans that involved fucking Býleistr up in front of his loyal subjects. In desperation, I thought back to times past when I needed concealment, before I'd created my chameleon spell—back when the cloak refused to cooperate.

Fog. I need to create fog.

"*Ceò*," I whispered, slamming the palm of my hand flat on the ground.

There was a time when casting such a spell would've required advance preparation, both to gather my druidic magic and to attune myself to the elements. But since bonding with Druid Oak, and after spending the equivalent of years inside the Grove honing my skills, releasing a fog bank was as easy as breathing air. Instantly, a thick cloud of mist sprang up from the earth beneath us, obscuring the entire floor of the arena, and the smoke trailing from my wounds as well.

"No!" Býleistr shouted, blasting the ground with lightning and fire.

But I was already gone, limping away to recover while I considered how I might end that fucker for good. He was strong, true, but so was I, and I believed that my magic was the equal of his any day of the week. I just had to channel it properly to get the effect I desired.

The problem was, the giant was twenty feet tall and immune to certain magical attacks. Fire wouldn't hurt him, so I had to assume lightning wouldn't do much good, either. And that was if I could hit him. He'd already proven to have enough mastery of illusory magic to conceal the origin point of his spells, leaving that tactic nearly useless.

"Drood, stop yer' hidin' now," Býleistr teased. "Yer' only makin' the sufferin' last."

In that situation, Cathbad's Planetary Maelstrom would've been the spell of choice. The only problem was, I didn't have the juice to lift the only loose stones around, which were the massive blocks that marked the boundary of the ring. The ground beneath us wouldn't work either, because it consisted of nothing more than smooth, hard clay.

At that moment, a lightning bolt struck nearby. It was

close enough to interrupt my thoughts, but thankfully far enough away for me to escape its effects. Soon, however, Býleistr seemed to lose patience, and lightning bolts began landing in random patterns all over the ring. There was no dodging them, because no one was fast enough to dodge lightning, so the best I could do was hope I didn't catch a lucky hit.

I needed to take him out immediately, or I was a goner.

Think, Colin. What's another heavy-hitting spell?

That would've been Mogh's Scythe, a spell that shot a super-compressed, molecule-thin layer of air out that would cut through anything in its path. It had worked well on the draugar, and it'd likely work on Býleistr as well. But again, I was limited by the fact that the spell required line of sight to aim.

Hmm... what if it didn't?

To cast Cathbad's Planetary Maelstrom, a druid had to direct the trajectory of multiple objects at once, causing them to simultaneously orbit around a central axis at speeds fast enough to kill. Thus far I'd managed to guide at least a dozen such missiles at a time—enough to ruin Hob's day, certainly. Could I do the same with multiple iterations of Mogh's Scythe?

I had no choice but to go for broke.

Fuck it. Time to invent Colin's Planetary Maelstrom of Scythes.

As fireballs and lightning bolts struck the ground in random patterns all across the dueling enclosure, I cast a druid armor spell on myself, just in case I got hit while I was working on my main offensive gambit. The Oak had taught me that spell on the fly by sheathing me in a protective, bark-like covering while I was fighting a dimensional shambler in the Void.

The armor trick worked great against physical attacks, but it was only so-so against elemental spells. Wood was a poor conductor but susceptible to fire, so it'd likely only offer one-shot protection if I got hit by a fireball. Meaning, I needed to make this quick.

I began by lying flat on the ground to hopefully avoid getting zapped. Then I dropped into a druid trance, a state of mind used in druidry to facilitate the casting of our most difficult magical workings. Less than a year ago, it would have taken me several minutes to achieve—and that was on a good day. Practice makes perfect, however, and today I reached my Zen state within the span of three full breaths.

Once I'd removed all external distractions from my mind, it was time to turn the atmosphere into weaponry. The spell required the caster to visualize the manipulation of a vast volume of air, compressing and flattening it until it became a semi-solid, razor-thin blade. Once formed, the druid would telekinetically launch the construct in a single direction at their very unfortunate enemies.

But I couldn't see my opponent, and one-and-a-half acres was a lot of space in which to hide, even for a giant. For that reason alone, I needed more than one scythe to cover all that ground quickly. Not to mention, a single cut might not kill Býleistr, especially if I just nicked him. I had to ensure his destruction the moment I cast the spell, else I might be dead before I spooled up a second casting.

Not wanting to disturb the fog bank and then give myself away in the process, I created my first scythe well above us, at the level of the highest stands. Seconds later, after repeating the process a dozen times, I'd fashioned a circle of invisible blades that were roughly arranged like teeth on a circular saw blade. I was about to set them spinning when a lightning bolt blasted the ground a few feet from me. My armor protected me from taking a jolt via ground conduction, but the impact nearly caused me to lose concentration and drop the spell.

Fuck, almost lost it. Focus, Colin-san...

A few steadying breaths later, I'd regained control of the blades I created, just as the giant crooned hatefully from somewhere close by.

"Drood, where are ye? Surely ya' hain't run away now!"

Fat chance of that, but Býleistr's voice sounded nearer to me than I liked. That was a definite problem. If he stood too close to me, I might chop my own self to bits when I released the spell.

Better finish this up, or else I'm dog meat.

Working through the complex hand gestures and finger forms for casting Cathbad's Planetary Maelstrom, I combined them with the patterns required to release Mogh's Scythe. I wasn't certain if it would work or not, but the blades seemed to be holding, and they quivered with restrained potential energy in my mind's eye.

Time to drop the beat.

"*Hairicín*," I said aloud, knowing that the giant would hear. However, a spell of this magnitude required a forceful recitation of the required trigger word.

"There ya' are," he sneered, as two fireballs hurtled across the field directly at my position.

Simultaneously, my blades dropped to about six feet above ground level and ten feet away from me in all directions, a distance they'd maintain until I changed their trajectory. I dodged aside as the scythes began spinning, starting slow as I struggled to control them, then faster and faster as I focused on pouring all my will and power into the spell. As the blades split the air, they created a vortex that sent the fog curling away all around me.

Aw, shit. I hadn't thought about that.

"What's this, then?" Býleistr said, chortling to himself. "Yer gonna kill me with a light breeze?"

Despite his amusement, the giant clearly caught on, because he sent a fireball right at the center of the area I'd cleared of fog. It was a direct hit, and the majority of the druid armor over my chest was incinerated on impact, staggering me but leaving me mostly unharmed. That pissed the Fomorian side of me off, as I'd been hiding and sneaking around for the better part of the battle—behavior quite unlike a Fomorian god-killer.

"Enough games, jötunn," I snarled. "It's time for you to learn why the Tuath Dé feared our kind."

"Find me then, drood!" the giant challenged. "If'n ya' kin."

I gave myself over to my Fomorian side then, allowing

it to harness and control the druid spellwork I'd so painstakingly cast. Instantly the simple, uniform rotating formations that I'd commanded the blades to follow turned into a dozen dizzying, intersecting patterns of invisible death. Likewise, the added influence of the Fomorian will on my druid magic hardened and reinforced the scythes, adding an efficacy to the spell I could never have achieved on my own.

Roaring a battle cry of bloody murder, I sprinted to the center of the arena, almost literally throwing caution to the wind as the blades turned the dueling ground into a killing field. With a thought, the orbital pattern of the scythes became a Gordian knot of decussating lines that covered the entire field. Somewhere behind me, I felt a blade hit something solid and heard a soft groan.

I spun in place just in time to see Býleistr shimmer into view not fifteen feet behind me. Apparently he'd been trying to sneak up on me and got caught in my spell. Blood spurted from his gut, and he clapped both hands over a wound that bisected him across his umbilicus.

"Drood, ya' ch—"

"Oh, shut up, already," I said, cutting him off by sending every blade I controlled through his body at once.

A dozen red lines crisscrossed his body, and blood flew in as many directions, spraying out an array of abstract crimson patterns on the ochre ground. Then, like a nameless extra in a samurai manga, Býleistr collapsed in a bloody pile of guts and body parts to the hard-packed surface of the arena floor. His severed head fell last, cut at an awkward angle that caused it to roll precariously in a wobbly path to my feet.

I dropped my druid armor and pulled off Gunnarson's cloak, making sure that I'd be the last thing Býleistr saw. The giant's eyes fixed on me, blinking once, twice, before finally staring up blankly at the steel-blue sky above. A hush fell over the crowd. Mothers covered their children's eyes, while others shielded their kids from the monster who'd just slain their king.

I wanted to say something witty, like, "Oh look, he fell to pieces!" or, "Some folk just can't keep it together when the chips are down." But instead, I swept my gaze across the audience, taking in their muted stares and the horrified looks on their faces.

That's right, get a good look. I'm the monster to monsters, bitches.

But I wasn't done. Flashing the crowd an evil grin, I retrieved Crowley's jar of shadow goop out of my waistband, then I unscrewed the lid and dumped it all over the giant's head.

"That's for pissing on me, you piece of shit."

I'd really just meant it as a final insult. Fact was, I had intended to blind him with it during the fight but never got a chance. To my surprise, the goop hissed and bubbled as it spread over Býleistr's face. Within seconds, the stuff had eaten every last bit of skin, hair, and flesh from his head, until only a stark white skull and jawbone remained.

Disgusted and caught off guard, I dropped the jar and backed away a step, readying a spell for safety's sake. Meanwhile, the black goop sent out a few probes to search for more food. Finding none, it sort of inch-wormed back over to the jar, crawling inside and pulling the top on after itself. The lid screwed itself down tight with a *scritching* sound, then the jar righted itself and went still.

Okay, that was fucked up. I am so glad that jar didn't bust inside my shorts during the fight.

The crowd gave a collective gasp, then they started jostling and fighting to leave the stadium. That was, all except for the guards and the ealdormen and ealdor-women, who all stared at me like I was a demon from the seventh circle of hell.

I locked eyes with Váli, who stood on one of the few boundary blocks that hadn't been blasted to bits. He smirked and winked at me, and for a moment, I could've sworn his eyes flashed from blue to violet. He gave the slightest nod of his head toward the exit, and that's when I knew it was time to go.

I gave a disgusted, weary wave to the ealdormen and ealdorwomen who'd served as jurors over the proceedings. "I'll be at the gate to Yggdrasil, waiting for you to deliver my companions and the Tuath Dé Physician. Be quick about it if you don't wish to suffer the same fate."

23

It didn't take long for the jötnar to deliver my people, along with a very confused Dian Cécht. As far as he knew, he had been in Jotunheim at the request of their king, to help with a very difficult delivery of jötunn quintuplets. Býleistr had known better than to create an inter-pantheon incident, so he'd concocted a story that was guaranteed to get the gentle-hearted Physician as far away from me as possible.

It had been a good plan, for the most part. So long as Býleistr kept us out of Jotunheim, he kept me from healing Finnegas. Failing that, he hatched his Plan B, which was supposed to be a lopsided trial and summary execution of yours truly. Either way, the old man would die, and he'd have his revenge. Too bad he hadn't counted on the meddling presence of not just one, but two, trickster gods.

I still had no idea what Loki had gotten out of the whole fiasco—besides a trip to Vegas, that is. The trickster mysteriously disappeared after all was said and done, and strangely, no one knew were Váli was either. Based on the dirty looks we were getting from Býleistr's royal guard, I decided it wasn't worth hanging around to find either of them.

As for the weregild, I gave the giants the lump of melted gold I'd snagged back in Jerrik's tomb. From the looks the ealdormen and ealdorwomen gave me, it probably wasn't enough. But they took it without comment, seemingly eager to see us go.

When Dian Cécht learned why I'd been trying to locate him, he agreed to portal us back to the Oak in Iceland immediately. When we got back to our campsite by the Druid Oak, Click was already there, cooking up one of his ten-course camp breakfasts. When he noticed our arrival, he set aside what he'd been doing, practically dancing a jig as he walked over to greet me.

"Holy shite, lad—that was feckin' amazing!"

I'd shifted back to human form while I was waiting for the jötnar to deliver everyone, after most of my injuries had healed. Despite taking time to recover, I felt beat up, both emotionally and physically, and more than a little used. I guess that's why I responded with a bit more of an edge to my voice than I intended.

"Don't even start, Click. First off, you might've told me what you and Loki were up to from the very beginning. Hell, either one of you could've portalled to Jotunheim and asked Dian Cécht to come heal Finnegas, but you didn't. Instead, you let me wander all over Iceland for months, all the while knowing that the old man was inside the Grove, dying a slow death."

Click's face fell, and his eyes grew sad. "Aw, lad, it's not that simple—"

"Sure it is," I replied with venom in my voice. "I appreciate all you've done for me, but for now, I think it's best if we parted ways."

"Boyo, ya' can't be serious—"

"Don't 'boyo' me. Just go, and while you're at it, take Crowley and Belladonna back to Austin. Shit, now that I think of it, we didn't even need to get them involved, did we?"

"Lad—"

"Click, leave," I said in a quiet voice that held much more threat of violence than any amount of shouting might convey.

"Right ya' are," he said as his shoulders slumped. "I'll be here when ya' have need o' me."

The quasi-god created a portal, revealing downtown Austin on the other side. Being Click, he took a moment to cast a spell that animated the cooking utensils so the food he'd been cooking wouldn't burn. Avoiding my gaze, he walked through the portal without another word, leaving it open so the others could follow.

Crowley and I exchanged a look that conveyed more than words could say. We might've mixed like oil and water, but we shared a bond due to both our lives having been completely fucked by the fae and the gods. I gave him a single nod of thanks, then he waited by the portal as Bells and I said our goodbyes.

Thankfully, Belladonna looked none the worse for the wear. The giants had treated her with a bit more respect after Crowley had shown them a bit of his magic—and after Bells had bared her teeth. Nobody really wanted to piss off a shadow mage and a naga—not even the jötnar.

"That was a little harsh, eh, *mago*?" she asked, glancing over her shoulder at the portal.

"I'm sorry you got dragged into this," I replied.

"Never a dull moment with you, *tonto*," she said, going on her tiptoes to give me a peck on the cheek. "Give those gods hell, and when you're done, come back and see us in Austin."

"I will, Bells."

After the two of them had exited through the portal, that only left Bryn and Ásgeir. I started to speak—whether to apologize or thank them, I didn't know. Regardless, the valkyrie stopped me with an open hand.

"Don't bother, druid," she said, whistling to summon Tordenvejr from where it had been grazing nearby. As she mounted the pegasus, she tossed me a wooden token that had a sword and shield on one side and a flying horse on the other. "Just to make sure you keep your end of the bargain. When you find that bitch Badb, you break that in half, and Tordenvejr and I will come running."

I had to chuckle despite my mood. "See you when I see you, Bryn."

"Not if I see you first." She spurred her heels, then horse and rider flew off into the night sky.

I cleared my throat to get Ásgeir's attention. He was busy making sure that Click's makeshift *tsukumogami* didn't burn the pancakes. Every time he'd try to snag one, the spatula would smack him on the wrist.

"Don't mind me, druid," he said without looking up from his task. "The job's not done until I get paid, and so long as I have a full belly, I'm content to tag along and see it through. That is, if you don't mind my company."

"Not at all, Ásgeir. But right now, I have something to attend to."

"See to your mentor, Colin," he replied. "I'll be waiting here between dusk and dawn when you return."

The odd thing about Dian Cécht was that he had silver eyes. Not just silver pupils—his eyes were solid silver, polished to a mirror finish. When we'd first made our introductions back in Jotunheim, he'd apologized for their unsettling appearance, explaining that he'd had to replace them several centuries before. His old eyes had been failing him, so he made himself a new, improved version that allowed him to perform microsurgery without the use of a microscope.

Magic was weird; god magic, even weirder.

Another strange thing about Dian Cécht was how he dressed, which was pretty much just like any middle-aged pediatrician you might meet in the States. Button-down blue shirt, red tie, sweater vest, white lab coat, khakis, and brown loafers. Combined with his tall, thin build, his kind face, and his neatly groomed salt and pepper hair, it was almost comical how much effort he put into looking like your typical family physician.

We didn't speak much after everyone left. Dian Cécht

was all business, requesting to see his patient ASAP, which was fine by me. After I portalled us inside the Oak, the Physician immediately approached Finnegas, proceeding to silently study him where he lay in Saint Germain's coffin.

Interestingly, he didn't ask about the stasis field, so I figured he assumed it was Click's work. Come to think of it, the two hadn't even acknowledged each other after we arrived at camp. It might've been because of the awkwardness of the situation, but I suspected it was probably because Dian Cécht didn't care for Click or his use of time magic.

Finally, after staring at my mentor for at least an hour, the Celtic god of healing spoke.

"His illness is beyond my ability to heal."

I grabbed Dian Cécht by the lapels, lifting him up on his toes. "What do you mean, you won't heal him?"

He glanced down at my hands with his creepy silver eyes, gently peeling my fingers from his sweater vest and lab coat. "I didn't say I wouldn't; I said I cannot. His injuries were not caused by magic, but by a *lack* of magic. And that, I simply can't fix."

As the immortal Physician's words sank in, I realized that he wasn't being maliciously fickle like a typical Tuath De. He was telling the truth. His tone was almost apologetic, and the fact that he hadn't used any of his Celtic god magic when I grabbed him only reinforced my hunch. Still, I couldn't believe it. After all that trouble, all that time, all my efforts, Dian Cécht couldn't heal Finnegas.

It was like someone took the air out of my lungs all at

once. I slumped bonelessly on a nearby bench, resting my head in my hands. After several long seconds, I looked up at the Celtic god of healing with tears in my eyes.

"I don't understand. Can you please explain it to me?"

His expression softened, as did his voice. "Certainly. Your master has lived a very long life—unnaturally long, in fact. And while that might not be an issue for a god, or for one who has chosen godhood, it is very problematic for a human."

"Hang on," I said, perking up slightly. "A human can choose to become a god?"

"In so many words, yes. But, to be honest, the term 'god' is relative. A more apt descriptor would be 'immortal,' although many immortals are worshipped as gods by mortal men and women." He glanced at Finnegas where he lay inside my stasis field. "The Seer could've taken that path, but he chose instead to remain fully human. Immortality always comes at a terrible cost, and he refused to pay the price."

"So, how did he manage to live so long?"

"He is a remarkable man, the likes of which this world will likely never see again. We were friends, once—did he tell you?" I shook my head. "Of course he didn't. We did not part on the best of terms."

"I'm sorry to hear that," I said, meaning it.

"So am I, child, so am I." Dian Cécht took a seat next to me on the bench, clasping his hands in his lap. "In any case, Finnegas extended his life via magic to watch over Fionn's line—your line. But without making the sort of Faustian bargain that grants one immortality, a human can only forestall death for so many centuries. That he lived this long astounds even me, and I've lived long enough to learn all there is to know about such magic."

I hung my head, thinking of the implications and what it meant for Finnegas. "Is that what the Tuath Dé did? Trade your humanity to become gods?"

He twiddled his thumbs nervously, a very un-godlike affectation. "My people were forced to do so, to ensure the survival of our race. We were already powerful mages when we encountered the Fomori, but our magic did little to prevent them from making us their subjects. They took our women for wives, and their female warriors even raped some of our men. It was a dark time."

I wiped my eyes before looking up at him. "So, you sold your souls to become immortal—a sacrifice that Finnegas wasn't willing to make."

Dian Cécht leaned forward with one elbow on his knee, gesturing at Finnegas as he spoke. "The Seer witnessed our mistake and swore to avoid making the same. Once you walk down that path, you can never go back. Death will elude you, and you're doomed to travel back and forth across the Veil for all time. Unless—"

"Unless you cease to exist completely," I said as I chewed on my thumb.

"I see that Fionn's supernatural cunning still lives on in his heir." He smiled sadly. "Yes, one can choose to end their life in such a manner, and many have over the millennia. Immortality takes its toll, often driving our kind mad."

"Like Click."

"Exactly. Gwydion chose the path of godhood when he was relatively young, and some would say that he had not matured enough to bear that burden. As you've seen, his madness comes and goes, mostly evidencing itself in harmless manic episodes. He is fortunate in that regard. More often, we are overcome by delusions of grandeur and extreme paranoia. Thus, the cruel and capricious nature of the gods."

"That explains a lot, and I appreciate that you shared that info with me." I clasped my fingers together, resting my forehead on my knuckles. "But it still doesn't tell me what I should do with Finnegas."

He laid a firm, bony hand on my arm. "You have to let him go."

Tears came to my eyes again, flowing in streams down my cheeks. "There's nothing I can do? I mean, there's really no hope?"

"Certainly, Gwydion can keep him frozen in this stasis field, perhaps for centuries. But that is no way for a druid of his stature to pass from this existence. I cannot heal him, Colin, but I can allow you to speak with him while he remains in stasis so you can receive his final wishes and say your goodbyes."

"I—I'm not sure."

Meaning, I don't know if I can trust you.

"If I were in your position, I wouldn't take my advice either. For that reason, I've summoned someone you know and trust." He cleared his throat nervously. "I, uh, hope you do not mind, but he's also the only god who can come and go as he pleases here."

A deep, mellow voice spoke up behind me. "Dian Cécht tells the truth, lad. It's for the best."

I stood and spun, reaching for my sword, only to find that my caution was unnecessary. There by my Oak tree stood none other than The Dagda himself.

He was much as I remembered him—a nine-foot-tall, hairy, brutish-looking man with a huge bushy beard, a wild mane of hair, and kind eyes. His club leaned against a tree nearby, and he stood with his hands clasped in front of him like an usher at a wedding—or a funeral. His smile was kind, but sad, and he approached with careful steps despite his bulk, as if afraid to disturb the old man's rest.

"I don't know if I can let him go," I whispered. "I don't think I'm strong enough."

The Dagda exhaled heavily, as if he were carrying a tremendous weight on his massive shoulders. "It's never easy, letting go of those we care for the most. But in this case, hanging on would be the cruelest choice you could make. The Seer was ever a proud man who walked his own path, head held high even when it seemed the whole world stood against him. Tell me, would you have him suffer a prolonged death, enfeebled and unable to move, just because you lack the stones to let him pass as he intended—as a warrior and master druid?"

Despite his kind tone, his words cut me deep. I raised my head and glared at him. "Are you saying I should've let him die in New Orleans? Or in Mag Mell?"

"Lad, no one is blaming you for doing your best to save him," Dian Cécht said. "But you've done all you can, and it's time to give the man his final rest."

"Nothing more can be done, Colin," The Dagda added. "Keeping him alive only prolongs his agony. Allow Dian Cécht to connect your minds, then speak with him and say your goodbyes. It is time."

I nodded once, choking back tears. Then, I stood. "I understand."

The Dagda gave a grunt of approval. "There's the man we've all placed our trust in, and Finnegas most of all. Now, lad, once Dian Cécht creates the link, we'll leave the Grove so you can say farewell in peace. But before we go, I have one final word of advice—you must return to Mag Mell and claim your due. And after it is finished, seek me out at my home."

I honestly had no idea what he was talking about, and frankly I didn't care. The gods were forever scheming, and they always had a ball in play. All I could think of was what I was about to do. There'd be time to consider The Dagda's words later, after—

Yes, after.

I looked Dian Cécht in his weird silver eyes. "Do it."

The immortal Physician hovered a hand over Finn's forehead outside the stasis field, then he brushed his other hand over my eyes. A sort of fog fell over me, and everything got really bright until the whole world whited out. Then, I opened my eyes and I was back in the Grove with Finnegas.

But instead of a body lying in a coffin inside a stasis

field, he stood in front of me in his faded jeans, scuffed cowboy boots, black western shirt, and battered straw hat. He looked as hale and whole as ever, and for a moment, I felt a spark of hope. But the look on his face told me it was just an illusion, a vision inside whatever shared mental space Dian Cécht had created for this meeting.

"This isn't real, is it?" I asked.

"Why ask a question if you already know the answer?" He smiled, causing his gray eyes to crinkle at the corners. "At some point, you're going to have to start trusting your own gut. Now, sit."

I took a seat on the same bench I'd sat on moments before, and he sat opposite me on a stool that hadn't existed in the real world. The old man leaned forward on his knees, clasping his hands as he watched me with the critical eye of a potter pulling his work from the kiln. I felt both exposed and comforted, because it was exactly the way he'd looked at me a thousand times before.

"Finn, I'm sorry—"

He scowled. "Stop that. You've no reason to be sorry, not for me, not for Jesse, not for anything. You've never given me any reason to regret taking you on as a student, and the only person who let anyone down was me."

"But if I hadn't gone up against those vamps in New Orleans, we wouldn't be here right now."

"Maybe, but I've been dying for a long time. And hell if I was going to let you meet your end at the hands of a bunch of half-witted undead. You'd have stood your ground, if only because you'd given your word, and they'd have kept coming by the dozens due to Badb's influence.

You weren't ready to face those odds then, so I made my choice."

"So, you knew she was there that day," I said.

"Of course. Her talon marks were all over that situation. The way Saint Germain planned things out, we should've had an easy getaway. Instead, every vamp in NOLA came down on our heads." He patted his pockets, giving up after a few seconds with a disappointed frown. "Fecking doctors. Figures that Dian Cécht wouldn't let me have one final smoke."

I laughed, despite myself. "Finnegas, I don't know if I can do this alone."

He spat to one side and stabbed a finger at me. "First off, you're not alone. I've spent the better part of a decade making sure of that. Second, you're the only one who *can* do this, and by 'this' I mean take on those evil, immortal pricks. Believe me when I say you have *everything* you need to prevail. And third, I'm tired, son. I've spent way too many centuries on this Earth, and my magic simply cannot sustain me any longer. You have to let me go."

"Somewhere deep inside of me, I get that. But first Dad, then Jesse, Uncle Ed, and now you—I can't help but feel like I failed you all."

He stood and crossed the distance between us in two steps, then he grabbed my face in his rough, nicotine-stained hands. The old man looked me in the eye from inches away. While his expression was fierce, there were tears running down his cheeks.

"You listen to me, boy, and listen good. In all my years

on this Earth, never have I been prouder of a pupil than I am of you."

"Finn—"

"Son, for once in your life, close that smart-assed trap and listen, because I have something important to say." He took a deep breath, and silver light shone from within his steel-gray eyes. "I, Finnegas of Assaroe, also known as Finn Éces and Finn the Seer, do hereby release you from my geas. Furthermore, I bequeath on you the title and respon- sibilities of Master Druid of the Mortal Realms, and duly transfer all my remaining power and authority as the reigning High Druid to you in full. Now, leave with my blessing, let me rest in peace, and go see your mother."

He kissed me lightly on the forehead, and suddenly it felt like a cold wind rushed into me from all directions. I heard a bell ring in the distance, but also inside my head, and a fog lifted from my mind as all sorts of memories came rushing back to me. Then, everything faded into white, and I fell into a deep, mindless sleep.

EPILOGUE

I awoke inside the Grove, in the soft grass right next to
Finnegas. He was already gone, but whether I'd lifted
the stasis field or The Dagda had, I couldn't say. The first
thing I did was to bury Finn, right there next to the maple
tree in the exact same spot where he'd rested all this time.

I didn't leave him in Saint Germain's coffin, as it didn't
seem at all proper. Instead, I had the Grove help me clean
him up, then I crafted a new coffin by shaping and forming
wood that the Grove provided, using druid magic. Once it
was finished, I laid him carefully inside, then I sealed it
and dug the hole for his grave by hand. His final resting
place didn't require a marker—the maple tree would serve
in that regard.

By the time I'd covered the grave and grown some grass
over it, I was spent. Later, I'd gather all his friends and
everyone who knew him, and we'd have a proper funeral.
But right now, I needed to rest and recharge, because I had
people to see and gods to kill. Thus, I slept.

After I awoke, I put on some decent clothes and packed and arranged my Craneskin Bag so I'd be prepared for any encounter. I armed myself thoroughly, because I was headed back to Austin. Not Austin proper, but I'd still be in Maeve's demesne, and I didn't know how she'd react if I ran into her. Plus, I had to worry about Aengus, Badb, and possibly Fuamnach.

One thing I wasn't concerned with, however, was being attacked at my old house. I had all this new information floating around in my head, and one tidbit that stood out about the house I grew up in was that it was a sanctuary, like a foreign embassy in hostile territory. The house and grounds were sacrosanct, and neither Maeve, nor any of the other Celtic gods, nor their agents would set foot there, on pain of death.

Finn had seen to that.

When the Oak dropped me in front of my house, everything was familiar, but different. I'd been here recently, hadn't I? No, actually, I hadn't. The old man's geas had kept me from recalling a shitload of things I knew about my house, my childhood, and, most importantly, my mother.

Mom—holy shit, this is weird.

I'd stayed here after Jesse's death, true, but the whole time I'd lived in my mom's basement, I hadn't interacted with her once. Why? Because it wasn't allowed. Seeing her could trigger memories that would interfere with the geas, and that would've fucked the old man's grand plan to keep me safe all to hell.

Appear harmless, or at least, average. Obscurity and flying under the wire, that was the plan. All while preparing me for a future where I was 99 percent likely to die before the age of twenty-five. Shit.

I didn't have the whole picture yet, not all of it, because the memories only clicked into place a little at a time. Standing in front of my old house, *click*. Walking up the front walk, *click, click*. Seeing all the photos on the walls and shelves as I strolled through my own house like a stranger, *click, click, click, click*.

Finding my mother sitting at the kitchen table, sharpening a huge-ass battle axe, *click, click*, infinity *click*.

Here was the woman who raised me alone after my dad had passed, with Finnegas and Maureen stepping in when it became too dangerous for me to know who she really was. This wasn't the woman who'd bandaged my knee when I fell, who tucked me in at night, or who consoled me when my dog died. Mom hadn't done those things, because those memories had all been manufactured when Finnegas had cast his geas. And she damned sure wasn't the addle-brained woman I remembered, who was more than a little loopy from being mind-wiped so many times. Nope.

This was the woman who put a dagger in my hand when I was three, a sword when I was five, and a spear not long after. This was the woman who'd made me drill and spar and drill some more, for hours and hours every day after school, in an effort to turn her sensitive, pudgy little boy into a warrior. This was the woman who had never nurtured me as a mother should, because by her very nature, she was incapable of doing so.

That just isn't our way. Fomorians don't coddle their children, even when they're half-human mutts who haven't evidenced a lick of Fomori DNA from the time they were born. Because ability doesn't matter to Fomorians, nor genetics, nor lineage. All that matters is this: You fight until you die. That is the way of the Fomori.

When I walked in, Mother didn't even look up from dragging that whetstone across the edge of her favorite battle axe. "Sit down, son," she said in an easy, confident voice that brooked no argument. "We have a lot to discuss."

―――――

This ends Book 11 in the Colin McCool Paranormal Suspense Series. But never fear, because Colin will return for more urban fantasy mayhem in Book 12, Druid Master...
Be sure to visit my website at MDMassey.com to download two free books, and to subscribe to my newsletter. And thanks so much for supporting my work!

Made in the USA
Monee, IL
05 March 2021

62011601R00167